FOR WHERE YOU GO I WILL GO

Destination Colorado

Bob Cox

authorHOUSE®

AuthorHouse™
1663 Liberty Drive
Bloomington, IN 47403
www.authorhouse.com
Phone: 833-262-8899

Published by AuthorHouse 10/31/2022

ISBN: 978-1-6655-7474-7 (sc)
ISBN: 978-1-6655-7473-0 (e)

CHAPTER ONE

Juame Castello awakened to the sounds of a squeaking wheel of a cart and the shouts of one of the laborers encouraging a reluctant ox along the path below his window. The scent of wild lavender invaded his sleeping room and separated him from his dreams. He fully expected his mother to appear in the doorway and encourage him to arise and begin a productive day. He was approaching his 13th birthday and was expected to begin taking on the toils of a man.

But his mother did not come to his room. In fact, she would never come to his room again. The Matron Castello had suffered from a severe bowel malady and succumbed to the illness nearly six months prior. The huge Castello house still had a noticeable void that had once been filled by Juame's mother. The house, located in the fashionable area of Girona, Spain survived, but the family seemed to be crumbling. The now widowed Juame Castello the elder immersed himself in his hidden assets, his support of the local mining industry and the use of slaves.

Juame's father amassed a considerable fortune as a result of his investments in iron mining, mostly near Ribes de Freser, but unlike so many of his peers, the elder Castello began to develop investments in shipping and new world trade markets. Juame was just becoming aware of what the trade markets were as a result of his father's ever increasing interest in Juame's education.

Juame arose and went to his window. Below he observed the source of the early morning noises. Several black men clad only in the bare minimum of clothing were leading three carts laden with rock through the street below. Their broad shoulders and huge biceps glistened with sweat and served as reminders of the hard labor that was required of them as slaves. To their owners, the slaves were valued above the oxen, only because they were able to speak.

Slaves were an integral part of Spain, and had been since the times of the Romans, when many of the slaves were Spanish, Eastern European and Christian. The slaves outside Juame's window were black, the result of newly established trade agreements, particularly a looming agreement with Havana, Cuba.

As a result of the family interests in world markets, Juame became proficient in the use of three languages. He of course spoke his native Spanish, but had also learned enough French and English to conduct comprehensive conversations in all three languages, an asset his father deemed very important, but often encouraged caution when Juame used his knowledge to become, not just communicative, but friendly with several of the slaves. It was those friendships that were on Juame's mind as he dressed and prepared for the morning meal with his father. He knew the meal, which consisted of some chocolate and a pastry, promised to be the venue for still another argument with his father regarding the slavery issues.

The elder Castello addressed his son as he entered the eating area. "Buenos Dias, Juame," he said in a somewhat passive manner. "Dor miste bien?"

"Good morning father," Juame replied in English. "Yes I slept very well, thank you. I have my tutoring session today with Señora Goya. Today, all my lessons will be in English," he continued in an effort to remind his father that they had agreed to advance their knowledge of English, in light of some recent dealings and trading with Ireland.

"Muy bien hijo," was the only reply given, and for several minutes nothing was said. Juame sipped on his chocolate drink and nibbled at the large pastry. He then broke the silence, which he knew would evoke a response from his father.

"Father, I spoke with Juana yesterday. She told me that Pedro has been forced to go to work at the mine. Father, he is less than one year older than me. Cannot you do something?"

Senor Castello met his son's eyes with a determined and almost threatening look. "Juame, I have warned you many times that your friendships with Juana and her brother were not to be tolerated. Their father is a slave. He works in the mine. His son is old enough to begin earning his keep. Pedro and Juana have Spanish names only so they can be readily identified. They are black. They are not Spanish. They know their place and you need to recognize that. Basta de charla. Enough!"

For the next several minutes Juame tried to reason with his father, trying to convince him that the ongoing use of slave labor was wrong, but he knew that the family business largely depended on the lower overhead costs that existed because of the inhumane practice of treating men like animals. As usual, his argument was not summarily set aside by his father, but rather rationalized as a sad, but necessary fact of life.

Juame's life was about to change. His father breached a subject yet to be explored during their conversations: "Juame, as we recognize that your friend, Pedro has reached an age in which he can become productive, we must also recognize that you, too should begin your adulthood. I have arranged for my business associates to begin visiting your tutoring sessions and to educate you in the ways of mining and mineral extraction here, in Ireland and in what is now being called the United Colonies in America. You will likely be required to deal with both of these places in the next few years of your life."

For the next two years Juame spent little time at home. He attended small tutoring sessions with several well-respected educators. He learned his father's business and made two trips to Paris accompanied by business associates. The 950-kilometer trip to Paris was grueling and culminated in long sessions with French clergymen who had little tolerance for anything that even resembled laziness. Juame was expected to demonstrate every aspect of his education, especially the use of the French language. His French mentors regarded their language to be the official language of the world. His Spanish and English associates disagreed and let it be known that, while speaking French would be beneficial, it was likely English that would propel him into the world of land ownership and industrial benefits. It was at that time that Juame first became aware of the extent to which his father had invested in the lead and copper mines of Ireland.

CHAPTER TWO

By the time Juame was 18, he had become an accomplished traveler and expanded his knowledge of both mining and farming in Spain, England and France. Early in the year of 1776, shortly after the death of his father, Juame began still another trip. The final destination was the copper mines of southwest Ireland.

Just weeks before the elder Castello died he called Juame into the study of his home.

"My son, you now know the secrets of our family's wealth, and you know that our wealth is depleting. It is essential that you go to Ireland and oversee our investments there. I have no doubt that our Ireland interests are destined to do great things. There are things happening that are going to make the mineral and textile industries flourish. I have sent missives to my business associates in Ireland. They will be expecting you. All the information and necessary funds will be found in the locked compartment of my desk. May God bless you in your journeys. I likely will not survive long enough to become aware of your success or failure."

Juame, to his own surprise, showed little reluctance to begin his role as head of the family business.

"Father, if this is your desire, then I will of course look upon my journey and upon the opportunity with the confidence that you and your associates have instilled in me; those basics of acquiring success. I know that my youth will be of concern to some, but rest assured that I have been dealing with that for some time now, and I will do justice to the family legacy."

As Juame was preparing to cross the English Channel traders and explorers were talking of a pending revolution in the American states. It was then he first heard about the young General Washington, who had placed canons above the Boston Harbor and forced British soldiers out of that city. Juame instinctively knew that, should the American states succeed in becoming independent of Britain, there could be great opportunity there. His father had befriended several Frenchmen who were involved in the fur trade in America and had assisted the Americans in their resistance to British authority.

At nearly every stop in England Juame heard more about the activities of the Americans. Britain was preparing for all-out war and Juame was thankful when he finally reached Holy Head and made the final arrangements to cross St. George's Channel and reach Ireland. He arrived in Ireland in the waning days of July 1776.

Ireland was a confusing country. Its economy was experiencing booms and busts like no other. A man known to many as Red Hugh basically controlled the Castello family holdings. His given name was Hugh O'Brien. O'Brien knew the Irish mining industry well and had encouraged Juame's father to become involved. The elder Castello and Hugh O'Brien met face to face on only a few occasions, but from the very beginning of the Castello/O'Brien partnership, there was a mutual trust that served as an almost tangible asset to the investment strategies. Men knew that O'Brien's word was unfailing. Hugh O'Brien met Juame at the docks in Dublin.

As Juame stepped from the gangplank and began a visual search of the crowds on the dock, there was little doubt that the man approaching him was Red Hugh. His red hair seemed to literally flow down his cheeks in large bushy sideburns that had the sheen and color of a new penny. His wool cap rested on top of his hair, rather than on top of his head. O'Brien's upper torso appeared as though it was clad in armor and the breadth of his chest necessitated his elbows to point slightly outward as he moved.

The Irish form of the English language flowed from O'Brien with a mixture of Irish words and subdued laughter as he stepped in front of Juame.

"There be little doubt that you are the young Castello," O'Brien announced. "How's about yee?"

"Very well," replied Juame. "I am very tired and my body and mind are ready for standing on some solid ground for a spell. You are Red Hugh, I assume."

"That I am. In the name of Jaysus, you are a young one. I do hope you are up to the tasks at hand. I understand you are knackered, but little have you seen yet. I just learned of your coming and of your father's death a few days ago. Your oul fella was a good one for sure. Now come along. There's a couple of lads collecting your trunks," O'Brien said, as he turned and started toward the town.

"We will stroll a bit to the inn. The boys will take care of the carriage and see that your trunks are secured. Yee have a bit of listening to do and that can best be done with a pint," O'Brien said, as he leaned forward a bit and picked up the pace. Juame was still getting his land legs and struggled somewhat to keep up with the man who was now his business partner.

Juame clung closely to the leather pouch that was strapped across his chest and hung to the left side. He had not let the pouch out of his sight since he had transferred the papers and money from his father's desk. The papers were mostly legal documents. The money consisted of a considerable sum in English pound notes and a few French gold coins. There were more coins secreted in one of the trunks, which were now in the possession of two of O'Brien's employees.

After securing rooms at the inn, Juame and Hugh sat at a corner table in the adjoining pub. Red Hugh was obviously well known in the pub. Several men greeted him, often with a slap on the back. Juame was introduced after each greeting, but often did not understand the exchanges that took place. The language mixture was confusing and often sounded more like the purring of a large cat than that of human beings communicating with each other. By far, the most common greeting to Juame was, "Fáilte go hÉirinn," or, "Welcome to Ireland." Most, but not all of the pub clientel spoke at least some English.

The pub had only the basic provisions for comfort. The tables were rough-hewn and the top boards were not evenly matched. They had been oiled, likely so they would better repel the countless pints of lager that had been spilled across the surface. The chairs were not chairs at all, but rather stools and the flooring was better than the tabletops, but not by much. Hugh ordered a pint of ale and a bowl of stew for each of them, and said little until he had drained almost half of the mug of ale.

After, what seemed like hours to Juame, Hugh started the conversation: "Tomorrow, we will venture over to Christ Church Lane. I have arranged to meet with one of the barristers that have represented us over the years. He will be rather busy in the law courts, but has agreed to meet with us and go over the paperwork that you have with you and the agreements between your father and I."

While Juame was very young, he had a unique comportment and knowledge base that belied his age. As he listened to Red Hugh outline the relationship between the Castello and O'Brien families, he recalled his last few conversations with his father.

"I must ask you about slavery. I know that my family holdings in Spain have made use of this practice, and while I will no longer have anything to do with those holdings, I must know, do the interests I am now involved in here use slave labor?"

O'Brien thought for a moment and then responded, "Slavery as you know it is not used in our mines or other endeavors; however what is known as indentured service has been used, but is being phased out as we speak. The Slave Trade Act is a very controversial law and is constantly being challenged. I look for it to be abolished at some point in the near future, but you need not be concerned with that. I think your involvement in our mutual interests will be such as to not cause you concern."

CHAPTER THREE

Early the next morning, after a small breakfast, Juame and Hugh met with the barrister, and Juame's life was about to change drastically. Owing to his young age, there were certain legal concerns about his function, but a plan was made to use Juame as an agent; one that could easily travel between the various countries and arrange mutually positive agreements among various business concerns. Juame would also return to France for some advanced studies.

After the papers were processed and left with the barrister, two carriages, one with Hugh, Juame and a driver, the other with Juame's trunks and two employees, started the trip to County Mayo, near Kilkelly.

Juame found the Irish countryside to be beautiful. Even the mine, which was so much a part of his future, seemed to have an aura of good luck surrounding it. The blue of the sky was dazzling and the night sky was filled with the glitter of stars and planets. Juame found that his favorite constellation, Orion, was particularly dominant in the sky above County Mayo. All those things had their own type of beauty, but there was another Irish beauty that literally made his heart beat faster.

On the day Red Hugh and Juame arrived in Kilkelly, arrangements were made for Juame to take up residence in a local boarding house. Red Hugh left Juame to await his belongings and get settled. The men who delivered the trunks were then to escort Juame to the O'Brien home for a late dinner. Juame dismissed the drivers while he unpacked, leaving one especially well built flat top trunk locked and placed near the bed. He placed one of the lanterns atop the trunk where he could control it from the bed. After washing some of the road dirt from his body, he rejoined the hired men and headed for the O'Brien estate.

It was that evening that Juame first laid eyes on Anne O'Brien. It was also the first time he experienced that increased heartbeat, dry mouth and difficulty in taking a deep breath. He found himself almost speechless; a condition that was completely foreign to him.

As was proper, Hugh O'Brien first introduced his wife to Juame, but Juame was unaware of the Mrs. O'Brien even being in the room. He could not take his eyes off Anne. Anne was obviously about the same age as Juame. Her red hair hung just to the top of her shoulders, shoulders that were broad and straight, but certainly not masculine. Her upper body tapered perfectly to a slim waist and just swelled enough to her hips to accent her long legs. And then, there were her eyes. Juame thought surely that they were a captured reflection of the green rolling hills through which he had just traveled. He had never seen green eyes like hers. They were penetrating and glistened with an orneriness that Juame would not completely witness for several more years.

Red Hugh noted the reaction of his young business partner, but continued with the introductions. "Master Castello, may I also present my young daughter, Anne," he said, putting just a little extra emphasis on the words "Master" and "young."

"Tá áthas orm bualadh leat," Anne said, as she dropped her eyes.

"I think our young guest would prefer English," Hugh said, again giving just a little extra emphasis on the word "young."

"Of course," said Anne, this time making eye contact with Juame. "I am pleased to meet you. I pray you will enjoy your visit with us."

Again Juame became enthralled with those green eyes. He had to force himself to not stammer as he replied, "Thank you. I am sure I will. There is much for me to learn but your father has certainly been accomodating in that regard."

As everyone was invited to sit at the table, Hugh again noticed that the two teenagers seemed to have already made a non-verbal connection with each other. "I must not let this progress unchecked," he thought to himself.

After Juame left that evening, Hugh admonished, first his wife, and then his daughter. Reminding them that Juame was basically an intern and, although he represented the Castello and O'Brien business relationships, they would be well-advised to remember that.

Three months later, after a non-stop familiarization of the mine and of the various monetary considerations of the countries in which business was being conducted, Juame returned to France, where his first order of business was to bank the assets from his father's desk and provide himself with a stipend for everyday expenses. Anne was conspicuosly absent for Juame's departure.

CHAPTER FOUR

It was in France that Juame first learned of the war between the American colonies and Great Britain. He was becoming more and more aware that the world was changing, and that trade between nations was becoming a very important aspect of his life.

Not long after arriving in France Juame also learned that, almost one year earlier, France began sending supplies to America's Continental Army. The French economy was shakey at best and Juame's continuing education included warnings that, should France become directly involved in America's war for independence, the currency of the French, the livre, would likely suffer. The Spanish dollar, however remained a strong form of currency, being of very high grade silver. Juame had amassed a significant amount of the Spanish coinage and used the milled dollars to his advantage.

Because of various British blockades imposed in the harbors of North America, trade with the colonies was difficult, but France had their ways of dealing with the problem and many of the French merchants were taking advantage of the fact. Among those merchants was a well-respected, but devious, Antoine Riviere. Riviere was involved in the fur trade and had holdings in St. Louis. He was an adamant supporter of the revolution. It was during one of his trips back to France that he and Juame met through a mutual friend. Riviere encouraged Juame to go with him and join up with the Continental Army. Juame declined, but stayed in touch as much as possible with Riviere.

When Riviere offered to sell a piece of land near St. Louis to Juame, Juame had began to think more and more about the possibility of some day going to America. He accepted Riviere's offer, with the understanding that he would only pay a portion of the asked price and balance would be paid if, and when, Juame could establish that the offer was a legitimate one. The final decision was for Juame to pay Riviere one hundred dollars upon delivery of the signed agreement and another six hundred when Juame confirmed that he was not being cheated. Ultimately Juame became owner of a piece of land in America; a piece he had never seen.

Juame informed Red Hugh of his acquisition via a missive. While he only received a curt response from Hugh, a letter from Anne came as a surprise. She explained that she, too had been keeping abreast, as much as possible, with what was happening in America. She wrote, "It is so exciting to learn about America and I feel so privileged to know someone who may actually be going there." Juame again thought of those penetrating green eyes, and decided to begin communicating, not only with Hugh O'Brien, but with Hugh's beautiful daughter.

His years in France were tumultious. After nearly three years Juame became convinced that he was destined to go to America. The Colonies had basically succeeded in gaining their independence and Juame anticipated that the economic possibilities in the new nation could prove to be enormous, but first he must return to Ireland.

Upon arrival in Dublin, Juame was elated to learn that both Hugh O'Brien and Anne O'Brien were there to meet him. Juame greeted his business partner with a quick handshake and turned to Anne.

"It is so good to see you again, Miss O'Brien," Juame said.

"Ó, ar mhaithe le Dia," interjected Hugh in Irish, then switching to English, "For God's sake, do yee not think I have not been aware of the correspondence between you two? What is with this Miss O'Brien foolishness?

Juame welcomed the correction and felt a blush. "I am so happy to see you here, Anne," he said. All the while not losing eye contact.

Almost in a whisper, Anne said, "I insisted on coming along with father to meet you."

That day, while taking a break during the trip to Kilkelly, Juame asked Red Hugh if he could formally court Anne. While Hugh had some reservations he agreed, but added the rules on which his consent was based.

"The lass has been speaking of nothing but America for several months now. I will allow this courting, and well, would welcome you into our family, but you must agree to allow some time before whisking me daughter off to America. I am sure she would agree to marry you this very day if you told her you were bound for America. If you agree to let things progress slowly, I will give my blessing," Hugh said, in his best professional, business like manner.

Juame readily agreed to the terms. He then informed Anne of the conversation.

"I likely should have talked to you about something before I mentioned it to your father," Juame said. "I have asked your father's permission to be allowed to court you, with the intention of asking you to become my wife." Juame stopped short and could think of nothing else to say at the time. Anne responded with a smile that seemed to light up the carriage they were riding in.

"Well, are you asking me to marry you?"

"Yes, I guess I am."

"Then, Bí ag éirí leis, be getting on with it," she teased.

"Anne O'Brien, would you do me the honor of becoming my wife?"

"I shall," Anne replied, "But only if you promise to take me to America."

"Anne, your father has given us his blessing, but only if I do not, in his words, whisk you off to America. I have agreed to take it slow, but I do promise you that you and I will eventually end up in America."

With that, the courship began. It was nearly two years before Juame and Anne were married. Each time the subject of America was broached, Hugh found a reason to delay things. Time dragged on. Juame and Anne were living in Kilkelly, but they felt as if they had yet to establish a home. Early in the year of 1784 Anne gave birth to their son, Michael.

CHAPTER FIVE

At about the same time Michael Castello was born, a man named Harry Cort was working on a furnace that would prove to be a more efficient way to refine iron, and a family very close to the Castellos in Ireland welcomed a new baby daughter, Nancy McDonald, into their lives. Both of these seemingly unrelated events would prove to have great impacts on the Castello family.

Shortly after Michael was born, the subject of going to America came up once more at the dinner table. Juame looked lovingly at his wife as she held the baby to her breast.

"Your father and I have discussed the possibility of going to America. We have arranged a business agreement with a mining company in Pennsylvania," Juame said. "This would be a life-changing decision and we must approach it with caution," he continued.

"Juame, we now have a new baby. This decision should have been made two years ago. A trip such as this will be very difficult with a wee one still in swaddling," Anne replied, her bright green eyes tearing up as she spoke.

"That is precisely what I am talking about," Juame said. "I have proposed to your father that we arrange for someone to go to Pennsylvania and make some advance arrangements so that, when we arrive, we can settle quickly and begin a whole new life. It will take two years or more to make this plan work, but by then little Michael will be much more able to travel. It will still be difficult, but we can make it work."

One month later Juame and Hugh O'Brien sat in a small office with one of their most trusted employees. Eamon McDonald grew up in the company. He knew every aspect of the mining and processing. He could handle a pick and shovel one day and work the accounts and arrange payroll the next. Over the past several years Eamon became more and more confident and had a reputation of making difficult decisions that, more often than not, proved to be the right decisions. He was much more hesitant with the decision he was being asked to make now.

"What do you know of America?" O'Brien asked.

"I know that the colonists committed acts of treason and escaped the hangman's noose with a new country. I know that The Crown is not too happy with the fact that a neamh-eagraithe militia succeeded in defeating the great British Army. I know that there is said to be untold riches to be had in these new United States, and I know that someday I plan on helping myself to some of those riches. Why do you ask?"

O'Brien could not help but smile at Eamon's response. He folded his arms and rested them on the table, leaning just a little closer to Eamon.

"Our business interests have recently expanded to America, but communication with our associates there is very difficult. The missives we send are often not answered. Maybe they are not even delivered. If our words do reach the intended person it is often months before we have a reply in our hands. We have learned that a system of posting letters has been developed in Philadelphia, making it more likely that we can be assured of delivery, if the packet makes it to Pennsylvania in the first place," said O'Brien.

At that point Juame joined in and placed a bundled package upon the table. "What we propose is that you go to Pennsylvania and become our proxy for the dealings we have with a mining company that we are sure will become a great success. The information is somewhat overwhelming, but we have, in cooperation with our barrister, managed to assemble a reasonable description and proposals in this packet. We are asking that you peruse the contents of this bundle and consider the offer we are making."

O'Brien then interjected, "Time is of the essence. While we encourage you to thoroughly examine our proposal, we must ask that you give us an answer as soon as possible."

Eamon hesitated for a moment before reaching for the large package.

"Gombeannaí Dia," he said. "I have prayed for such an opportuntiy, but I must confess, this comes at a most inconvenient time. My wife has recently given birth to our daughter and my departure would not be a good thing. Would I be expected to take my family, or would I go alone? How long would I be gone?"

"I think you will find all the answers to your questions in these documents. It will be a life-changing decision and you must make it only after careful consideration and discussion with your wife," said Juame.

Over the next several days Eamon pondered over the massive information contained in the package. He was astounded by the preparations O'Brien and Castello had made. They seemed to have more knowledge about America than anyone he had ever known. The information about Pennsylvania was both overwhelming and enticing. It was obvious that the Irish mining industry had provided a link to the mining of both coal and iron in Pennsylvania. During those days he often sat at the table with his wife and read to her the accounts of the American industrialists, with whom his employers had evidently had extended relationships. Eamon's wife caught herself daydreaming as he silently read page after page. When he paused to read a passage to her, she could not resist a brief smile. She knew what his decision would be days before he himself knew.

Iron was the future and Eamon knew that its production was going to be the foundation on which a new nation would grow. Pennsylvania already had numerous iron making facilities, and they had the coal necessary to fire the huge furnaces. From the largest pieces of iron rail to the smallest carpenter's hammers, Pennsylvania was producing the base metal needed to manufacture a bright future.

CHAPTER SIX

The economy in Ireland showed signs of a decline and the tensions between the Catholics and the Protestants seemed to be escalating. There were rumors of entire families leaving, some as indentured workers with only one thing in mind: Go to America where they could experience religious freedom and take advantage of the possibility of owning their own property and making a decent home for their families.

Eamon McDonald was very aware of the problems that Ireland was facing and knew, without being told, that Juame Castello was very close to making the decision to leave Ireland himself. Eamon knew that the generous offer made to him was offered because Juame needed him to lead the way to America and he intended to do just that. The only question in his mind was whether he could make that decision without harming his wife and child. He needed to talk to Juame one more time before he decided once and for all. He arranged for a meeting and once again sat at a table with Juame Castello.

"Sir," he began. "Your offer to finance my trip to America is a most generous one. The proposal that I represent you honors me and I assure you I can carry out your wishes, but I must have answers to just a few more questions."

"By all means, put forward your questions," said Juame. "I will answer them to the best of my ability."

"When would I be expected to leave? asked Eamon.

Juame thought for just a moment before answering. "The trip is a long one, and once you arrive in Philadelphia, you will have a journey of more than 100 miles overland to the banks of the Susquehanna River, where you will be met by our representatives. The ideal time for your departure will be about three months from now."

"And, what of my family?"

"You are advised that the best thing is for you to go and get settled. We will arrange passage for your family when it is appropriate. Keep in mind that you may not be impressed with the United States and will just want to return to Ireland. Should that be the case, we will finance your return and you will stay in our employ for the time being, but my plans are to slowly remove myself from what I perceive to be many upcoming problems here in Ireland. I also have some interests near St. Louis, and may well turn my attention there. That remains to be seen," Juame said.

Eamon was somewhat surprised at the way his wife received the announcement of his decision. She appeared to be, not just in favor of relocating to America, but enthusiastic about it. She began acting as though the family would be leaving the next day. She flitted around the house like a newly emerged butterfly, touching everything just for a second, announcing what needed to go with them and what needed to be given away or sold.

"Slow down, woman," Eamon said at last. "They want me to leave in about three months. That gives us time to get prepared and organized for my departure. It saddens me, but you cannot leave with me. I must go on ahead and make the necessary arrangements for you and for Juame and Anne. Juame has promised me that he will make haste and that he will see to it that you and the child are provided safe passage to Pennsylvania. I caution you that the trip will be long and hard and you must plan on taking only the necessities. We will provide for the comforts once we are settled."

The remainder of the year passed slowly for all those involved in the plans to relocate. Ireland was showing more and more signs of conflict. The Irish Volunteers were resisting the British government more every day. The British Parliament was discussing a number of so-called reforms and there were a significant number of Irish leaders who feared that France could once again rise and attempt an invasion.

Finally, as the summer of 1787 was drawing to a close, Eamon began his journey to America. He had the bare necessities of comfort, all of which could be compressed into a pack sewn together by his wife. At the insistence of those advising him, a new pair of shoes was placed at the bottom of the pack. He was likely destined to do a lot of walking. After arriving at the Port of Philadelphia, Eamon, according to the information provided by his employers, faced a journey of over 100 miles to the edge of the Susquehanna River, and much of that might be on foot.

Eamon was pleasantly surprised that he could part with a small portion of some Spanish silver coins in his possession and procure a strong horse and necessary tack from a livery in Philadelphia. The gelding had been well fed and his grey coloring reminded Eamon of the right-hand horse that pulled the warrior Cu Cualinge's chariot as described in the Book of Leinstar. The price of the horse did not include a name so Eamon immediately dubbed the horse Sir Leinstar. The liveryman simply shrugged his shoulders. "Never did like the idea of hanging a moniker on a horse. Makes a man become too attached. Hell, if I named all my horses I would feel like a slave trader when I sold one. Now, get out of here and leave me to my work," he said.

"I will come by early in the morning to get Sir Leinstar," Eamon said. "I need to acquire the necessary supplies for my trip."

The next day Eamon visited a mercantile where he purchased what he anticipated needing for a three-day trip, including a fine .40 caliber Pennsylvania long rifle, a possibles bag, 100 balls, the necessary patching material and three pounds of black powder, along with other accessories.

He went to the livery, obtained a small sack of grain and paid the livery for the horse, tack and grain. He placed the new shoes in one saddlebag and some salted pork and pemmican in the other, leaving room in his pack for a small skillet and coffee pot. His pack and bedroll was secured behind the saddle and the long rifle found a home in a deerskin scabbard on the right side of Sir Leinstar. He studied the map provided to him before he left Ireland. He had mostly memorized the nuances of the map, but he felt better after referring to it one more time.

Judging by the time, the sun and the speed Sir Leinstar walked, Eamon estimated that he had progressed over 30 miles by the time he picked a small clearing near a stream for his first night. Prior to leaving

Philadelphia, Eamon had procured a breakfast at the rooming house. It had been his only food that day. The salt pork, some dry bread and a cup of coffee served as his dinner. There was plenty of grass for the horse and the small fire gave Eamon some comfort, but he realized that, for the first time in his life, he was truly alone.

Eamon had not fired a gun for nearly three years, and that was a worn-out musket that belonged to his father. He removed the long rifle from its leather scabbard and held it in his hands. It was a finely finished firearm and gave Eamon a certain sense of security, but he needed to become familiar with it.

After swabbing the barrel with a dry patch, Eamon, following the instructions given to him by the mercantile owner, carefully measured 40 grains of powder and poured it down the barrel. He then used a short-starter to force a ball and some patching material a short distance into the barrel. After trimming the patch he pushed the patch and ball down the barrel the length of the short-starter, then pushed it to the bottom of the barrel with the ramrod. After charging the pan with powder, the rifle was ready to be fired for the first time. Eamon picked out a small light colored rock on the steep bank on the opposite side of the creek, took careful aim, and fired the rifle. To his surprise and satisfaction the rock shattered. After two more shots Eamon was content with the accuracy. He cleaned the rifle, loaded the barrel with another round, and slipped the unprimed rifle back into its scabbard.

Early the next morning, after some coffee, Eamon once again started his journey. He was pleasantly surprised to find a well-traveled trail that led him in the direction he wanted. It was obvious that someone had hauled trees that had been harvested from the dense forest on both sides of the trail. The further he travelled the more pronounced the trail became. As the sun was just past its peak Eamon was able to shoot a blue grouse that stood just a few yards from the trail. While he was plucking the feathers from the bird he heard some noise in the trees not far from where he had tied his horse. He returned to Sir Leinstar, reloaded the rifle and silently worked his way on foot through the trees toward the noise.

He circled the area for nearly an hour before deciding that he probably was letting his imagination run wild. He returned to Sir

Leinstar and removed the saddle and bedroll, deciding that he was hungry and would call it a day. As the sun began its trip through the afternoon sky, Eamon started a fire and was engrossed in roasting the grouse on a makeshift spit when he heard another sound, this time behind him. His rifle was leaning against a log, just out of reach. As he made a lunge for the rifle, he became aware of the fact that he was not alone. Standing less than 20 feet behind him was a tall, muscular Indian.

In perfect English, the Indian said, "Please do not get excited. I am not here to harm you. The Indian held up a handful of mockernut hickory leaves, together with some dandelion leaves. He continued, "I heard you shoot and watched you remove the feathers from the bird. You can add these leaves to your fire and help the taste of the bird."

Eamon relaxed. "I would welcome your advice and ask that you share my dinner," Eamon said. "I am Eamon. What are you called?"

The Indian slowly moved to the opposite side of the fire. "I am called Shikwine. I am of the Lenape, but I was long ago accepted into the family known as O'Conley. They raised me as their own. I have only a faint memory of my family, but thanks to others of my kind with whom I have become acquainted with, I have retained and learned more of my heritage and my Lenape language. I do know that my people know that bird as tepahtuiyok," he said pointing at the plucked grouse, "In English that means stupid."

"Put your branches on the fire and seat yourself. We will make a small feast of this stupid bird," Eamon said with a chuckle.

"I am honored to be your guest. My horse is hobbled nearby. I will go get him and return to your fire." With that Shikwine turned and walked into the woods.

CHAPTER SEVEN

Eamon was immediately comfortable in the company of Shikwine. He raked some of the hot coals of the fire to the side and fashioned a spit of two forked branches and a long skewer. When Shikwine returned with the horse, Eamon slipped the bird onto the skewer and placed it above the hot coals. He then assisted Shikwine in staking the horses in a small grassy area nearby. Eamon gave both horses a small amount of the grain.

"You will spoil my horse," Shikwine said jokingly. "He is not accustomed to such pampering."

"He is a beautiful horse, but I notice you have no saddle. I fear I would simply fall off without the stirrups to balance me," said Eamon.

"This horse has never been introduced to the saddle or mouth bit. I have other horses at my family's home. Some of them may be saddled at times, but this one, whom I call Xinkwchal, has never been ridden with anything but a bridle and blanket. I have fashioned a small pouch on one side of the blanket for my ball and powder and another longer one on the other side for my rifle," Shikwine explained. "The name, Xinkwchal, in English means 'big nose.' I use this horse when I am traveling because he smells things others do not. He has often warned me and aided me in avoiding danger. Others, including men, might have the sense of smell, but Xinkwchal seems to know how to use it effectively."

As the two sat near the fire, Eamon knew in his heart that they were destined to become friends. He sensed that Shikwine was an honest man and was convinced when Shikwine took his first serving of the roasted grouse, held it upon a square of leather and raised it up while obviously saying a prayer. Eamon too offered his thanks to God before they started eating. He wondered if all the native people were like Shikwine, or did he just have the good fortune of being in the company of a unique man?

"I noticed that you prayed before partaking of our meal," Eamon said. "Are your prayers the result of you being raised by a Christian family?"

"Your question can be answered with both a yes and a no. My people, the Lenape, believe in an almighty creator of the heavens and the earth. The Lenape believe that the earth provides for us in the way of meats from the animals and the goodness of the things that grow from the soil. It is unfortunate that not many of us remain, but those who do, know that most white men also believe in the Creator. I have never fully understood my adopted family's belief in Christ, but I understand why they believe the way they do." Shikwine explained.

Eamon pressed for more information. "Tell me more of your people and how you became to be raised by an Irish family. I assume by the name, O'Conely, that they are Irish."

Shikwine smiled and replied, "Yes the O'Conelys are from Ireland. They are well respected in this entire territory and most of the Lenape, who are better known to the whites as the Delaware, consider the O'Conelys as friends, but others condemn them for violating the earth. I have been part of both their family and the people of my Lenape ancestors."

"What do you mean violating the earth?" Eamon asked.

Shikwine continued, "This trail you follow was once only a game trail used by deer. Those from Europe came into the area and began cutting down the trees, first for their homes, and later to fire their large furnaces used for the making of iron. They are now digging deep into the earth to take the black fire rock and iron from those diggings."

"The Lenape people have been in this area for thousands of years. They called themselves Lenni-Lenape, which translates in English to mean Original People. They survived by using what the Creator made available to them, and many believe that this digging for iron and coal violates what the Creator intended and there is also the belief that the people who came into our lands brought with them curses in the form of diseases never before seen by the Lenape. It was one of those diseases, called smallpox, that killed most of my original family and resulted in my adoption by the O'Conely family."

Eamon listened intently, interrupting his attention only to add another stick or two to the fire, as Shikwine continued: "I have spent the past years learning of my heritage and trying to renew the trust that the whites and my people once had. Many years ago, the man you know as Penn sat with my forefathers at Shackamaxon and agreed to allow each other to exist. The whites know the agreement as the William Penn Treaty. Simply said, my people call it the peace agreement. The elders known to me tell me that the treaty was to last as long as the rivers run, the sun rises, and all the stars of the Creator shine, but that has not been the case. Many of the whites have violated the agreement, and so too have those of my people. I hope to someday mend the wrongs of both sides."

Shikwine then added more wood to the fire and squatted close where the fire lit up the ground. "I talked of the trail you follow. I must now reveal my reason for being here. You have very limited knowledge of where you are. Am I correct?"

"I have maps, which were provided by my employer and I am following them closely," replied Eamon.

"And, those maps are supposed to lead you to a rendezvous with your friends near the big river?"

"Yes, that is true," Eamon, said, somewhat surprised at the question. "How do you know of this?"

Shikwine smiled and replied, "The O'Conelys are friends and business partners with those who work the mines and the people you were sent to meet at the Susquehanna. I was sent to find you and safely guide you to your destination. It is good that I found you when I did, because you have taken the wrong trail and your travel on this path will not get you where you want to be. I did not tell you this before because I wanted to visit with you and determine if you could be trusted. I believe that we are destined to become friends and I will, at the dawn, lead you to the rendezvous with your people."

CHAPTER EIGHT

With Shikwine guiding the way, the new friends arrived at the Susquehanna on their second day of travel and met with the Castello business partners late that afternoon. Eamon learned that Shikwine performed other duties for the mining companies, one of which was to deliver and pick up missives in Philadelphia. The Pennsylvanians had developed a remarkably efficient means of receipt and delivery system for letters and small packages. Eamon immediately penned a letter to his wife and to Juame, telling of his safe arrival and the trust he had in his new friend.

It was six months before Eamon received a reply. By that time, Eamon had established himself in a small borough called Wyoming on the bank of the Susquehanna River and near the mining enterprises of the Wyoming Valley. Everything was seemingly going right, but Eamon yearned for his wife and child. It was another three months before he heard from his wife. She wrote of her loneliness and begged Eamon to do what he could to arrange for her and young Nancy to go to America. About that same time, Eamon received a missive from Juame advising that arrangements were being made, and that it was likely that Eamon would see his wife before he and Juame would see each other.

While immigration was constant, there was a significant drop in the numbers of persons entering the United States through Philadelphia. More and more, the New York harbor was the entry point for those seeking a life in America. The winter of 1789 was harsh. Eamon had been in America for nearly two years. His daughter was five years old and he was entering into a deep depression over the fact that he had not been with his wife and daughter. The spring of 1790 brought good news, along with some information that troubled Eamon. An American gentleman, hired by Juame was escorting his wife and daughter to America, but they were going to land in New York. Their journey was to continue in a stagecoach reputed to make the trip from New York to Philadelphia in three days. Eamon and Shikwine were to meet them and bring them to their new home.

Ryleigh McDonald had the perfect name as far as Eamon was concerned. In Irish folklore the name denoted a courageous person. Her parents must have recognized that trait immediately. When she and Eamon married, it was not without problems, but Ryleigh pushed back against every attempt to prevent her from spending her life with the only person she had really loved. She had other potential suitors, some of which her parents preferred over Eamon. As a young woman, she was not strikingly beautiful, but her demeanor was intoxicating; her smile was one that made others smile as well. She was strong and eagerly prepared to make a new life in America. When she and her daughter boarded the ship with her new bodyguard and guide, she at once became one of the more popular passengers. Everyone seemed to gravitate toward her and they seemed to always leave her company with a smile on their face. During the long journey to New York Ryleigh often renewed the spirits of others and made their trip a little less stressful. Her escort, whom she knew only as Phillipe, was obviously a well-traveled man. Having been born in Illinois, he was a citizen of the United States and the Castello family knew his father. Those few facts, along with the fact that he was constantly by her side and displayed a true affection for young Nancy, was about all Ryleigh knew of Phillipe. The trip to New York took just over 30 days and Ryleigh had often tried to learn more, but Phillipe avoided any conversation that would reveal the details of his life.

New regulations relating to immigrants to the United States were confusing to Ryleigh, but Phillipe's status as a citizen made the process relatively easy, although Ryleigh was concerned that some of the people involved seemed to think that Ryleigh and Phillipe were man and wife, and Phillipe did nothing to dispel the assumptions.

Once through the immigration process, Phillipe arranged for a carriage to take them to a hotel, where they would spend one night and have a luxurious meal. As the carriage worked its way through the streets, Ryleigh was amazed at the number of street vendors lining both sides of the streets. She saw evidence of large amounts of produce, fowl and fish products being sold. Ryleigh hugged little Nancy and whispered into her ear, "We have truly arrived in the land of opportunity."

At the hotel, Phillipe acquired two rooms and informed the clerk that they would require arrangements for baths in the rooms before they went to the dining room that evening. The bath, while simple, was as far as Ryleigh was concerned, an absolute luxury. She felt as if the stench of bodily odors and the staleness of the ship were magically replaced with the smell of fresh soap. She could sense the joy of the bath being experienced by her daughter.

Ryleigh and Nancy met Phillipe in the large dining room. Nancy ran to Phillipe and hugged him saying in her best English, "Thank you for bringing us to this wonderful place."

That evening they dined on beefsteaks and a side dish of fresh oysters. Ryleigh, having never eaten oysters, was reluctant to try them, but soon determined that Nancy and Phillipe would eat them all if she didn't take a couple soon. The texture was foreign to her palate and she declared that oysters would not be common in her kitchen. Phillipe assured her that obtaining oysters was not something possible from the waters of the Susquehanna River. The beef, however, was becoming more and more popular and replacing the wild game meat. After a fitful sleep in a down-filled bed, the trio once again met in the dining room for coffee and pastries. They once again hired a carriage to deliver them and their luggage to the coach station. One hour later they were in a stagecoach and headed for Philadelphia. Ryleigh found herself talking almost constantly to Nancy, recalling every description she could recall from Eamon's letters, and telling Nancy how lucky they were to be on course to becoming true Americans. In three days they would be re-united with Eamon, and in one week's time, they would be at their new home. Nancy bounced up and down in her seat with joy, her anticipation showing as she stared out the window of the coach. Every few minutes she asked, "How much further now, Mother?"

The stagecoach was becoming a staple in the new country, but the roads were just beginning to see improvements. The ride was, in Nancy's words, "bouncy." The coach stopped every ten miles to replace the four horses with fresh ones. During some of the stops, privies and refreshments were available, but the ride soon became tiring. Ryleigh looked forward to each stop so she could climb out of the coach and stretch her body. When they stopped at the station where they spent the first night, Ryleigh and Nancy fell into the bed totally exhausted. The bed was nowhere close to the comfort of that in the hotel, but it felt like a cloud under their shaken bodies. She reminded Nancy that they would have one more overnight stop and reach Philadelphia on the third day.

At mid day on the third day of the journey Philadelphia came into view. Ryleigh marveled at the number of buildings, most with a plume of smoke rising from their rooftops. The city was much larger than she expected. Phillipe explained that there were more than 40,000 people living in and around Philadelphia and that it was the center of government for the young nation.

As the stage pulled to a stop Ryleigh noticed a large group of people gathered at the window of the nearby Federal Gazette newspaper building, but her attention was quickly diverted when she recognized Eamon standing at the platform. She stepped down from the stagecoach as soon as it stopped and literally jumped into his arms. Nancy also left the stagecoach without assistance by turning on her belly and sliding to the platform. The three embraced each other. Tears were streaming down Ryleigh's face and Nancy was jumping up and down. The luggage was being transferred to a heavy wagon nearby when the reunited family finally calmed.

"What is happening across the street?" Ryleigh asked.

"It is a sad time for Philadelphia and the country," Eamon explained. "Ben Franklin died yesterday, the 17th of April. The Gazette has posted in their window the page announcing the death and giving a synopsis of his life. He was a great statesman and had much to do with the establishment of this nation. He will be missed."

Eamon and Phillipe had a short conversation, and then Phillipe kissed Ryleigh's hand and gave Nancy a hug as he helped her into the wagon next to her mother. As Eamon slapped the reins to start the horses moving, Ryleigh said, "Phillipe is such a gentleman. He was very attentive and Nancy just loves him. Why was he chosen to accompany us?"

"Phillipe is the son of Antoine Riviere, who sold some land near St. Louis to Juame several years ago. He is going back to St. Louis. Juame made all the arrangements and I believe it is Juame's intention to someday soon go to St. Louis to see the land. Her curiosity satisfied, she held her arm around Nancy and settled in for another three days of travel.

CHAPTER NINE

Eamon and Ryleigh were barely settled in and becoming used to being together once again when Eamon received word that Juame and Anne Castello were en route. Eamon was instructed to make ready the small house that was built for the Castello family. The house was located nearby and Eamon and Ryleigh made short order of preparing it.

As Christmas approached and the decade was coming to a close, Eamon and Juame spent most of their time managing and improving the growing iron industry in Pennsylvania. The waning decade brought many significant changes to the young country. The District of Columbia was established in 1790, mostly as a result of the nation's slavery stance. The Continental Congress, on July 16 of that year passed the Residence Act, which according to many, was an effort to appease the pro-slavery states who feared that maintaining the capitol in Philadelphia showed a bias to a state that was too far north and sympathetic to those advocating the abolition of slavery.

Juame was adamant in his opposition of slavery. He failed to understand how one person could own another. His conversation at the dinner table one night aired one of his concerns.

"Anne, I have told you before of my dealings with Antoine Riviere. There are some things that I must discuss with you, and with my business associates," he said.

Anne placed her hand on top of Juame's and replied, "My dearest Juame, you have made me a very happy woman by bringing me to this new nation, but I have discerned in the past weeks that something is bothering you. Pray tell me what it is."

Juame sat quietly for a moment and then said, "This news of the pending move of the nation's capitol bothers me in two ways. First the reason for this move, as conveyed to me by our solicitor is shrouded in the shame of slavery. It moves my heart that this nation of freedom is tarnished with the cruelty of forcing a human being to serve another human in this manner. That brings me back to my dealings with Riviere. Some time back, and I will not get into the details of why; I purchased a piece of land from Riviere. I anticipated that being a landowner in a newly forming nation would allow me the freedom to come here and give my family new opportunities. The iron industry dictated that I come to America and to this place. That is not what I originally planned. My intention was to go to the land many miles south of here and make my home near the great river that divides America from lands controlled by France. My missives to and from Mr. Riviere led me to believe that America would expand to the west of the Mississippi River.

"You have spoken of this land before," replied Anne.

Again, Juame hesitated and then said, "I know I have, but circumstances are changing rapidly here and that causes my second concern. A man named Thomas Jefferson is now the Secretary of State. He is adamant in his belief that the United States should expand to the west as much as possible. It is very likely that Mr. Jefferson will some day be president. If that happens it could be that his expansion will include the land that was granted to Riviere by France and then sold to me. I do not know if Mr. Jefferson, or any other president for that matter, will honor my ownership. Jefferson's relationship to France gives me hope, but I must stay informed in this matter because I still intend to some day go to the Missouri Territory."

As the thought of becoming part of America's expansion continued to dictate many of Juame's decisions, he called upon his solicitor and confided his status and concerns. The solicitor agreed that title to the property in the Missouri Territory may or may not remain under the control of Juame and his family. He also encouraged Juame to draft the necessary documents to pass his estate, including the Missouri property to his only heir, Michael, who was not yet seven years old. Juame, with the assistance of his solicitor, prepared a will but purposely left some loopholes. Should he pass before Michael came of age, his holdings would be held in trust under the guidance of Eamon McDonald until such age was reached. Meanwhile, Juame continued to control and expand the iron industry in Pennsylvania. More and more canals were being built to divert water to the crops and many of the canal companies began to use rails and horse drawn machinery along those canals. Both the rails and the machinery provided significant profits to the Castello holdings.

On March 4, 1793, President Washington was sworn in for his second term. He gave a short speech, which was printed verbatim in several newspapers. Juame, within a few days of the event, sat at his evening meal with the latest copy of the *Gazette* and read the words of the president. He conveyed his impressions to Anne, saying, "This address given by President Washington contains less than 150 words, and yet it says so much about the man and what this new nation requires of it leaders. Listen to what he said about his responsibilities. '*Previous to the execution of any official act of the President, the Constitution requires an oath of office. This oath I am now about to take, and in your presence: That if it should be found during my administration of the Government I have in any instance violated willingly or knowingly the injunctions thereof, I may (besides incurring constitutional punishment) be subject to the upbraidings of all who are now witnesses of the present solemn ceremony.*'"

Anne could see the sincerity in Juame's eyes and hear it in his voice. "My dear husband, I see that you are happy to be here in America, but I also see that other things are bothering you. Pray tell be what things make you toss and turn in your sleep and lose yourself in thought."

Juame knew his wife was right, but he chose not to answer. He rose from the table and retired to the small desk in the corner of the room. He lit the lamp, procured pen and paper from the drawer and began to write. He did not divulge what he had written. He placed the page into an envelope and sealed it with his personal wax seal. On the outside of the envelope he wrote the simple statement: To Be Opened Only Upon My Death, J. Castello.

During the next year Juame became almost obsessed with the politics of the United States, but was often frustrated over the fact that information was scant, especially when it came to the Senate. Shortly after Washington started his second term, the Pennsylvania legislature appointed Albert Gallatin to be their senator. Juame and his business associates were concerned about the appointment of Gallatin, largely because of his economic beliefs and his opposition to the policies of Alexander Hamilton, but Juame was not sure that Gallatin was all that bad. He wanted more information.

Juame learned from the *Gazette* that the controversy over Gallatin had resulted in the Senate changing their closed door policy and that the Senate would be open to the public for the 1794 session. During a subsequent meeting with some of the business partners Juame stood in front of the group and told them of the new policy: "I believe that, as industrialists and investors in this new nation, we must be more involved in the political actions taken by those now seated in Philadelphia. The Senate, which until now has met in secret, will now be open to the public. I intend on being there and encouraging those in charge of the presses to be more active in reporting what happens at these sessions."

Ignoring the bitter February cold, both Juame and Anne traveled to Philadelphia, Juame to attend the first day of the senate session and Anne to explore the newest clothing designs. Michael, now nearly ten years old, was left at home in the care of a young woman whom had functioned as his tutor for the last four years. Anne was at first reluctant to leave the boy at home, but soon admitted the advantage of having his already above average reading, writing and mathematics skills further advanced during her absence. Juame expressed no misgivings about the arrangement.

On the morning of February 11, 1794, Juame Castello sat in the gallery of the United States Senate, and for the first time, really began to understand the amazing dynamics of the government. He was to talk about that day many times over the next years.

CHAPTER TEN

Over the next year Juame became more and more concerned. A major concern was the state of affairs in Ireland, where he still maintained a significant investment in the production of iron ore. The year brought many Irish immigrants to America and many of them came seeking work in the Wyoming Valley. Those immigrants brought with them the stories of increased unrest. The few French immigrants also seemed full of doom and gloom.

"Based on my communications with our friends in Ireland and those in France and with Phillipe, it seems that every country in Europe is either in rebellion, or contemplating some sort of rebellion or invasion," Juame said, stating the obvious to his business associates during a meeting held at a local pub.

The meeting was called specifically to discuss the holdings in Ireland. The consensus was that the Castello group should divest its interest in the Irish holding as quickly as possible. A missive was prepared and sent to the necessary people in Ireland shortly after Christmas of 1794.

By the spring of 1795 Juame was more convinced than ever that the holdings in Ireland were in jeopardy and he was frustrated with the lack of action on the part of those who were entrusted with managing those holdings. He knew he would likely have to travel back to Ireland and was in the midst of planning a trip when Phillipe Riviere showed up unexpected. He rode up to the front of the Castello home in a travel carriage. He was alone, but had obviously loaded the carriage with ample provisions and equipment for a long trip.

"Phillipe, what brings you to our home?" Juame asked as he stepped out onto the porch.

"I come for many reasons," Phillipe replied. He stepped down from the carriage and grasped Juame's extended hand. "I bring well wishes from my father and others in St. Ferdinand, Phillipe" said.

"Well, I welcome you and eagerly await a conversation, but first you must come into the house and join me in a dram. I have just received some of the best usce beatha from the Old Bushmills Distillery," Juame said as he stepped to the door, holding it open for Phillipe.

"Aye, usce beatha, the water of life. It has been a time since I have heard any of the Irish words spoken to me, and it has been just as long since I have savored the taste of a good distilled spirit." With that, Phillipe stepped inside and was followed by Juame, who went directly to the cabinet and obtained two glasses and a bottle of the famous Irish whiskey. After each took a small sip of whiskey from their glass, Juame placed both hands on the table, palms down, as if he needed to prevent the table from floating away. He stared directly in Phillipe's eyes and waited. Phillipe diverted his gaze for a brief moment, and then took a deep breath.

"My father has just recently attained the age of 50 years" Phillipe began. "While he is still in generally good health, he has informed me that he wished to guarantee that his legacy and fortune is properly looked after, should he suddenly be called to heaven. He has confided in me that his service in the revolution, the battle that took place in St. Louis and his capture and subsequent escape took a toll on both his body and his mind."

"And why does this mandate bring you to my home?" Juame inquired.

Phillipe took another sip of whiskey and replied, "You and my father had some business dealing some years back. He wishes to speak with you and convey information that he believes only a one-on-one conversation can accomplish. He has asked that I beseech you to accompany me to St. Ferdinand and meet with him."

"I must tell you," Juame said, "much of what you speak of has been in my thoughts almost constantly for the past months. Not only do I wish to speak with Antoine, I fear I will have to travel to Ireland in the near future. I confess I do not look forward to either trip, and the fact is that the 900 miles you are asking me to travel with you will likely be much more difficult than a trip to Ireland."

As Juame and Phillipe continued their conversation, Anne and Michael entered the room. Michael, now 11 years old, stood closely beside his father and looked at Phillipe, as if expecting Phillipe to acknowledge him.

"You have grown to be a strapping young man," Phillipe said, finally.

"Thank you," said Michael. "I am almost as tall as father."

"Yes you are, and I hope you will someday be able to also fill his shoes," Phillipe replied.

Michael seemed somewhat confused by the statement and looked down at his feet, obviously comparing them to those of his father.

Anne interrupted: "You have some chores to complete before darkness makes them difficult young man," she said. Then directing her attention to Phillipe she asked, "You will be dining with us this evening, I assume?"

Juame answered for Phillipe. "Yes of course our friend will take supper with us and he is also encouraged to share Michael's bed chamber."

After their meal, Juame and Phillipe continued their conversations. Juame asked Anne and Michael to join them. He directed his attention first to Anne.

"I have decided that I will accompany Phillipe to a place that the French refer to as Fleurissant, located near St. Louis. Phillipe's father, Antoine Riviere transferred part of a land grant to me in that place. The Spaniards have since called the place St. Ferdinand. It may be that my ownership of the land will be invalidated. The only way I can assert my claim is to go with Phillipe." He then turned his attention to Michael. "I do this for your future. It is my prayer that you will someday be able to go to this land and make a home there. I believe this nation is destined to expand beyond our imaginations, and I hope and pray you will be a part of that growth, but first I must ask you to act beyond your years and take charge of this household while I am gone. Can you do that?"

Michael smiled and nodded with obvious enthusiasm. Two days later Juame and Phillipe were en route to St. Louis. Among Juame's possessions packed for the trip was a single piece of parchment paper; the only record of his purchase of the land near St. Louis. Since the purchase, a family who farmed it had occupied the land; sharing what meager income they obtained with Juame.

CHAPTER ELEVEN

Over a month passed before Juame and Antoine met in a small meeting room in the St. Ferdinand church. Their last meeting had been in France many years ago. It was during the France meeting that Antoine sold the parcel of land in what was now the Missouri Territory.

The two men first talked in a mixture of French and English, then settled on English.

"As you instructed, I have with me the document you signed regarding the land," Juame said. "I must say the intrigue has been with me since Phillipe requested that I meet you here. What, pray tell, is the sudden urgency?"

Antoine began talking. "Please allow me the privilege of relating to you what brings us together. As you are aware, I chose to stand with the revolutionaries during the war with England. My only real battle experience was with the San Luis Militia at the Battle of St. Louis. I believe that victory will ultimately prove to be a keystone in the expansion of the United States. I was captured during that battle and taken to a prison in Illinois. The British proved to be poor jailors and I managed to escape and return to St. Louis. I have since gained the respect of many people. I know that makes me sound pompous, but it is a fact."

"Our correspondence with you and with the family that occupies the land I am here to talk about has proven that you have some significant influence in this area," Juame said.

"That may be so," Antoine continued, "but I have also amassed a certain amount of detractors, some of whom have blocked a declaration of citizenship. There are those who want to declare the land transactions such as this one null and void. The fact that France turned this territory over to Spain only complicates the matter at hand. Many of these transactions were made only through oral arrangements and no bona fide record exists. Our business on the other hand is sealed with the document you have with you."

At that point Antoine retrieved the parchment from his satchel and placed it on the table between them. They discussed how things have changed since they first made the agreement. At that time France controlled the land where the property was located. Spain now controlled the region, but Antoine said he had reliable information that the current situation could change at any time. Juame looked at the document, which had been written in French, but the amounts noted were in terms of the Spanish dollar. The Spanish milled dollar was commonly used because of the consistency of silver in the coin. It could easily be cut into pieces to satisfy debts in any amount. Juame smiled at the amount written in an eloquent French hand: "Cent dollars en main et six cents dollars à payer plus tard." In English the phrase was "One hundred dollars in hand and six hundred dollars to be paid later." Juame recalled that part of the six hundred dollars was paid to Antoine in the form of shaven deer hides provided by the people he allowed to use and live on the property. He reminded Antoine of the arrangement.

"I remember it well," Antoine said. "My payment actually came from Manuel Lisa, who is an upcoming fur trader. Your tenants gave the hides to him and he, in turn, paid me, but we now have to take the next step. I have contacts in France and in Spain and my association with the American government is significant. I propose that we make an official record of this transaction, both to enhance your chances of maintaining ownership and to help me in other ventures."

Antoine went on to describe what action he would take and why he thought those actions necessary.

"I think there is a good chance that France will again gain control of this area. I also think it is very possible that proposals being made by Thomas Jefferson may lead to America getting that control. I have at my disposal the minds of two barristers, both of whom will guide me in these actions and decisions. I must ask you to trust me. Your trust will prove, I think, a benefit to us both.

After several days of meeting with the barristers and recording the various documents, Antoine and Juame parted company. Juame began the long journey back to Pennsylvania, where he knew he would find more problems to solve.

Upon his return to the Wyoming Valley in Pennsylvania, Juame was pleasantly surprised to find that things were in relatively good order. His biggest surprise was the maturity achieved by his young son. Michael was not yet a teenager, but he sat with Juame and Anne during many discussions and participated as if he were much older.

"Father," Michael asked during one of the after-dinner discussions, "I have read in the newspapers that there is considerable problems developing in Ireland. Some of my friends, who are also from Ireland and are older than I, are saying that it is likely that a rebellion is in the making. What will happen to our holdings there, should that occur?"

Juame sat back in his chair, the surprise and pride showing on his face. He smiled and replied, "Son, your grasp of knowledge belies your years of life. It is true that problems are present in Ireland. It is also true that our family has some significant investments in Ireland, but those concerns are being addressed. It takes time. Communications are very slow. You need not be concerned."

Michael was not satisfied. "But Father, Nancy says that her father has said that we may be returning to Ireland. Is that true?"

"Eamon McDonald has acted on my behalf during my recent absence, and he has performed well, but maybe I should caution him about discussing business in the presence of children," Juame replied.

"But Father, is it true? Are we going to Ireland? Will I be required to leave Nancy and my other friends?'

Again Juame was impressed by the maturity of his son and decided to explain as much as possible.

"Michael, I have no intention on taking my family back to Ireland. Circumstances there, as near as I can determine, are not good and are getting worse. That being said, Eamon and I have discussed the fact that I may have to go to Ireland, but I will go only to finalize some business there and will stay only as long as necessary. Final decisions are yet to be made. We are awaiting further communication from the solicitors in Ireland."

As Juame and Michael carried on their discussion, Anne sat quietly and listened to the exchange. She finally decided to join in.

"Husband, you tell your son that Eamon should not discuss business in the presence of his children, and then you go on to do the exact thing you expressed concern over. Michael and his friends, especially Nancy McDonald, study together and attend church together and that became even more a fact during your absence. They are bound to breach these limits of discussion at some point, after all, they are still children."

Later that evening Anne pressed Juame for more information.

"I know that you and your associates do not believe in women being involved in business, but your activities have a direct influence on how our family and the many families dependent on the Castello holdings live. I do not cherish the idea of our returning to Ireland, nor do I wish for another separation if you should choose to go. I think I am entitled to be kept abreast of your plans."

Juame responded, "You are right, and I will try to keep you informed, but the fact is that my plans change constantly. As for me leaving you alone, a certain amount of that is inevitable. I know now that I must go to Philadelphia and meet with our barristers there. I will leave within the fortnight, but I shall be gone for only a few days. It is these meetings that will have a bearing on my future plans."

Anne replied, "Could you not arrange for one of these barristers to go to Ireland on your behalf?"

"That may be a possibility," Juame said. "But I need to know how much authority I can give to a representative. My inclination now is to divest entirely. Ireland is in turmoil and procrastination might well prove to be fatal to our business interests."

Juame's trip to Philadelphia and his meeting with the barristers resulted in his return home with some positive ideas. He was still convinced he may have to return to Ireland, but expressed his belief that the trip was not something he had to accomplish with any haste.

Many of the Castello employees in Ireland became members of a republican revolutionary group being called the Society of United Irishmen. Juame learned from his barristers that many smaller revolutionary groups had recently aligned themselves with the United Irishmen, making the organization stronger than ever. There was increasing hostility against the British government. He also learned that the lack of timely information from Ireland was largely due to the British Insurrection Act and the fact that British General Gerard Lake had confiscated the private arms of many Irishmen and had suppressed the *Northern Star*, a newspaper that was sympathetic to the society.

In the early months of 1798 Juame was forced to make a decision. A winter trip to Ireland was not going to be easy, but he knew he had to go. He arrived in Ireland in March of that year. The trip had been extremely difficult and Juame had a severe lung infection by the time he arrived.

By the time Juame had divested the Castello holdings, he was mostly bedridden and not improving. The British arrested many of the persons who became owners of the properties early in the spring. Juame arranged for the funds he accumulated through various transactions to be forwarded to the Bank of Pennsylvania. Less than one week later, on May 24, 1798 an all-out rebellion started. Before the end of the month Juame went to his bed for the last time. His consumption claimed his life during a very cold night. He was only 38 years old.

CHAPTER TWELVE

Michael Castello, at the young age of only 14, found himself in a situation that he was having a difficult time dealing with. With his father dead he was being expected to understand things that should be left to adults. He was too young to make legal decisions and yet expected to understand the decisions that were being made by others. Within weeks of being told of his father's death in Ireland, he was seated at the table in the McDonald home with his mother and Eamon McDonald.

Eamon began by explaining exactly why Juame went to Ireland. "Michael, your father was blessed with an ability to look beyond what the day was holding and plan for the future. As long as I have known him, I have been in awe of that ability. He anticipated the trouble in Ireland and knew for some time that he needed to divest his holdings there. He and I had a trust between us that few men will understand and he often confided in me. Years before we came to America, I knew that your father was planning on doing just that. When he entrusted me to come here and begin preparations, I had little doubt that I was doing the right thing by accepting that challenge because I knew that he would not forego the dreams he had created in both my family and his. America is the future and we are a significant part of what is happening here."

Michael could only nod. His head hung low. He was still mourning the loss of his father and could barely hold back the tears. He knew if he looked up and caught the eyes of his mother they would both give into their continued grief and the tears would be held back no longer.

Men did not cry and he was being forced to be a man. There had been no traditional funeral for his father. Juame was laid to rest in Ireland. A service of sorts was held at the local church, but it had left Michael with the feeling that life had betrayed both he and his mother.

"Not so long ago, your father divulged still another of his dreams to me," Eamon continued. "Juame developed many friendships and acquaintances over the years. One of those persons was Antoine Riviere who, among many other accomplishments, was instrumental in the founding of St. Louis in the Missouri Territory. When your father went to St. Louis some time back, it was to meet with Mr. Riviere and firm up the ownership of a piece of land there. Your father's intention was to someday expand his holdings by involving himself in the iron and lead mining future in the Missouri Territory. Mr. Riviere, many years back sold your father a piece of land there. The circumstances are complicated, but suffice it to say that I hold the documentation and control of that Missouri land with instructions that it be given to you when you reach legal age."

"What is legal age?" Michael asked.

"That is why I have asked you here today," continued Eamon. "There have been recent decisions on the part of government officials that indicate that you can become a landowner at your age if your father saw fit to leave the property to you in his final will and testament. The law also recognizes that, when a man dies, his property becomes the property of his heir, regardless of age. I have arranged for the barristers that represent our holdings to meet with you and make the necessary arrangements. You are about to become a significant land owner here in Pennsylvania as well as in the Missouri Territory, assuming that title of the Missouri property is validated."

"But how will I...? Michael started to ask. Eamon interrupted:

"There are many questions I cannot answer. The legal ramifications are many and only those trained in the law will be able to answer. Your father requested that I oversee his estate but we will have to determine to what extent when we meet with the barristers. For now please help yourself to some tea and biscuits. I must return to my other duties." With that, Eamon put on his coat and hat and left the house. Anne stood, put her shawl around her shoulders and told Michael that she needed time alone and would walk home, leaving Michael seated at the table alone.

Michael was lost in thought when he felt a hand on his shoulder. He turned to face Nancy. Her smile made him feel much more confortable. Nancy had become a close friend and confidant over the past several months. She put a cup and saucer in front of Michael, placed another at the head of the table so she could face Michael. She filled both cups and pushed a plate of macaroons toward him.

"Michael, I am so sorry about your father," she said. "I want you to know that I am here for you. I think we both know that the coming months, and maybe years, will be difficult for you and that, because your youth seems to have been taken from you, you might find times when you need to be young again. I will provide those times, should you ever have the need." She slowly raised her cup to her lips and waited for what seemed forever before Michael responded.

"Things are just starting to soak in," he said. "My mother will be dependent upon me. I knew and accepted that immediately. But now, I am being told that I am all of a sudden going to be a landowner and at the least an ex-officio taskmaster of more than one business venture that, truth be known, I know nothing about. I do thank you for your concern and rest assured that I will probably ask you to help me be both a teenager and a man. I only hope that I do not become too much for you to handle. Your friendship is important to me and I will try to not take advantage of it."

When Michael returned home he found his mother seated at the table, staring into the flames of the fireplace. She had obviously stocked the tinderbox from the woodpile outside and Michael felt a surge of guilt for not having completed one of his chores before going to the McDonald home. Anne was still dressed in her black silk dress that bore only a light pattern of evenly spaced stripes on the skirt, which hung to the sides of the chair. She had an empty teacup in front of her and the table bore no signs that she had eaten anything recently. Michael noted that the stewpot was on the sideboard. He kissed his mother on the cheek and left the house, going to the small root cellar, where he filled a basket with carrots and various other vegetables. He then took a jar of recently potted venison from the shelf and returned to the house.

"I think I have what is needed to prepare us some supper," he said to his mother as he entered the kitchen.

"I am not hungry," Anne responded.

"Well, I am," Michael said. "And, as I prefer to not eat alone, I will ask that you join me." With that he scooped the beef fat from the top of the jar of meat into a small cast iron pot and began laying out the vegetables. He was slipping a knife from the stand when his mother reached over his shoulder and took the knife.

"I will not have you being both the man and the woman of this household," she said. "Now go pay attention to your studies and I will have a dinner for you, or I mean for us, shortly."

Anne quickly chopped the vegetables, placing them into the large pot with some water. She then placed the smaller pot of beef fat near the fire. She scooped some coals from the fireplace and put them into the small cook stove, adding two pieces of wood on top. The stove warmed quickly and Anne placed the pot of beef fat on top of it and began to add water and some slices of onion. An hour later Michael could hear the table being set. He stepped back into the warm kitchen area and watched as his mother carefully ladled the venison stew onto the plates and poured two cups of tea from the teapot.

"Well, don't just stand there," she said. "Sit down and eat."

Michael sat at the table, bowed his head and repeated the Catholic blessing. "Thank you oh Lord for these, thy gifts, which we are about to receive from thy bounty. Amen."

Anne had taken only a few bites of the stew when she placed her spoon on the table and put her face into her hands. "Oh Lord, what do we do now?"

"We will be all right," Michael replied. Eamon and I are to meet with some barristers who will explain what happens next."

Anne looked up, looking almost surprised. "Your mention of barristers has caused me to think of something. My mind has been muddled of late."

With that Anne rose from the table and went into the small enclave where Juame kept a desk. From a shelf above the desk she removed a book, opened it and removed a key held in place by sealing wax. By then Michael was standing beside her.

"When your father left for Ireland, he was not confident as to when he would return, or for that matter, if he would return," Anne explained. "Just prior to his departure, he showed me this key and I watched as he secreted it in the book. His instructions were that, should he not return for any reason, you and I were to open the locked desk drawer and retrieve what was in it."

With that, Anne inserted the key and slid the desk drawer out. Inside was a single sealed envelope with the words: *To be opened only upon my death, and only by my loving wife, Anne and my son, Michael.* There was also another key.

Anne slowly sat down in front of the desk. Michael pulled up a small stool and sat next to her. Her hand was shaking as she handed the envelope to Michael. Small tears were beginning to flow from her eyes. "Please, you read it."

Michael broke the seal and removed a two-page document from it. He began to read:

MY DEAR WIFE AND SON,

> *I am to assume that, your holding this in your hand means I failed to return from Ireland. For that, I am sorry, but your lives must go on and the Good Lord will guide you, but I intend on helping him.*
>
> *Eamon McDonald has been given my power of attorney for the purposes of handling my business interests. He is fully aware of my desires in that regard and has contact with the solicitors that represent our holdings. For his loyalty and efforts on our behalf, he will receive a fifty percent interest in all of our holdings in Pennsylvania. The agreement in which Eamon and I have entered applies only to the Pennsylvania interests, but he has agreed to also mentor you, Michael, and oversee what is necessary for you to assume my share of the Pennsylvania holdings.*
>
> *Eamon and the involved barristers are in possession of my Last Will and Testament. I have also arranged for a copy of that document to be sent to a Pennsylvania lawyer, Hon.*

William Rawle. Both of you will need to contact Mr. Rawle at his offices in Philadelphia as soon as possible. He will explain to you how we came to know one another and what my directions to him have been. You must understand that he will represent you, not our companies.

Lastly, Eamon is in possession of a strong box that is to be given to you when you ask for it. The box contains a significant amount of silver coinage and other money. It is intended for use by you to maintain the household for the time being, including the hiring of a person to help you, should that be necessary. The contents of the box are not included in the will or any other documentation.

Please know that I have loved you both so much.

Sincerely,
Juame

Michael handed the letter to his mother. She took a few minutes to read the letter silently, and then she placed it back into the envelope, placed it back into the drawer and closed the drawer, leaving the key in the lock. The next morning Anne went to the McDonald home where she met Eamon as he was leaving for the mine. He waited for Anne to come up on the porch. He took both of her hands and, once again, expressed his condolences.

"I assume you are here to ask me for something," Eamon said.

"Yes. I am supposed to ask you for a strong box you are holding for my son and me."

Eamon held the door open for Anne and they both entered the house. Nancy was standing near the stove and turned to address Anne.

"Good morning Mrs. Castello. May I offer you a cup of coffee? Father is fond of his coffee in the morning and I have come to like it as well. Mother is feeling a little ill this morning and is still in her bed, but I can tell her you are here."

"No, do not bother your mother," Anne said. "I am hear to get something from your father, but I would enjoy a cup of your coffee. It has been some time since I had coffee."

Eamon returned to the room with a strong box that was obviously heavy. Placing it on the table, he said, "I was instructed to give this to you only when you asked for it. Juame told me that you would have the key and that you and Michael would know what to do next. The box is quite heavy. I will hook up our small wagon and Nancy can drive you back home. I know it is just a short distance, but I must attend to my other duties and the box is too heavy for you to carry home."

Anne sat with her coffee and noticed that Nancy seemed to have an air of maturity very similar to that of Michael. She was a good hostess and carried on an articulate conversation. After several minutes Eamon drove up to the front door in the wagon. He came in, but said little. He took the box from the table and put it into the wagon. "Be sure and give the horse a little grain when you return," he said to Nancy. "She hasn't been in harness this early in the morning for some time."

When Nancy and Anne arrived back at the Castello house, Michael met them outside, where he had been splitting some wood. He carried the box into the house, but showed little interest in it. Anne noticed a little smile and maybe a glint in Michael's eyes. Michael then volunteered to drive the wagon back and help Nancy unharness the mare. He reminded his mother that it was the gentlemanly thing to do, climbed up on the wagon, smiled at Nancy, and gave the reins that little subtle movement that tells the horse it is time to start moving. He headed toward the McDonald house, letting the horse take a very slow walk.

CHAPTER THIRTEEN

The last year of the century was well into spring. Michael Castello, now nearing his 16th birthday, was seated next to his mother in the Philadelphia office of William Rawle. The renowned lawyer was arranging various papers on his desk. He looked over the top of his spectacles and smiled at Anne.

"Now, let us get down to the business at hand," he said. "First, I must explain why Juame directed you to me." He directed his comments to Michael. "Your father and I met in France many years ago. It was his association with Antoine Riviere that brought us together. Your father and I were of similar dispositions on various matters, primarily our complete disagreement with the practice of slavery. We also agreed that the women of most countries were not appreciated. In many instances they were, and are, treated as though they do not have minds and can only do the will of some man."

Anne sat demurely, her gloved hands resting on a handbag in her lap.

"My husband always treated me as an equal in our marriage, but I will say that is not true of many of his business colleagues. I was often asked to leave a room because they were discussing business," she said.

"Sadly," Rawle continued, "what is happening in Ireland right now has more to do with slavery than most people realize and the problem continues to exist here in America. We will likely see the day in the not to distant future when slavery will become a major issue here. I also believe that women will see the day when they are treated as equals under the law, but it may be a long time before either women or colored people will be seen as societal equals."

Rawle then went to great length to explain the nuances of Juame's will and other documents in his possession. While Anne could not be the owner of the Castello properties, the documents explained in detail that Michael was to consider the counsel of his mother in the years to come, and that half of the holdings in Pennsylvania were being transferred to Eamon McDonald, and that, while Juame did not consider the arrangement to be a partnership, he had expressed a desire that Michael consider him both a friend and a business associate. Eamon would have the final say on business matters until Rawle finalized the legal requirements giving Michael actual ownership. He explained that he was of the opinion that the law would allow that to happen, but it would take a judge to make the final decisions.

Meanwhile, the property in Missouri remained in somewhat of a limbo, also awaiting judgment as to the validity of Antoine Riviere's ownership of the land in the first place.

It took nearly one year for a more clearly defined arrangement was finalized, and it became apparent to both Michael and his mother that, if Michael was to be a successful businessman, they needed to further his education.

With the help of Eamon McDonald, the Castello holdings now included a small investment in the iron production in Pittsburg. As the fall of 1800 approached, Michael found himself enrolled in the Pittsburg Academy, where he could receive an education, not only in the basic academic sense, but also further his knowledge of the mining industry. He and his mother made two trips to Pittsburg prior to his enrollment. The round trip of nearly 550 miles was difficult and proved to be almost more than Anne, now over 40 years of age, could endure. The years were hard on her, and after returning to her home following the second trip to Pittsburg, she spent several days confined to her bed.

The strongbox left by Juame contained ample funds for Anne to hire a young woman to assist her and also enough money for Michael's upcoming expenses in Pittsburg during the interim until Michael began receiving funds from the estate.

Prior to Michael's departure, he asked Nancy McDonald to inquire among her acquaintances and find a suitable live-in caretaker for his mother. The plan came to fruition when Nancy introduced Michael to

Dianna Harris. Dianna Harris was 16 years old. Her mother died when she was only 12 and she had become quite efficient in keeping house and providing assistance to her father, but things changed in the Harris household when Mr. Harris remarried. Dianna explained that she didn't dislike her stepmother, but she felt much less important. She was eager to take the position that was ultimately offered to her and agreed to move into the Castello home upon Michael's departure.

On a day when Dianna was getting acquainted with Anne, Michael walked to the McDonald home. He knew that Eamon would be away and thought it a good time to talk to Nancy and her mother. When he arrived, he learned that Mrs. McDonald was running some errands and Nancy was in the house alone. Nancy met Michael on the front porch and invited him to sit with her on the porch.

"It is interesting that you chose to come here at this precise time," Nancy said as she sat. "Just minutes ago, my mother told me that she anticipated your coming to visit. She told me that, should you come while she was gone, it would be inappropriate for you and me to be in the house alone. She rattled on something about us being of an age when we should be chaperoned."

Michael grinned. "Your mother is right, and I have been subjected to similar censure by both my mother and your father. I must assume that they are more keenly aware of our affections now that we are on the cusp of being adults, but I come today to once again ask for your assistance and I had hoped to speak to your mother as well. I will be leaving a few days hence to go to Pittsburg and it will likely be some time before I can return. I like Dianna Harris and I think I can trust her, but it would put my mind at ease if I knew that you and your mother could keep abreast of how things are going with my mother."

"We must talk about this when my mother returns, Nancy said. "She should be here within the hour. Meanwhile, I must tell you that I too will be leaving very soon. My parents have arranged for me to go to Philadelphia to a small boarding school, which is managed by some so-called matron. I really do not want to go, and at times feel that I may become Clarissa if I fail to pay attention to my life."

"Who is Clarissa? I don't recall anyone of that name," asked Michael.

"Oh, she is just a character in a book I managed to read, or at least read most of it. My mother discovered it and took it from me. I suspect she did not return it to the girl that gave it to me. I think she probably read it herself. At any rate, it seems I must go to Philadelphia and learn how to act like a lady, I guess part of acting like a lady is not being alone with some good looking lad that I have known all my life and who now suddenly becomes a threat."

Michael felt a blush rising in his face when Nancy referred to him as being good looking, and almost without thinking, he found himself responding. "Well that is a tall compliment coming from a beautiful young lady, and probably a little forward for one who sits without a chaperone with a man she confesses to be good looking. I think we should avoid such scandalous activity," he said with obvious sarcasm.

They looked at each other and laughed out loud, admitting they were mimicking their parents, but when the laughter subsided, they looked at each other in a different way than they had in the past. They held each other's gaze until it became awkward. Michael attempted to get the conversation back on topic.

"The Pennsylvania authorities are at this moment encouraging the continued construction of the pathway, now being called a road, from Philadelphia to Pittsburg. My mother and I have twice traveled part of this road and I have learned that it may soon be further improved as a toll road. If that happens, it will make travel somewhat easier, but I fear I will still have many obstacles to overcome in traveling from Pittsburg once I have settled into my studies and business obligations."

Nancy assured Michael that her mother would certainly be willing to keep an eye on what was happening in the Castello home and that she thought it appropriate for both her and her mother to communicate with Michael through regular letters. She told Michael to advise of his address as soon as he was established in Pittsburg. Mrs. McDonald returned to find the young people seated on the front step. She affirmed that she would stay in touch with Michael's mother, and then instructed Nancy that things needed done before her father came home. Michael felt somewhat clumsy saying goodbye, and made sure he addressed Mrs. McDonald first. As his eyes met Nancy's, he stepped backward down the steps, turned and headed home.

Even with the slightly improved road, the trip to Pittsburg took four days. Stops were beginning to spring up along the way and gave Michael the opportunity to rest his two horses and give himself a rest. The small wagon was loaded with the necessary articles for Michael to establish himself in a rooming house in Pittsburg. The road was hard on the horses and the wagon as well as on Michael. During the long hours of staring at the behinds of two horses, Michael often found himself in deep thought about his future and about his separation from his mother. He was also realizing that he was going to miss his companionship with Nancy McDonald. Nancy's going to Philadelphia meant an additional distance that was difficult to traverse, especially in the winter months. The relationship with both Nancy and his mother was destined to be limited to what could be written in letters, but even the letters had to make a long journey and replies would take weeks.

Michael settled into his studies and his other obligations within days of arriving in Pittsburg. He had been there less than a month when he received his first letter. The letter was from Dianna Harris. She had been instructed to report on Anne's condition every two weeks. Her report was neither good nor bad. She advised Michael that his mother remained somewhat weak, but had improved slightly over the past several days. The letter gave Michael hope. Although the December weather could change his plans, he intended to go home for Christmas.

CHAPTER FOURTEEN

In fact, Michael did not make it home for Christmas. He spent the cold holiday by attending church services and remaining at the church among several others who had no immediate family in the area.

As the months passed and the year of 1801 began to see vast changes, Michael literally became a Pittsburg resident. Any time away from his studies he worked in the office of the small mining venture in which his family held controlling interest, but he continued his education.

In the fall of the year Michael made his first trip back to see his mother. He found her well and determined that she and Dianna Harris were more like mother and daughter than woman and servant. On the day Michael arrived at his old home he found Dianna assisting a young man hired to cut and store wood. They already had at least six cords stacked in the shed. Anne pointed out a small addition recently added to the house, specifically to provide quarters for Dianna. There was also a new cook stove in kitchen area. Anne explained that she and Dianna worked together baking bread, cleaning house and tending to various chores. They shared those tasks equally.

Anne arranged for a large dinner and invited the McDonalds. Michael found himself truly longing to see the McDonalds, in particular that one McDonald who thought him to be "good looking." She did not attend.

As the McDonalds pulled up to the Castello house, Michael's disappointment immediately showed in his stature and his voice. "Is Nancy not coming?"

Eamon answered with a slight smile, "I am afraid not. She is now preparing to take a more involved position in the girls' school, in which, until recently, she has been only a pupil. The matron of the school has asked Nancy to assist with a few younger ladies, so she will be both student and teacher. She will likely stay in Philadelphia for some time. I think she has dreams of becoming a matron of a school of her own. Her mother and I have expressed our support, should that become a possibility."

After dinner Eamon invited Michael to sit on the front porch. "How are things in Pittsburg?" Eamon asked.

"The city is growing rapidly," Michael replied. "There are many entrepreneurs, some not so honest I fear, who are calling Pittsburgh the gateway to the west. Some of the miners whom I have become acquainted with say that the rivers will soon become even more important than they are now, and as you know, there has been a growing interest in mining coal and limestone. My friends say that we should divest and become more involved in the coal mining."

"I agree with your friends," Eamon said. "With President Jefferson now in charge, it is likely that he will begin to take steps to advance his concept that the United States should be expanded greatly. That means moving west, and it also means that some other countries will not take kindly to the idea. As for this so-called gateway to the west, it seems to me that Pittsburgh has a significant adversary for that title. The area around St. Louis is also expanding their interests, and you, lad, have the potential of having a very valuable holding there."

Michael thought for a moment, and then replied, "I receive notices that funds from those who live on the land near St. Louis have been transferred to the bank in Philadelphia. The money for the most part does not make a difference in my life, but each time I receive that notice I cannot help but try to envision what that property is like, and even if it is my property. The lawyers caution me that the title may never be without problems. They have even advised me to rid myself of the property and let someone else worry about it. I just cannot do that."

"I will never presume to advise you to ignore William Rawle and his associates," Eamon said. "But, were I in your shoes, I would hold on a little longer. There is rumor that Jefferson is communicating at this very moment with his French acquaintances, and that he is organizing a survey party to assess a large portion of our continent."

"I, too, think I should take things slowly," said Michael. "At the same time, I am concerned about things here at home. My inclination is to finish this term at the school and then come back to this valley, which I love so much. If I continue to prosper, there is no reason I cannot have a home here; maybe even a home independent of my mother, but close enough to provide her any assistance she may need."

Michael and Eamon continued to converse for another hour. Once again Eamon was impressed with his young associate's grasp on life in general and on the business interests he was involved in. Eamon knew that Michael had that deep-seated common sense necessary for success in any endeavor.

Michael was determined to return to the Wyoming Valley. He was also determined to be an independent person. He knew that would not be possible if he simply returned and occupied a room in his mother's house. By the same token, he felt a deep responsibility to his mother. During a visit with the lawyers in Philadelphia, Michael had been impressed with the growing trend of building with bricks. The law firm itself was housed in a new brick building that had a feeling of strength and durability. Now there were several brick buildings in and around the Wyoming Valley.

The day after his visit with Eamon, Michael made arrangements to purchase a small plot of ground just a few hundred yards from his mother's home. Two days later he sought out the architect of one of the more impressive brick buildings in the area. Ultimately Michael secured a contract with the architect and arranged for funding of a new brick home. If everything went right, the home would be completed in the spring of 1802. Michael felt a surge of confidence as he left to return to Pittsburg, but his happiness was somewhat tempered by the fact that he had not seen Nancy.

The winter passed slowly and it was cold, colder than Michael had yet experienced. The severe weather slowed everything down. Production at the mines was at an all time low and communication with Nancy had nearly stopped. Michael hoped the weather was to blame for the lack of letters from Nancy, but he feared there were other reasons.

He delved into his studies and tried to damper his feelings by seeking the company of some of the local girls, but it did not work well.

As the spring of 1802 finally started to warm things up, Michael accepted the fact that he wanted to return to the Wyoming Valley. His new home was nearly complete, but his dream of sharing it with Nancy was fading quickly. He returned in time to help with the final construction of the house.

Nancy McDonald was now 18 years old, an age when many women were already married and starting a family, but Nancy loved her life at the girls school. She was officially one of the youngest matron's assistants of any girl's school in Philadelphia. She prided herself in helping young girls become young women. She taught them to sit properly, to walk upright and speak proper English. She frequently talked to the owner of the school about selling her the property and the school, which was well regarded by both middle class and the more affluent women, but was looked on with some concern by many influential men. The young Miss McDonald was venturing into topics that were beyond what most men considered appropriate for her students.

Nancy, using all her charm and acquired sophistication, managed to convince the controlling men of the Library Company of Philadelphia to allow her access, and at times loan, of the library's impressive volumes. The library was founded by Benjamin Franklin and housed some of the most important documents of the Revolutionary War and the establishment of the United States of America. Nancy considered the country's history to be important in the education of the girls at the academy. She spent hours at the library copying many of the documents and then including the information in her curriculum.

After being rebuked several times for her promotion of higher education for women, Nancy made a trip home to talk to her father. Depending on how her father received her ideas, Nancy's future depended on the scheduled one-on-one talk with Eamon McDonald.

Shortly after their evening meal, Nancy asked her father to sit with her in his small room, affectionately called his study.

"Father, I need to talk to you about something very important," she began.

Eamon acted as though he had not heard his daughter. "Michael is back and has built a new house just up the street from his mother," Eamon said.

Nancy scooted to the edge of her chair to get closer to her father. "I know that," she said. "But father we need to talk of something very important to me."

"He was very disappointed that he was unable to see you when he visited last, and he tells me that you have not answered many of his letters."

"That is true. I have neglected the correspondence lately, but..."

Again, her father interrupted her: "Michael thinks very highly of you, Nancy. You know that, do you not?"

Nancy was determined to take charge of the conversation. "Father, listen to me. I will talk about Michael later and I will make a point of seeing him tomorrow, but I must tell you that I have been having some interesting conversations with the matron of the school and I have breached the question of asking her if she would be willing to sell the house, which I would continue to maintain as a school, but would be in a position to establish my own curriculum. Of course, I cannot simply reach into my handbag and procure the funds. The property is actually owned by Madam's father, anyway, and I am being told he would not likely sell to a woman, especially a very young woman."

As Eamon started to say something, Nancy held up her hand in a stopping gesture and continued. "That, by the way, is one of the reasons I want to take charge of the school. It is about time that people started to realize that women can also be business people and I can do something about that by teaching young women more than just how to stand and walk and cook for a man."

Eamon shook his head. "I think you may be asking for more trouble than you think, but I do not disagree with you. I will do this. I will consider what you are asking for, understanding that you are asking a man..." He smiled and continued, "This would be a big step for both of us, so I ask that you consider everything until the end of this year. I suggest you make a list of the advantages and disadvantages of your proposal. Start the top of the list with your age. We will discuss this again on Christmas. Can we do that?"

Nancy agreed and went to her room. One hour later she was sitting on the front porch of Michael's nearly completed house. Michael was seated next to her. He could feel her closeness, but sensed a distance in her demeanor.

"Its a little chilly," he said. "We could go inside."

Nancy looked at Michael and could see the sincerity in his eyes. "I think we should not do that."

"But I would love to show you the interior and get your advise on some things that are yet to be done."

"Michael, I do not think it would be appropriate."

It was then that Michael could hold his feeling no longer. "Nancy, you must know how I feel. If you give your permission, I will run to your father's house and ask if I can formally court you, with the full intention of marrying you, say next June."

Nancy's lips quivered and a tear formed in one eye. She carefully wiped her eye with her sleeve and turned toward Michael. "I think I do know how you feel, you silly boy, but you have never even kissed me. Besides, I have to make some other decisions and I promised my father I would not make things final until he and I could agree on those things this coming Christmas. I am making a list and..."

Michael did not let her finish. He held her face in his hands and gently pressed his lips to hers. She responded, but slowly pushed him away. "You just added another thing to my list." With that she stood and almost ran toward her parents' house.

CHAPTER FIFTEEN

Christmas came and went. Nancy and her father made arrangements to purchase the house and the school in Philadelphia and Michael settled into his lonely house. The next year passed too quickly. Michael and Nancy saw each other only twice during the year and, once again, Michael was waiting for an answer.

In mid February of 1804, Michael received a letter from the Rawle law office in Philadelphia. The letter was short and to the point, asking that Michael come to Philadelphia and meet with William Rawle. The letter expressed urgency, but was not specific as to why Rawle was requesting Michael's presence.

Owing to a much-improved road, Michael was able to secure passage on a stagecoach and travel to Philadelphia. He felt nervous, yet felt some hope that he would also be able to see Nancy and maybe better understand her desire to be a teacher. He decided to visit with the attorney before he contacted Nancy. He rationalized that something important was about to take place and that maybe; just maybe, it would be something that would bear weight on Nancy's reluctance to marry him.

As he settled into the chair in front of William Rawle's desk, Michael felt his stomach churning. He noticed his hands were shaking ever so slightly, but shaking nonetheless. Rawle placed a large file folder on the desk and took his seat.

"Michael, you will no doubt recall that I have, over the past years, counseled you to rid yourself of the property that your father purchased from Antoine Riviere. It has been my belief that, while the property has certainly provided some additional income for you, it would in the long run cause you more grief than it is worth."

Michael interrupted, "Mr. Rawle, if you summoned me here simply to rehash your opinion, you have wasted both my time and yours. Others tell me that there is great potential in that holding and I will not be convinced easily to rid myself of it. I understand that my legal possession of the property may well prove to be denied to me, but until that happens, I plan on keeping what I have."

Rawle leaned forward and opened the file. "I have not asked you to come here so I could convince you to abandon your interest, but rather to admit that I may have been wrong. A close friend of mine now sits in the House of Representatives in the Federal District. He has forwarded to me something that may well turn out to be a good thing for you, but you must act quickly." He pushed a two-page document across the desk. Please read the second page of this," he said.

Written in a smooth hand, the top of the page contained the words; "The following is my transcription of a notification to the House received from President Jefferson on January 16. As you are no doubt aware, President Jefferson has managed to expend a large part of the national treasure to purchase the vast area called Louisiana from France.

The Jefferson letter explained that the United States had taken possession of Louisiana and was establishing a temporary government. It summarized that Governor Claiborne of the Mississippi Territory and General Wilkinson were appointed commissioners to receive possession of the territory and that Claiborne had been appointed Governor of the Louisiana Territory. Michael's attention was drawn to the last paragraph of Jefferson's notice. It read:

"On this important acquisition, so favorable to the immediate interests of our Western citizens, so auspicious to the peace and security of the nation in general, which adds to our country territories so extensive and fertile and to our citizens new brethren to partake of the blessing of freedom and self-government, I offer to Congress and our country my sincere congratulation."

Rawle waited for Michael to peruse the document and then said, "If you are still determined to establish your title to the land, you must do it as soon as possible and see to it that the proper documents are provided to the territorial government now being formed. I have prepared what you need to get this done." He handed Michael the portfolio of papers, then added, "Another thing that may interest you is that just within the last few years there have been significant findings of something called galena in the area of which we are talking."

"I know of galena," Michael said. "It is a very desirable type of lead. Eamon McDonald has briefed me on its uses and encouraged some research into our becoming more involved in the mining of lead and silver. Our associates tried just last year to send people down the Ohio River, hoping to get to the area near St. Louis where the lead is being mined. The people we sent met with unfriendly operators on a barge and only one returned."

After nearly two hours of conversation with Rawle, Michael left the offices and hired a carriage to take him to the girls school. Nancy met him in the parlor and provided tea for both of them. "I received your letter just days ago," Nancy said.

Michael sat near the edge of his chair. "I have recently become aware of some information that will likely cause me to be gone from Pennsylvania for a lengthy period of time. I want you to be aware that I am still very much in love with you and I would marry you today if it were possible, but I know that is unlikely to happen and I understand your commitment to this school. So, I plan on going back to Pittsburg and meeting with some of my associates there. Then I will likely take passage on one of the commercial barges and find my way to St. Louis"

"Michael" Nancy replied, "I am certainly not prepared to marry you today, and you are correct in your assertion that I am dedicated to this school. As you probably know by now, my father has funded my purchase of this property. Ironically, the property could not be recorded in my name alone because I am a woman and some of the idiotic laws we live under require that a man be the primary on any legal document. That, precisely, is one of the reasons I must continue here, at least for the time being. I wish you well in your planned journey and look forward to our meeting again before too long."

With an obvious assertion of dismissal, Nancy rose. Michael too rose to his feet, leaned forward and kissed Nancy lightly on her lips. He waited for a more passionate response, but received none. He donned his hat and coat and left the school.

As the warmth of spring began to bring about a renewed activity for everyone, Michael was once again in the rooming house in Pittsburg. In a few short weeks after his arrival, he arranged to escort the shipment of a small forge that was to be loaded on a barge and shipped to St. Louis. The trip promised to be an adventure, productive and dangerous. Those operating the barges were known to be less than law-abiding. Michael learned that ignoring the law was not really what the barge operators were doing. In fact, they traveled through areas that, for all intent and purpose, had no law. The rivers they traveled often were the borders of various jurisdictions and those jurisdictions often, themselves, were ignoring the law rather than be involved in a confrontation by other entities.

Companies shipping merchandise and equipment on the barges were trying to counteract the problem by sending their own representatives, and when they could they even procured their own barges. The Castello industries and associates with whom they did business acquired the exclusive use of the barge Michael was scheduled to travel upon. Those companies then sold passage to others. Michael and two other Castello employees were charged with keeping the shipments from being taken by the outlaws of the various settlements by which the barge would pass or temporarily dock.

At each of these dockings Michael learned more about the increasing trade being promoted by the forward-thinking business people of Pennsylvania and other burgeon settlements. There was talk of people who were exploring the possibility of making upstream travel easier by using sails on the barges. Those conversations were of special interest to Michael, largely because he knew he would need to return to Pennsylvania. He did not cherish the idea of such an arduous trip. That trip would prove to be delayed for quite some time.

When Michael arrived in St. Louis he immediately inquired as to where he could meet with Antoine Riviere. It seemed nearly everyone knew, or knew of, Riviere. He was considered a co-founder of St. Louis. Michael had been in the area mere hours before he was meeting with Antoine's son, Phillipe. Together Michael and Phillipe met with

98-year-old Antoine at his home. Michael was impressed with the apparent vitality of someone who was nearly 100-years-old. Despite Antoine's commitment to America he had, just recently, attained citizenship.

Antoine assured Michael that the land involved in the transaction between Antoine and Juame Castello was a valid transaction. The land was originally granted to Antoine by the government of France. In highly accented English, Antoine reassured Michael that there was a very clear understanding with the Jefferson-appointed people that the grant would be honored, and that any transaction regarding the property prior to the purchase of the territory would therefore prove to be valid.

While awaiting final decisions, Michael met regularly with the family that was farming a large portion of the land in question. He noted that the family was well respected and regarded by others to be very competent. Michael assured them that their arrangement with the Castellos would remain in effect. He also arranged to occupy a small cabin situated on the property for the duration of his stay. His stay proved to be a long one. Correspondence between St. Louis and France often took several weeks and even months. St. Louis had no newspaper and that made information even harder to obtain.

The cabin was in an area known to the French as Fleurissant, and included the settlement of St. Ferdinand. As more settlers came into the region, the English spelling, Florissant, became prevalent. Michael settled into a routine of helping with farming, visiting the lead mining holdings, and attending regular church services.

July 4, 1805 was a special day, but it was late in July before Michael knew how special it was. July 4, 1805 was the day the Louisiana Territory became official and the deed to the Castello land was accepted. Michael was ready to return to Pennsylvania.

CHAPTER SIXTEEN

Michael was back in Wyoming Valley, Pennsylvania just as the trees were beginning to show their fall colors. The white oaks that surrounded his house seemed especially beautiful. On one fall evening Michael's mother came to his house for supper. They sat on the porch and watched as the sun was lowering in the western sky. Neither Anne nor Michael said anything for several minutes. Anne broke the silence.

"Michael, I am now 45 years of age. I know that is not really old, but it is not really young. You are only now a man, in terms of age, but there are times when I feel that you are every bit as old as I am."

Michael turned to his mother. "Where did this come from?"

"Well," Anne continued, I think I would like to be a grandmother while I can still enjoy it, but I see little movement on your part. I know how you feel about Nancy, but she too has excelled beyond her actual age. She is now teaching in a school that is owned by her. You are a very successful businessman with a large estate and a beautiful house, which you live in all alone. I do not understand."

Michael seemed almost irritated with his mother. "Mother, Nancy McDonald knows very well how I feel. She knows that I would marry her at any time. She has made her decisions, just as I have made mine. It was Father's wish that, by the time I became 21 years of age, I would have proven myself and could honestly say that I was ready and willing to expand both my knowledge and my business capabilities. I think I have lived up to his wishes and I intend to continue to carry on with what he started."

Michael ignored an attempt by his mother to interject. "Mother, I know you once stood by my side on the bank of the river in Pittsburgh. I do not believe either of us could have comprehended what that river offered. I now know of the potentials of the Ohio and of the Missouri and the Mississippi. I now know that the people of the United States will not be deterred. They will seek out the lands of the west. They will not give up. As we sit here now, there is an expedition ordered by President Jefferson and headed by Meriwether Clark and William Lewis that will likely give cause for a vast expansion of this nation. We now have one foot on the trail beginning in St. Louis and I will someday take another step on that trail. Mark my words. Antoine Riviere told me during one of my visits with him that Lewis and Clark's efforts will forever be part of the history of this nation. I truly believe what he said. Antoine himself contributed to the expedition and provided Meriwether Clark with a rifle that will also be a unique part of history."

Michael had succeeded in capturing his mother's attention. "I am very curious to learn more about this expedition and to listen to your accounts of meeting with Mr. Riviere. What is this about a rifle?"

"The rifle he gave Clark is unique, "Michael said. According to Antoine, it would have proven to be a deciding factor in many past battles had the fighters on either side taken steps to procure some of the rifles. It was invented by an Italian named Girodoni and fires with the use of air compressed into a tank in the stock. The rifle is capable of firing as many as 20 shots, one after another, without reloading. I have asked Antoine to attempt to procure one of the rifles for me."

He told his mother all he knew about the Lewis and Clark expedition and told her that he would someday return to St. Louis. He also informed her that he was now owner, or at least the tantamount owner, of a mining claim not far from St. Louis.

Michael spent the remainder of the year deeply involved in his business dealings. The Castello companies now owned significant coal and iron mining interests in Pennsylvania and held an impressive lead mine in the Louisiana Territory. It was the Louisiana holdings that sent Michael back to Philadelphia to visit with William Rawle

Rawle greeted Michael in his ornate office. "For you to make the trip here, you must be concerned about something Mr. Castello, "What can I do for you?"

Michael noted at once that Mr. Rawle did not greet him as a naive teenager, but rather as an adult - Mr. Castello. Michael felt a surge of importance upon hearing the greeting. He was invited to sit, and did so before beginning his conversation.

"First of all, I must thank you once again for your efforts on my behalf with the farm land in the Louisiana Territory. I am confident that there will be no further problems associated with that land, but now we have another problem. I arranged for the purchase of a lead mine near St. Ferdinand. With the help of Philippe Riviere I also arranged for the current operators of the mine to lease it from us and continue operations. It is my opinion and the opinion of Phillipe and his father that this will prove to be a good investment."

Rawle leaned forward. "And just what is it that you need from me?"

"The purchase and lease were handled by an attorney retained on my behalf by Phillipe. I assumed, probably in error, that the title to that property would not be questioned, but it turns out the property was part of a land grant from Spain and was not formally assumed by France, or for that matter, by the United States. A relative of the man who sold us the property is now attempting to regain control."

Rawle smiled and leaned back in his chair. "I do believe that you have the key to good fortune hidden in those britches of yours," he said. "Only recently, I have come to know a young man that may well be the answer to your problems in the St. Louis area. I have his calling card here in my drawer."

With that Rawle retrieved a card from the drawer and handed it to Michael. Inscribed upon the face of the card in old English script were the words, EDWARD HEMPSTEAD - ATTORNEY AT LAW - RHODE ISLAND, UNITED STATES OF AMERICA.

"Okay, but just how is an attorney from Rhode Island supposed to help me with a problem in the new Louisiana Territory?"

Again, Rawle smiled. "He is no longer a Rhode Island attorney. When I met this enterprising lad, who is but a few years older than you, he was on his way to your prized Louisiana Territory. I do believe that he fully intended to walk all the way, if necessary. I know of no other person who exudes the energy and determination, as does Mr. Hempstead. I did my best to keep him here in Philadelphia, but he had his sights set on this new westward expansion and he intended on starting in St. Louis.

Before Michael left the office, he and Rawle composed a letter to Phillipe Riviere, asking that he attempt to locate and meet Edward Hempstead. The letter was posted that same day.

Time passed slowly. Michael returned to his home and tended to business in the Wyoming Valley. He exchanged several letters with the Riviere family. Coincidently, it turned out that their involvement in the politics of the St. Louis region brought them to know Edward Hempstead. William Rawle's assumptions about Hempstead proved to be quite correct. Hempstead wasted no time becoming acquainted with the right people at the right places. He had barely had time to settle in St. Louis when he became acquainted with several influential French inhabitants and already had some of them as regular clients.

While the title to the farmland had been handled with relatively little problem, the new mining property was an entirely different thing. The French people in the area did not want anything to do with trying to deal with Spain, and the French government was too deeply involved in an all-out war with England.

Nearly two years passed before Edward Hempstead secured a settlement with those who were trying to establish claim to the mining property. The settlement was costly but not nearly as costly as things to come.

River travel was constantly gaining in popularity and the shipping of materials, including the iron produced within the Castello holding was becoming commonplace. Even more important was the lead ore. France and England were in an all-out war. The United States government was trying to stay out of the fray, but it was proving more and more difficult, and France wanted the lead ore, but their shipping problems were hindered by Britain.

President Jefferson resisted at first, but finally realized that Britain would not hesitate to make matters worse. In the early days of February, 1807 the House of Representatives passed a bill providing funding for defense of the harbors. On February 10, 1807 Jefferson sent his missive to the House and Senate, advising that he had put into motion the actions required by the bill. He ordered gunboats to be distributed in the harbors and movable artillery pieces to be provided to oppose any enemy. Britain was becoming more and more aggressive against American ships, often boarding them and taking crewmembers away, claiming them to be British citizens.

It seemed to Michael and his associates that nearly everything that happened would first prove to be beneficial and then turn against them. Their investments were experiencing a significant boom and bust economic situation.

When a man named Fulton succeeded in navigating the Hudson River from New York to Albany, those involved in various kinds of trading, both within the United States and with other countries, started investing heavily in shipping. Their fortunes looked promising at the start, but came to an abrupt end thanks to the war between England and France.

The excitement waned considerably when, on December 22, 1807, Congress passed the Embargo Act, which effectively closed down international trading from or to the United States. While Michael kept up to date as much as possible, he did not hear about the Embargo Act until mid-January of 1808. The one positive thing that occurred was a contract between the War Department and a bullet manufacturing company that obtained most of their lead from the mine in the Louisiana Territory.

Michael and Nancy McDonald had not seen one another for more than a year when Michael, while on business in Philadelphia, called on Nancy at her school. She seemed very excited to see him and invited him to dinner that evening. Four young ladies that were students of the school accompanied them.

"I was under the impression that you had more students," Michael said as he and Nancy sat with glasses of sherry after dinner.

"Yes there were six more, but the father of two of my girls was taken captive by British troops and the family returned to England. Another family found it necessary financially to return their daughter home. Another young lady is getting married. Quite frankly, it has taken a toll on my finances. If I am unable to recruit more students, my little enterprise here may be in jeopardy."

As Michael was preparing to leave that evening, he reached out and held Nancy's hand. "You know if you need anything, you just have to ask. You could just give up the school and marry me."

He received only a nod and left. He and Nancy did not see each other again for a long time.

CHAPTER SEVENTEEN

Thomas Jefferson and his administration succeeded to keep America neutral during his term as president, but there was a substantial buildup of military might. When Jefferson left office in March of 1809 his expansion of the defenses of the United States directly impacted the several enterprises that Michael Castello was involved in.

Michael, for the most part, supported Jefferson and was not adverse to seeing Jefferson's friend and Secretary of State James Madison being Jefferson's successor, but there was one thing that Michael did not like. Jefferson was a slave owner. Michael and his mother often discussed the fact. Anne recalled that her late husband, Juame Castello, left Ireland largely because of his distaste for slavery and indentured servitude.

The next three years were trying. While Madison continued for some time to keep the United States neutral, his efforts were often in vain. Britain continued to harass commercial shipments and several indigenous tribes, especially in the north, were siding with Britain.

Anne Castello, now approaching 51 years of age, was openly concerned about her son, who at age 26 had still not married. She worried that his constant travel and obsession with business dealings would be detrimental to his health and she truly wanted grandchildren. Michael kept company at times with young ladies. He attended a few picnics and social events, but never seemed to develop a sincere relationship. His female friends soon lost interest and set paths that led away from Michael's.

When Anne and Michael attended a Christmas celebration at the McDonald house on December 25, 1811, she finally thought that there were some positive things happening. Nancy McDonald was present and still as beautiful as ever, and more importantly, she was paying a lot of attention to Michael. While the outside temperature was below freezing, Nancy quickly agreed to take a walk with Michael. Anne was sure she sensed a blush in Nancy's face as Michael helped her with her shawl. Michael smiled as Anne put on her hat that was designed to keep her ears warm. He handed her muff to her and almost forgot to don his own coat as he opened the door.

The couple had just left the house when they heard the joyous sounds of carolers just down the street.

"Oh, let's join them," Anne said and pulled Michael down the walk.

As they walked from house to house raising their voices in the joy of the season, Michael could feel the old feelings beginning to reignite. He felt Nancy's arm as it looped through his. Her hands were buried deep within the muff. He wished one of those hands held a wedding ring.

Michael brought their walk to a halt and turned to Nancy. "Nancy, is there a special man in your life? I do not want to be presumptuous. The town is celebrating the new year with an evening social followed by fireworks and a dance. I would be honored if you would accompany me to the festivities."

Nancy's face displayed that youthful blush. "Well, Mr. Castello, I should ask you the same. Is there some special lady in your life? Perhaps one that you desire to make jealous by being seen with a schoolteacher that some would say is becoming an old maid? An old maid I might add that certainly does have a special man, but he has not shown much interest in me for quite some time."

Michael replied, choosing his words slowly. "I have kept company with a lady or two, but none have stirred the feelings that I have had for you for these many years. I hope you will tolerate my giddiness and say you will spend the last day of this year at my side."

"I shall, yes I shall," Nancy said as she almost skipped up the walk. "Now hurry up, they are about to sing the last carol for the evening."

They rejoined the group and sang a melodic version of Silent Night. That night, as Michael stretched out in his bed, he decided that he would once again ask Nancy to marry him, and if she declined, he would never breech the subject again. The next day he went to a jewelry store and purchased a fine diamond ring.

On New Year's Eve Michael and Nancy attended the social and the dance. They gathered with the crowd to sit in a park and watch fireworks. Michael was having little luck getting Nancy alone. Finally, as the new year was announced, he kissed her gently and guided Nancy to a nearby bench.

"Nancy, you told me that there was a special man in your life. I guess I need to know how special he is," Michael said.

"He is very special. In fact, he has asked me to marry him, but I did not respond affirmatively. If he were to ask me again, I would likely say yes," Nancy said.

"Well," Michael said hesitantly. "That makes things a little awkward."

Michael had the ring hidden in his hand. He reached out and put his hand into Nancy's muff. "I had really planned on asking you to marry me tonight, but..."

Nancy interrupted. "You silly man. That special man in my life is sitting here holding my hand at this very moment."

With that, Michael gently pressed the ring into her palm and said, "Well, I am asking now."

Nancy pulled her hands from the muff, placed the ring on her own finger, threw both arms around Michael and almost screamed, "Yes. Yes. A million times yes."

She broke from the embrace and kissed Michael passionately. They leaned against each other as they walked together. Michael hailed a carriage and escorted Nancy to her father's house. He was almost giddy as he returned home. He resisted the urge to stop by his mother's house so he could tell someone the news.

The next day Michael and his mother were once again guests at the McDonald house. Nancy had arranged for an afternoon tea. Because it was a Wednesday both Eamon and Michael were working. Both took time to honor Nancy's wishes. Michael knew why Nancy made the request but Eamon arrived showing a little frustration over being taken away from his duties.

As Ryleigh McDonald poured the tea and settled back into her chair, she looked at her daughter and could see the anxiousness that reminded her of times when Nancy was very young and had something she deemed important to say or do. Eamon noticed the fidgeting and he also noticed that Nancy was clasping her left hand with her right and seemed to be massaging it. Finally, Eamon spoke.

"Okay girl, why have you summoned both Michael and I from our duties to come sip tea with you and your mother?"

Michael held up his hand, signaling Nancy that he should speak. "Mr. McDonald, I have asked Nancy to marry me and I sit here now to ask for your and Mrs. McDonald's blessing. I know I should have asked you before, but I had to know if Nancy would say yes."

Ryleigh literally jumped from her chair, grabbed Nancy's left hand and held it up before her. "Oh what a beautiful ring!" Turning to Michael, she said, "It is about time. I am not getting any younger, you know." She then turned to Anne and gave her a hug.

Eamon then spoke. "First of all, let me say how proud I am to be associated with you, Michael. Never in my wildest dreams would I have predicted how fast you matured and how much of an efficient businessman you have turned out to be. Secondly, it is about time you and I treat each other as equals. Please start calling me Eamon. Thirdly, and most important, by all means I give you my blessing, but you, Nancy and I need to sit and have a long talk before any other arrangements are made."

Michael reached out and clasped Nancy's hand. "Of course. Perhaps this coming Sunday after church services we could meet at my house. Would that be agreeable to you?"

After Eamon agreed to the meeting, Michael and his mother took their leave. Anne embraced Michael's arm tightly as they walked to her house. As she started to enter the house and let Michael return to work, she said, "Your father would be so proud of you right now."

The next Sunday following church services Eamon met with Michael. Michael poured each of them a small glass of sherry.

Eamon began the conversation. "Michael do you know what a spré is?"

"You mean like an ocean spray?

"No," Eamon smiled, "It is an Irish word spelled s-p-r-e. If it were translated to English and defined, it would mean 'fortune.'" In Ireland it means 'dowry.' Do you know what a dowry is?"

"I know exactly what it is," Michael said with some emphasis. "I am of the opinion that a man and a woman should marry for love, not because the woman's father wants to sell the woman to a man. Just what are you getting at?"

"Don't misunderstand me," Eamon said. "What I am getting at here is that Nancy has confided to me that she wants to divest the property in Philadelphia. Because of some archaic laws, I am the registered owner of that property, but it rightly belongs to Nancy. I propose that, when you two marry, the proceeds of that property be placed in your name, with an agreement between us as gentlemen that it is Nancy's, not her spré, but her property, and that you hold it in trust for her and expend it only at her direction. Can we agree on that?"

"I would have it no other way," Michael replied.

Eamon finished his sherry and stood to leave. "When I get home Nancy will come to see you."

That evening, Nancy was somewhat humored when Michael related his conversation with her father. She asked for and received Michael's indulgence in setting an exact date, pending the sale of her school. It turned out the delay in setting a date was much longer than either of them anticipated.

CHAPTER EIGHTEEN

The spring of 1812 found Michael once more on a barge headed for St. Louis. A letter from the law office of Edward Hempstead predicated his trip. The St. Louis attorneys, especially Hempstead, were involved in the politics of the region to the point that very little government activity took place without Hempstead and his associates knowing in advance.

The Louisiana Territory was about to be split into other territories and the mining and farming properties Michael held in the area were once again coming under scrutiny. The attorneys advised that Michael should be dealing with some of the consequences in person. The mining properties, which were mostly in the Potosi area, were of special concern. Lead mining was becoming more and more important as the United States built up its arsenal. Canon balls and bullets were being manufactured at a rate that was almost unbelievable.

The crops being produced on the Castello farmland were also in great demand. Transportation and trade links were improving greatly, but Britain was more of a problem than ever. It was becoming more and more apparent to Michael and his advisors that war with Britain was a distinct possibility.

Michael arrived in St. Louis in late April. He learned that one of the most recognized figures in the lead mining region, Moses Austin, was also showing up in person to the various meetings and political conferences being held. Both Austin and Michael were present in a meeting when they learned, just a few days after it happened on June 4, the Territory of Missouri was officially designated and a territorial government was already formed and taking charge. For the next several days Michael spent his time with an attorney ensuring that his holdings, both mineral and agricultural, were recognized in the new territory.

Just two weeks after the official designation of the Missouri Territory, the United States declared war against Britain.

Meanwhile, Nancy McDonald was becoming more and more frustrated. For the past few years she tried to instill an education for young women that focused on more than just how to become a good wife or a teacher. She believed that both of those pursuits were admirable and that most of the young women she dealt with would ultimately become one or the other, and maybe both, but she also believed they needed to be more aware of politics, and business practices.

Nancy was looking forward to her marriage, but she certainly was not looking forward to being a subservient wife, who just went along with the decisions of her husband just because he was a man. Her attempts to sell the school made her even more convinced that women needed to be recognized in a much greater way.

She was adamant that any sale of the school must be made to a woman, and that the buyer must be of the same mindset as Nancy and continue to teach women to do more than needlework and housework. Time and again she found herself dealing with a man who claimed he was interested in the school on behalf of his wife or his daughter but showed little interest in letting his wife or daughter be part of the negotiation. Many times the men would not deal with her at all unless her father was present. Because her father's name was on all the legal documents, Nancy was hard pressed to have him directly involved in any negotiations, but she was determined to make her father understand that the final decisions would always be hers.

With the nation now at war, Michael's return to Pennsylvania was delayed several times, giving Nancy more time to sell the school to someone who fit her criteria. When she received a letter of interest from Mademoiselle Annette Boche, she was encouraged. Mlle. Boche described in her letter that she had been educated in France, spoke fluent English, French and German, and had the necessary funds to purchase the Philadelphia property. She was a recently naturalized citizen of the United States and was living in Philadelphia. Nancy answered the letter immediately and asked Mlle. Boche to meet with her as soon as possible. The meeting took place less than two weeks later and included only the two ladies.

Nancy greeted Mlle. Boche at the door, relieved her of her shawl and escorted her into the parlor, where she had a pot of tea and some small cookies arranged on a table between two chairs.

"Mademoiselle, I am Miss McDonald. I welcome you to my school. Please be seated and let us become acquainted before we speak of any specific business things," Nancy said, indicating the seats.

Mlle. Boche smiled. "Thank you Miss McDonald," she said as she carefully sat on the edge of the chair and folded her hands in her lap. "First of all," she continued. "I am trying to leave the formality of being called a mademoiselle. I would prefer you call me Miss Boche, at least for the time being."

The two ladies spent the next hour exchanging personal information. As they talked, Nancy noticed that both of them had relaxed and slipped back into the chairs. The attention to propriety was dissolving. Nancy learned that Miss Boche was currently teaching at another school; one that dwelled heavily on the so-called proper way a young lady should act. Miss Boche's father had recently passed away, leaving her with a substantial inheritance, which she planned on investing. She asked Nancy to provide details on the property.

"The house sits on three large lots that would simplify expansion," Nancy began.

"We have five bedrooms on the upper floor, each adequate for two young ladies. Presently, we attempt to place a newer student in a room with one that has been here for at least one year. The second floor also has two large powder rooms. I believe the shared use of those facilities encourages compromise, but arguments do develop. Here on the ground floor I have my quarters, which includes a private water closet. This room, the parlor, functions as both a place to entertain guests and a study area. You will notice how well lit it is during daylight hours and the abundance of oil lamps for use in the evenings. Visitors, with the exception of parents on certain days, are not allowed upstairs. And young men are never allowed to be alone with our students and must remain in this room unless they are invited to a special dinner, which is arranged both as a social event and a lesson for the ladies. I will show you the entire facility in a few minutes."

"How many students do you now have?"

"At this time," Nancy continued. "We have six young ladies. We can accommodate ten. Two new girls are enrolled now for the upcoming fall term. One of the girls is in her final year here and now serves in a part-time teaching capacity in return for her tuition and board. Thanks to the underhanded tactics of the British Navy, we do not have a full compliment of students at this time, but I anticipate that will change soon."

Nancy then asked Miss Boche if she would join her and her students for the evening meal. "I am not promising anything unique," Nancy said. "I assign the girls in pairs to prepare the meals. The pairs change frequently and scheduling is a challenge. This evening two of our youngest students are in charge of the dinner. They are both relatively inexperienced in the finer points of etiquette, but their mothers have done an admirable job in teaching them how to cook. I have the menu that the girls submitted right here." Nancy went to a nearby table and picked up a sheet of paper that displayed exquisite handwriting.

She looked at the page and said, "It seems we will be having a small portion of Humkessoep, a main course of roasted venison and a raspberry tart for desert."

Miss Boche replied with a smile, "I am familiar with Humkessoep. Our Dutch people here in Pennsylvania have turned soup making into a fine art. I could make a meal of Humkessoep alone. I would be pleased to dine with you and your young ladies."

The meal was served in a family style with the girls in charge placing the soup tureen near one end of the table, and then placing the covered roast and a large bowl of potatoes near the center. The deserts were placed above each plate and then the girls all gathered around the table. One of the girls in charge said a blessing and Nancy introduced Miss Boche. They all sat in unison and began the meal.

Miss Boche, after finishing her soup, and as the roast and potatoes were being passed, started a conversation. "That was delicious. I was telling Miss McDonald earlier that I was very fond of Humkessoep and this is some of the best I have tasted. So tell me, ladies, how do you like being here?"

After a round of lively conversation, in which each of the young ladies spoke in turn, never interrupting each other and always placing their utensils properly on their plates before speaking the entire group retired to the parlor. By the end of the evening Nancy knew she had a perfect buyer for the school.

Two months later Nancy returned to her father's home in the Wyoming Valley. The school property had sold to Miss Boche and Nancy anticipated Michael's return.

Return he did and the couple wasted no more time in preparation for their wedding. They were soon settled in Michael's house and Nancy immediately began to make it a home.

CHAPTER NINETEEN

As Michael and Nancy settled into their home, they frequently shared newspapers and openly discussed what was happening in America. Michael was passively sympathetic of the natives, but was disturbed when he learned that some of the tribes were actually fighting on behalf of Britain.

War proved to bring financial gains to the enterprise that Michael controlled, but he had begun to remove himself from the mining industry and was more and more involved in taking care of the small farm on which they lived.

Americans overall, Michael thought, probably came out for the better as the war came to an end. Louisiana became the 18th state and, not long after the treaty of Ghent was signed the war finally ended when the British were soundly defeated in New Orleans.

Michael sat at the dinner table reading the latest Philadelphia newspaper while Nancy tidied up the kitchen. "Listen to this," he said to Nancy. "There are plans being discussed to build a canal that will connect the Great Lakes and Ohio and Mississippi valleys with the Hudson River. Do you know what that would mean?"

Nancy sat down. "It would probably mean you would want to go off on some sort of business venture and try to be among the first men who managed to make a trip from Lake Erie to the Atlantic Ocean," she said sarcastically.

"Well, they are just now talking about it, so it would be some time before they can actually do it, but I will not deny that I could make a few plans just in case," he said, obviously trying to tease Nancy.

"Nancy reached out and grasped Michael's hand. "You should start making some plans pretty soon," she said. "But what you should be planning is how you will do your best at being a father."

"Are you telling me that you are...?"

"That is exactly what I am telling you. I am fairly confident that I am pregnant, and I am sure that means you will be a father before this year is out."

Michael felt a series of different emotions stirring through his body. His stomach growled, his head pounded and his hands started shaking. He stood up, encouraged Nancy to stand also and he embraced her so tightly that she had to literally force him away.

"We must go tell my mother at once," he said, his voice shaking noticeably.

"Just settle down," Nancy replied. "I am not absolutely sure. It is too soon to make any grand announcements. Just promise me that you will try very hard to stay close to home for a while. I am of an age when pregnancy might be difficult and I need you here by my side as much as possible."

"I promise, in fact I fully intend to become a real farmer and stay right where I am," Michael said, again giving Nancy a hug.

The days seemed to pass slowly before Nancy finally told Michael that she was sure that a baby was imminent. They arranged for Nancy's parents and his mother to get together for dinner the next Sunday. With the blessing said, the group started to settle into their seats. Nancy spoke up. "There is one more blessing that is to be bestowed upon our family."

Everyone turned to look at Nancy and she noted that the soon-to-be grandmothers were already smiling.

"Michael and I are soon to become parents."

She barely got the words out before the two older women rushed to Nancy and gave her a big hug. Eamon shook hands with Michael.

"I told you so," Ryleigh said, directing her exclamation to her husband. "I told you she had that glow about her."

"I, too noticed the glow of an expectant mother," Anne said. "But frankly, I was beginning to think I might be wrong." She held out her hand and took Michael's hand in hers. "Oh how I wish your father was here right now."

As expected, Michael and Nancy welcomed a new baby into their lives. James Michael Castello was born without complications, but he was only weeks old when Michael began talking about another farm, this one near St. Louis. He watched as Nancy nursed the baby and broke the silence.

"I have received a missive from those taking care of the farm ground in the Missouri Territory. They are faltering largely because they are following my wishes to not use slave labor. I cannot condone the owning of slaves and we may need to make some life-changing decisions soon," he said.

A worried look came over Nancy's face. "I hope you are talking about selling that property, and not talking about going there right now."

"I do not want to sell. After all we have gone through to keep the property, I feel that I would be betraying my father to sell it without at least trying other things first. As you know, I have all but removed myself from the mining interests here, but this small farm will only provide a meager income for us. The mining properties in Missouri will continue to help considerably, but I must determine what our options are before long."

Nancy again looked worried. "Are you saying that you are considering moving us all to the Missouri Territory?"

Michael thought a moment before answering. "I guess I am saying that relocating there might well be one of the options. This nation is going to grow and St. Louis is proving to be a starting point for those wanting to move west. This property, which is near St. Ferdinand, could well be a very valuable asset. River travel is becoming more efficient. The farm has great potential and if subsidized with funds from the mine, I think we can eventually make it pay its own way."

With a note of finalization, Nancy replied, "I am not taking a newborn baby on a long 900 mile trip on boats. The prospect of doing that scares me to death."

"You and James will be the first consideration before any decisions are made. Now, I have some chores that need attended to," Michael said as he walked to the door and put on his coat.

Michael tended to his chores, saddled a horse and rode to the McDonald home, where he found Eamon McDonald just returning from the mining offices nearby.

Michael handed the letter from Missouri to Eamon. "I hoped, at least for the time being, that my headaches involving this old Riviere property were over with, but it seems another problem has arisen. I come to seek your advice."

Eamon read the letter, held it to his side with one hand while massaging his temple with the other. "I also feel a headache coming on. Am I to assume that you are contemplating uprooting your little family and heading for St. Ferdinand?"

"Not at this very moment," Michael responded. "But I must confess that the option of moving there and managing the farm ground in my own way has crossed my mind. I think I could be happy as a farmer and I also think a farm would be a good place to raise my son."

Eamon hesitated, and then became very serious. "You asked for my advice and I will give it to you, but the decisions must be made by you and Nancy. Let me say first of all that moving such a great distance will be a very big challenge for Nancy and the baby. Secondly, do not doubt for a minute that taking that child away from his two grandmothers will not set well with either of them. Thirdly, I have watched you over the years and mining is in your blood. I predict that you will become more involved in the mining in the Missouri Territory and that farming will be a sideline for you. My advice is to talk this over honestly with Nancy before you even think about talking to Ryleigh or Anne, and I do not envy your position with either of those women."

Michael thanked Eamon and headed home. His head was spinning with various scenarios, none of which he decided would be easy.

As the next spring thaw turned to an early summer, Michael was on his way to the Missouri Territory. He was going to prepare for his family to once again become pioneers.

When Michael arrived in St. Louis, his first impression was one of awe. The town had become a city. The Creole buildings, which were dominant in his last visit, had been expanded, many with large wood additions. The most obvious sign of growth was the many brick buildings.

As Michael walked to a rooming house where he planned to stay for a day or two, he encountered another sign that St. Louis was growing. A street hawker was peddling copies of the Missouri Gazette. Michael enthusiastically purchased a copy. Once settled into his room, he spread the paper out on a small table and noted that it contained detailed information regarding the political environment of Missouri. He read with interest some of the accounts of immigrants and the news stories from various parts of the world from which those people came. The paper also displayed an ad for an upcoming slave auction. He put the newspaper aside; retrieved pen, paper and a small vial of ink from his travel bag and prepared a letter to Nancy.

August 15, 1815

My Dearest Wife,

I have arrived in St. Louis and will be here for a day or two so that I can meet with certain persons who will likely influence my decisions of the immediate future.

I pray that you and young James are well. Know that I miss both of you intensely and that my purpose for being where I am is to provide our son with a future. Please give him my love.

The city has changed dramatically since my last visit. It seems to vibrate with people who are preparing to go west. The fur trade is still active and is proving to be an important industry, especially for the Creoles. Mr. Lewis and Mr. Clark have quite literally blazed a pathway into a frontier that we can only imagine.

I will meet tomorrow with my advisors before heading out to our land near St. Ferdinand. I fully intend to do whatever necessary to make this land productive and to do it without forcing people to work the land. I think it can be done.

I will also meet with a lawyer regarding our interests in the lead mine. I do not plan on becoming personally involved in the mine, but I must oversee the operation to the extent that it will provide us with subsidy for the farming.

I promise that I will send daily missives to you.

Your loving and devoted husband,
Michael

Michael's association with the Riviere family once again proved to be beneficial. Within a few months he was trading furs and acquiring a small herd of cattle. A trusted friend of the Rivieres took over the day-to-day management of the farm. A modest house was located on the property and Michael arranged for the house to be upgraded and ready for his return. He had made his decision. Now it was time for Nancy to realize the benefits of leaving the Wyoming Valley. He returned to the Wyoming Valley shortly before Christmas.

Once again, a family dinner was arranged for the purpose of informing Eamon, Ryleigh and Anne of Michael's plans for his family's future.

Nancy agreed that moving to the Missouri Territory was a logical move, but she insisted they wait until James was a little older. Not only did Anne agree with the plan, but she also asked if she could go with them. Their destiny waited.

CHAPTER TWENTY

James was in his fifth year; about the same age his father had been when Juame Castello brought his family to America. Now the youngster was standing between his mother and his grandmother as a few pieces of luggage, a large trunk and a small wooden desk were being unloaded onto the dock in St. Louis. Although now on dry land, James could still feel the movement of the barge and boats on which he had been confined for weeks. His steps were tentative and he held on to both of the women's hands firmly.

Michael, Nancy, Anne and James left their home in Pennsylvania as soon as the spring of 1820 would allow. The small farm, both houses and most of their possessions had been sold shortly before they left. The only furniture they took with them was a small wooden desk Nancy had acquired while managing the school for girls in Philadelphia. As the desk was offloaded to the dock Nancy recalled the conversation she and Michael had, a conversation that was the closest thing to an argument they had experienced in their years together.

"We must be as prudent as possible in limiting the number of possessions we take with us," Michael had said to the women who were engaged in packing clothes and personal belongings. "We do not want to take anything heavy or bulky. We will be charged extra for such things"

"I hope you are not intending to sell my desk," Nancy replied.

"Once we get settled we can get you a new desk," Michael said.

"I will not be settled without my desk. That is where I compose my letters, and now that I will be a world away from my parents, I intend to compose many letters. That desk is where I have started to teach your son to read. That desk is my link to a world I left to marry you and I will find some way for it to go with us. That is all that I have to say on the subject."

Anne smiled as her son started to say something, thought about it, and then replied, "As you wish, my love."

Michael arranged for a wagon and driver to transport the trio to their new home. As he and the driver made arrangements, Michael noted that a newspaper hawker was nearby and summoned him. He purchased the latest edition of the *Missouri Gazette*, but did not take time to read it. They had a short but challenging trip to St. Ferdinand and their new home nearby before their adventure reached a conclusion.

Acting upon the recommendation of the wagon owner, Michael went to a nearby livery where he purchased a lighter wagon and two draught horses. When he returned to the dock, the desk and other items had been loaded onto the hired wagon and the driver left for the farm. Michael explained to his family that they would follow in the smaller wagon after procuring some basic provisions to tide them over until he and Nancy could do some trading for other necessities. Two hours later they were on the road with salt, flour, dried venison, a smoked turkey a few garden greens, and other items picked out by Nancy and Anne. Some of the miscellanies seemed frivolous to Michael, but he was out voted quickly and ridded himself of some silver each time the women made a decision.

A surprisingly well-traveled road led from the western edge of St. Louis to the Castello property near St. Ferdinand; a distance of just over 20 miles. The horses were fresh and the wagon not overly heavy, but the trip took over three hours. Michael drove the horses and experienced one of his most enjoyable minutes of the trip when young James sat beside him on the seat. Most of the time James rode behind Michael in the arms of Nancy or Anne.

Michael had yet to see the newly renovated house. The drawings exchanged between him and the man contracted to do the work gave him some notion of what it would look like but he was anxious, hoping that Nancy would approve of the new home. To make that approval a little more likely Michael had arranged for a very special commodity that had been shipped in at a huge expense. Cast iron cook stoves were considered a luxury, but it was a luxury that Michael felt necessary. Adding that special touch to make Nancy's life just a little easier was worth the cost.

There was also his mother to consider. A small addition to the original house provided for a private area just for Anne. Michael smiled as he anticipated his mother's response to the room. Anne was easy-going and in relatively good health. With the exception of her illness several years before, she was in relatively good health for a 60 year-old woman. Michael had little doubt that she would approve of the entire farm, but she appeared very tired. The trip from Pennsylvania had taken its toll.

As they pulled up in front of the house, the hired wagon driver and his assistant had just finished taking everything into the house as they had been instructed to do so by Michael. The driver accepted final payment and left the family standing in front of the house.

"It is beautiful," Nancy said as she looked at the house. "This front yard needs some flowers and that porch needs some chairs, and..." Michael interrupted her.

"There is a lot to be done, but let's go inside. It is getting late and we have to get through our first night here with very little comfort. I have arranged for much to be done prior to our arrival, but there are still many things which I must do before I can retire for the night."

When Michael opened the door for Nancy her eyes fell first upon her desk, which had been carefully placed against a wall across the room. "It is perfect," she said, turning her attention to a window on the east side of the room. "Oh, the light from the rising sun will fall perfectly on the desk. It could not be more perfect."

Just then she noticed the cook stove. "Michael, how did you do this? It is perfect."

Michael smiled. "Well before you completely wear out the word perfect, let's all get inside and shut the door. We can do a quick inspection and then I will unload the wagon and get the horses to their corral where some well-earned grain awaits them."

As soon as Michael unloaded the wagon the women retrieved the smoked turkey and began preparing their first meal. Michael started a fire in the stove and left to take care of the horses. By the time he returned, the house felt much warmer. As the sun settled in the west two lanterns were lit and Michael sat on the rudimentary bench at the table. For the first time he opened up the newspaper. The headline seemed to jump from the page. Why had he not noticed it when he bought the paper? In bold type were the words, "Statehood at Last?"

The Missouri territorial government had applied for statehood two years earlier. The application was denied mostly because those in the north who were anti-slavery feared they would be outnumbered if the slave-holding Missouri Territory became a state. According to the article, Main was admitted as the 23rd state on March 15, 1820 and, as part of a compromise, Missouri would be admitted the next year, and all the remaining Louisiana Purchase north of Missouri would be considered non-slavery. The news was bittersweet to Michael. He would have liked to see Missouri become a non-slave state, but he knew that it was unlikely from the start. He considered it a positive move that the compromise exempted the rest of the Louisiana Territory from the practice.

Antoine Riviere died about four years before Michael and his family arrived. He was believed to have been about 110 years of age. Within weeks after his family's move to Missouri, and as a direct result of Michael's friendship with the Riviere family, he met Auguste Chouteau, a renowned fur trader who maintained several trading posts; one not far from the Castello farm. Michael knew of Chouteau's reputation for dealing fairly with the Osage inhabitants of the territory and he immediately liked Chouteau on a personal level. That meeting also resulted in Michael befriending a family of Osage Indians who maintained a small farm. Michael learned that the Osage people were basically part time farmers. They planted their small areas of beans and pumpkins in the spring, and then left the farmland to go to their hunting grounds, returning in the fall to harvest whatever remained. They practiced no cultivation and their yield was typically very low. Michael saw this as an opportunity and offered to take care of the small crops during the Indian's absence. He, in turn, would share their crop. A deal was made that benefited both Michael and his new friends. It also started a lifelong relationship.

When Anne learned of the arrangement between Michael and the Osage, she was pleased. "Your father had a special relationship with the Lenape, who were natives of the Pennsylvania area. He never accepted the treatment that the natives received, as a whole, from the white immigrants. He would be proud of your relationship with these people, and he would condone it with ease."

Nancy also agreed with Michael's actions. "I, too, learned of the plight of the Lenape from my father. It is my understanding that the Osage are people of peace and it is my prayer that your dealings with them will be a guide for others," she said.

Michael thanked his mother and wife for their kind words. "There is another thing that makes me want to know the Osage people more intimately," he explained. "They have a long history of taking lead and other minerals from the mines. In fact, early exploration of the mining property, which we are invested in was done by the Osage and a few of the offspring of those early miners are working at the mine as we speak."

CHAPTER TWENTY-ONE

After the Missouri Constitution was officially adopted on July 19, 1820 the first general assembly met at a hotel in St. Louis. The assembly selected St. Charles as a temporary home for the state capital. Michael was present for the announcement.

From that day forward the population of St. Louis grew in leaps and bounds. A number of companies were formed with the sole purpose of leading people west, but Michael was where he wanted to be, at least for the time being. He became more and more involved with the politics of the area and was instrumental in the formal name change of St. Ferdinand to that of Florissant in 1829. By then, James was 14 years of age and often accompanied his father to various meetings. He had also become a very efficient farmer and displayed knowledge beyond his years when it came to livestock.

Not long after Christmas of 1830 Michael sat with his family in front of the fireplace. He looked as though he was trying to determine the thoughts of his mother and his wife.

Anne Castello was now 70 years old, but in remarkable health for her age. She sat in a large chair, which had become known as 'Grandmother's chair,' and was not used by anyone else. As Michael looked around, he and his mother's eyes met.

"Michael, you have something on your mind," she stated. "I can always tell when you have some idea or announcement you want to make. So what is it this time?"

"Don't tell me that you are off on another adventure," Nancy said. "Please don't tell me you want us to move west."

Michael sat up on the edge of his chair and looked at Nancy. "No I do not want to move west, although I believe those doing so have the future of this nation in their hands. As for me being off on some adventure, I do not know if I would say it is an adventure, but I am planning on a little trip. James has come to the age when he can handle things here for awhile, and he and I have talked about that. The manager of the mine has been in contact with some of his kin in the north. Owing to the fact that railroads are being built and will quite likely some day lead to an amazing amount of travel, he and his family are considering some other mining possibilities in an area of Wisconsin in the Michigan Territory. As we speak there are some serious problems with the natives of that area, but I am told that there are some promising lands there. I have agreed to meet some interested parties later this month."

"I knew it," Nancy said. My father told me that you would eventually expand your mining interests. He said mining is in your blood and that you would not resist the promise of riches buried deep within the earth."

"Perhaps you are right," Michael said. "But understand that I am not saying we need to pack up and head for the Michigan Territory. I am not going to Wisconsin. I am only going along with some fur traders to a small outpost located about 270 miles north of here on the Mississippi. There I will meet with others who are interested in both the fur trade and the lead mines of Wisconsin. This is only an exploration on my part and the trip back here will be much quicker that than of going. Bear with me."

So, even before winter had released its hold, but later than originally planned, Michael was traveling on the slow trip up the Mississippi River. He arrived in the small village later called Davenport where he met with several other potential investors over a period of one week. The information imparted during those meetings was largely based on two of the more prominent fur traders and politically connected men in the area, Antoine Le Claire and George Davenport.

The investors were told that the lead mining industry was producing millions of pounds of lead each year and that much of the land where both lead and iron could be found in Wisconsin had been ceded by the

Sauk Indians in 1804 and that negotiations were active with the Ojibwa, Ottawa and Potawatomi tribes that could result in lands to the south and west of Milwaukee being available for mining. The government of the United States was already issuing mining permits that could result in huge profits. At the conclusion of the meetings Michael agreed to make a substantial investment in procuring the permits and establishing ownership of some of the mining properties.

When Michael returned to Florissant, he found that the spring planting was nearly done and that James had suddenly become a young man, often both working and supervising the activities on the farm. The small cowherd was growing. Two heifers had already given birth and five more were ready to calf at any time.

As they sat at the dinner table, Michael expressed his satisfaction with both his trip and with how well things had been taken care of in his absence.

"James, I want you to know how proud I am of you for the way you have taken care of things," Michael said as he placed his hand on James' shoulder.

After a brief pause, Anne spoke. "Michael, your son has all the best qualities of you and his grandfather. Your father at times placed what I thought was undue pressure on you at a very young age, but you always stepped up. James has that same desire to do whatever is necessary. He is up at dawn and will not retire of an evening before the day's work is done and done properly. Your pride is well founded, and while we are dishing out accolades, let us not forget this wonderful wife of yours. She is destined for sainthood."

James let out a short giggle. "Saint Nancy, the patron saint of chickens," he said. "She spends so much time with those chickens that I sometimes think she may just build a nest for herself in the henhouse," he said with another giggle.

Nancy accepted the sarcasm, but replied, "I don't hear any complaints when you sit down to your bacon and eggs or when one of my hens gives her life to provide you with a chicken dinner. Now, my dear Michael, tell us of your adventure upriver."

Michael explained his decision to invest in the Wisconsin mining industry, saying that it was largely speculation, but promising.

"We will have to wait and see," he said. "A lot depends on the negotiations with the indigenous people of the area. As always, I do not want them to be mistreated, but we all have to admit that the expansion of this nation seems to be inevitable and I see this as a true opportunity to see that young James here has a future in that expansion."

For the next several months Michael sent and received missives from his associates in Wisconsin. He routinely discussed the contents of the letters with Nancy and James. James was becoming increasingly interested in the ventures and told his father that someday he would like to go to Wisconsin.

In early October of 1833, Michael received a large packet from Wisconsin. It contained a manuscript of the Treaty of Chicago, which was the second such treaty, the first being made in 1822. Michael read over the words carefully and discussed the provisions at length with Nancy and James. It seemed to Michael that the men responsible for negotiating the treaty had done so in an appreciative manner. Michael knew the commissioners, George Porter, Thomas J. V. Owen and William Weatherford, only through his correspondence with fellow investors, but regarded them as reputable.

The treaty, as it read, provided what seemed to Michael at the time to be an equitable exchange in that the United Nation of Chippewa, Ottawa and Potawatomie Indians would be given a large portion of land west of the Mississippi River.

Michael sent an affirmation to his associates, agreeing to release some further funding in anticipation of being able to actively engage in mining in the areas allowed.

By early the next year land offices were being opened in Mineral Point, the area of interest in which Michael's funds were being directed. His associates had clear and encouraging acquaintances with those in charge of the land offices. Ultimately, the Mineral Point public land sale resulted in promising holdings. Michael received a map of the area, explaining where, and to what extent, the mining was to take place.

Michael sat with James in a rare meeting where they were the only two present.

"What I have started in Wisconsin, you will likely have to carry on. Some day all the decisions regarding that venture will be yours to make. For the time being, all of those decisions will be made by me, but with your knowledge and input. Am I assuming too much here? Do you agree with me that you are now a man and that you will make good decisions based, first on what is good for your family, and secondly on what is good for the people who will bestow their trust on you?"

"Father," James replied. "I am without words to describe what your trust in me means. I confess that I do not yet fully comprehend what is happening, but I know that your mentoring will provide that understanding. I have listened to your stories and those of Grandfather Eamon for many years now. I think I have known for a long time that I will be expected to carry out the legacies that you, mother and the McDonald family have built. I will take on that responsibility and carry on to the best of my ability, that I promise you."

James' response made tears well up in Michael's eyes, but he went to bed that night knowing that his family's future was going to be in good hands.

CHAPTER TWENTY-TWO

Only a few months had passed when James' life took a new path. Michael was getting more and more involved in Missouri politics and decided that a trip to Wisconsin was not prudent at the time.

Once again, Michael sat down with James. "Son, the time for me to ask you to go beyond your current horizons has come much quicker than I intended. Things are happening here in Missouri that I feel compelled to be part of, maybe to the point of seeking public office. But there is a need for me to go to Wisconsin. In lieu of me going, I could send a trusted representative. I believe you can be that representative, but I must know if you can put your heart into the task."

James felt a nervous growl in his stomach. "What would you have me do? I must say that I had hoped for a trip to Wisconsin, but I assumed that, should that come to pass, it would be a trip with you."

"I, too, hoped to take you with me so we could both see the properties there together," Michael said. "However, circumstances are such that I hop- you will take the responsibility upon yourself to represent our family and our business holdings, not just as a representative, but as a full partner in what we are trying to accomplish."

"How soon would I have to leave?"

Michael smiled as he realized James was going to take on the task. "I will arrange for proper documents to be prepared in the next several days. I will also see to it that you have the bank drafts necessary to satisfy our obligations to our existing associates. You also will have sufficient money to take care of other expenses as you see fit. We will talk again in a few days."

With that, and a very business-like handshake Michael got up and left the room he used as an office, leaving James alone to think.

Travel in general had become easier but James' trip to Wisconsin was not without its problems. While Milwaukee had what amounted to a natural harbor, large ships were not able to dock there and much of James' travel was overland. One month after leaving his family in Missouri James was seated at a table in the back of a small pub in Mineral Point, in what was soon to become the Wisconsin Territory. James felt like a child sitting with much older adults.

At first, the men in the room assumed they would merely tell James what to do and he would do it. They found out rather quickly that James was their equal in nearly every way. He demonstrated that he understood the task at hand and was quite capable of being a productive part of the association. The purpose of the meeting was to plan a strategy beginning with the acquisition of mining claims. The men planned on going to the first government land auction at the Mineral Point Land Office the next day. They planned to purchase as many claims as possible, using individual names. After the proper deeds were executed, the group would combine their interests under one umbrella company and proceed with mining operations.

It was during these discussions that James introduced an amendment to the plan. He pointed out that the bank drafts he had in his possession amounted to significantly more than each of the other investors intended on spending. He proposed that at least one of the claims would be the sole property of the Castello family and, at the discretion of the family, might later become part of the other properties.

There was a heated discussion following James' proposal. James, in a bold move, intimated that denial of his proposal might well jeopardize the monies he had being invested in the larger proposition. Ultimately, the group agreed on a contract whereby a corporation would be formed with all the properties purchased, and that the Castello family would have a controlling interest in the corporation. The attorney present informed the group that he would have the paperwork completed and ready for signatures the following day prior to the auction.

The land auction was intense, but few of the potential purchasers had prepared as well as those involved with the Castellos and even fewer were as prepared to start mining. Most of the properties acquired by James and his fellow investors were properties that already had some sort of mining, mostly for lead, which had taken place earlier by indigenous people. The group needed only to modernize the operations and get miners to work for them. Before James was ready to return to Missouri miners and families were already on their way, or had already arrived. Many of the ones who had failed to purchase a claim were now seeking employment with those who were successful in doing so.

James stayed in Wisconsin somewhat longer than he intended. In lieu of a personal account of the various dealings, James prepared a letter to his father:

October 1, 1834

My Dear Father,

I know that you are anxious to hear the details of my effort here, but there are still some tasks that must, in my opinion, be completed before I return to Missouri. With the winter sure to come soon, I may quite possibly need to stay in this area until at least next spring. I will keep you informed as to my actions and my intentions.

I was successful in acquiring, what I am told are some promising claims, and have, as you directed aligned with other investors. I must tell you that I expended the entire amount of money you entrusted to me. There was some confusion over the lands available and there are a notable number of people who would prefer that more of the land be set aside for the raising of crops. I do not necessarily disagree with their arguments. It is obvious that the area is going to grow in population very quickly and the development of flourmills and other agricultural related industries can only add to the comfort, and value of our endeavors.

I have learned that there is adequate population now for Wisconsin to be an official territory of the United States. I find that interesting, but I certainly do not want to be a citizen of this territory. I am not overly impressed with the surrounding in which I have found myself, but will continue efforts to ensure that our investments become successful.

There has already been a great amount of mining in this area. I have befriended a few gentlemen who have agreed to allow me to accompany them to the mines in which we are now invested. I look forward to that experience, but I certainly would favor not living in this area any longer than is required. I miss you and mother and our friends, and I will return as soon as it is practical.

Give my love to Mother and to my grandparents.

Respectively Yours,
James

Michael sat pensively for a minute after he read the letter from his son. He handed the letter to Nancy.

"I think our son has become his own man," he said.

Nancy read the letter and placed it on the table as she replied to Michael.

"That seems to be the case for sure, but he certainly is not impressed with Wisconsin. I do believe, however, that he will stay as long as it is necessary for him to complete his tasks. He has your tendency to think he must be directly involved once he has involved himself at all, and he will not make decisions without knowing in his own mind what those decisions will mean to everyone involved. He will make this family proud of him and his work. You can count on that."

"I agree wholeheartedly," Michael replied. "I will send him a letter first thing tomorrow morning and advise him that he needs to decide who he trusts and allow them to carry on, with or without him, but you must get used to the fact that you may not see your son for some time. I can read between the lines in that letter and I know that he feels he has things to do and must get them done."

Nancy let one of her giggles escape. "The other thing that boy must do is think about finding himself a good woman and including her in his future. We are getting older every day and I would love it if I were blessed with a grandchild or two before I get too old to enjoy them."

"That will happen soon enough. Now, I have some chores to attend to," Michael replied as he stood up, kissed Nancy on the forehead and put on his coat.

For the next three months James imbedded himself into the mining operations. He worked the same hours and received the same pay as the other miners. His advantage was that he could leave at any time. He was recognized as a part owner of the properties without question, although he noted that some of the miners seemed rather aloof, especially during times when the miners socialized at a local pub.

The other investors were cordial and James spent Christmas Eve with two families, both of which had moved and planned on staying in Wisconsin. John Ballard and James became good friends almost immediately. Both were of the same age, and shared the fact that they were in Wisconsin representing their fathers. John, however, was newly married and he and his wife were expecting their first child. The Christmas Eve activities included the baby announcement from the Ballards and quickly separated the festive group into ladies discussing homes and children and men discussing mining and politics.

James addressed the other men in the room. "As soon as the weather permits, I will probably return to Missouri," he said. "I am encouraged with the quality of men we have working now and I think that I will be leaving our holdings in good hands. I also think that we should select some experienced men from that group, men that are capable of being foremen and will be respected. I know that I am looked on as the young pup and I do not have enough experience to expect those miners to always do my bidding."

John and the others agreed, almost too quickly, James thought, but assured James there were men among the miners that were true leaders and that they would converse with the other investors and pick some of them to act as foremen and shift bosses. With that the men rejoined the women and, one by one, encouraged their wives to quit talking about babies and go home. James was the last to leave, after thanking the Ballards for including him in the little party. By mid-February he felt comfortable in preparing to go back to Missouri.

CHAPTER TWENTY-THREE

When James returned to Missouri he was met with some disturbing news that his father's health was failing. He was bedridden and having trouble breathing.

Nancy sat with James outside his father's bedroom.

"He has had his good days and his bad days, but lately he seems to have more bad than good. He has become overly concerned with the political activities of this area and I think he suffers some anxiety over the fact that he and his friends seem to try so hard for so little. The anxiety leads to his becoming ill. Of course, he will deny that he is trying to solve all the problems and does not recognize what it is doing to his health," she explained.

James held his mother's hand and asked, "What is he so concerned about?"

"In his mind, all the problems in our lives boil down to the conflicts between pro-slavery and abolitionists and he has pretty much identified with the latter. Crime is becoming a big problem and he is convinced that the state government is corrupt in several ways. Just recently he learned there have been several conflicts in Texas and that it may come to pass that Texas will revolt against Mexico. He believes that could mean that Texas could eventually become a state, and that would mean a very big slavery state would become part of the United States," Nancy said, as tears welled up in her eyes.

"That seems a little excessive for him to be concerned with Texas," James said. "I understand his beliefs, but why would Texas mean anything to him?"

"It's not just that," Nancy replied. "If Texas becomes a state, it would be on the pro-slavery side. That bothers your father, and to make things worse, a number of the miners here have gone to Georgia, where they discovered gold a year or so ago. Some of the mines in this area are already using slave labor and having the free miners leave just adds to the problem."

In October, Texas revolted against Mexico, resulting in an all-out war. While Michael was not fully recovered, he managed to go to the mine most days. He was directly involved in the local politics and never missed a meeting, whether one with state and town officials or one of the many abolitionist gatherings; many of those erupted into violent confrontations.

Not long after hearing the news about Texas, Michael was sitting quietly in front of a fire, a book resting in his lap, when Nancy and James entered the room. He did not acknowledge their presence until Nancy interrupted him.

"Your thoughts were miles away," she said. "What in the world were you thinking about?"

"I recently received this book, which I arranged to be sent to me from Paris where Charles Gosselin's company published it. I first heard of the book at one of the meetings I attended earlier this year. This one is in French and only 500 copies were printed. I understand that it will be available in English, but I felt a need to read what this man had to say. I will confess that my French is lacking some these days, but this man's words are enlightening to say the least."

James reached out and took the book from his father's hands and read the front cover: *DEMOCRATIE EN AMERIQUE ALEXIS DE TOCQUEVILLE.* He read the title in English: "*DEMOCRACY IN AMERICA.*"

He lowered the book into his lap when Nancy asked, "Why is a Frenchman writing about democracy in America?"

"As I understand it," Michael explained. "Tocqueville came here about four years ago to study the penitentiary system. France has had some significant problems when it comes to penal institutions. In so doing, he was impressed by the unique way that our founders approached democracy. He traveled around the country for nine months before returning to France and publishing this book.

James opened the book and paged through it. "Thanks to you, Father, my French is still acceptable," he said. "I see here in the early pages that this man was impressed by the fact that our government, unlike any other, has endured to give power to the people, rather than being powerful in and of itself. I must read more when you have finished." With that, he handed the book back to his father.

Michael thought for a short time and then began once again to refer to the book. Holding it up, he said, "Mr. Tocqueville may well have traveled to the United States to study the penal system, but he managed to absorb what this union is really about. He recognizes that France has, what is termed a democracy, but he said that any advances toward true freedom of the people have largely come by chance, while here in America we have formed what is a truly representative style of government. He says it is a style that is becoming more and more important to the people and causing them to be more and more confident in defending this new concept. He saw that our constitutional framers, after much debate and thought, put into words that which if defended properly, will serve the people of this nation for generations to come."

Michael then went on to say, "We sit at the beginning of what I believe will turn into a mass exodus of people moving into the western territories. I have no thoughts about joining them. I would rather stay here and enjoy any profits we might realize from the inevitable settling of the west. We have learned just recently that Texas is in the midst of a revolution. The people of Texas have risen up against the Mexican government for some of the same reasons that Americans rejected the monarchy of England. While I cannot condone war in and of it, I do understand the thought process of men who desire freedom of the individual. The one thing that still bothers me is that all of this thought and knowledge; all of these proclamations of individual freedom still leave us with the idea that one man can be owned by another. I believe this will cause problems that are yet unseen as this nation expands."

The conversation and the late hour obviously took a toll on Michael. He excused himself and retired to his bedroom.

"Father does not look well," James said to his mother.

"He is tired, but he will not give up," she replied. "I will tell you that he is depending on you to lead the family forward. He has already prepared a will and directed his lawyers to make arrangements for you to become the primary head of all his business dealings. That is why he has put everything relating to the Wisconsin properties in your name."

"Wisconsin," James said with a sigh. "I suppose I will be obligated to once again go there, but I will put it off as long as possible. I did not observe anything during my time there that made me want to stay any longer than was absolutely necessary. What I need is to find a woman like you to share my life with. I feel as though I am 18 going on 40."

Nancy smiled. "You are a fine looking, intelligent young man. Do not wish your life away, but I also caution you to recognize love if it comes to you. Your father and I did not do that. I think we waited too long to declare our true commitment to each other. I take most of the blame for that, but the other side of the coin is that I have experienced that freedom he so often talks about. I was unique in the world of women and I am proud of my contributions to the education of young women. They all have a better chance of being individuals. I truly believe that. Now bank the fire for me and get back to your own home before the night advances any more. I love you."

James returned the compliment, added some wood to the fire and walked out into the night, his father's words repeating themselves in his head as he walked the short distance to his house.

CHAPTER TWENTY-FOUR

In 1836 the U. S. Congress passed the Gag Rule. The rule prevented abolitionist petitions from being considered. The rule upset Michael and he made it known to his colleagues and those who were active in politics. He openly discussed, and was often vilified for his stance on slavery. When Arkansas was designated as a state in June of that year, Michael was in a solemn mood one evening at the supper table, where James again joined him and Nancy.

"I truly fear that this nation has some of the greatest opportunities of any nation in the history of the world," James said. "But I also fear that we are creating our own problems. Arkansas is now a state, making the number of states 25. It is another state that lives with slavery."

Looking to Nancy he continued, "It is though you were sewing one of your beautiful quilts, but intentionally tearing the fabric along the way, making it easier in the future to rip the entire quilt apart."

Nancy reached out and covered James' hand with her own and bent slightly forward, looking him in the eyes. "The fabric I worry most about this moment is the fabric of your life. You look tired. Your sleep is not restful. You need to pay more attention to your health and worry less about what is happening in the world around you. We are strong people, but we must remain strong by taking care of ourselves."

The next morning a courier awakened James at an unusually early hour. The courier handed James a brown envelope that was sealed with a red wax seal of the office of an attorney in Wisconsin. It was marked "URGENT."

James, knowing that the envelope may contain life-changing information, brewed a pot of strong coffee before sitting at his table and opening it. The envelope contained one sheet of paper embossed with the name Robert Walton. Walton was on retainer by James and his associates in Wisconsin and had, in the past several months, brokered several transactions, none of which warranted a special courier to bring James up to date. Upon reading the opening sentence, James knew his apprehension was justified.

Following the normal salutation, the first line read, "Your presence is needed as soon as possible." The short letter went on to describe that Wisconsin was on the verge of an economic depression. One of the banks in which the Castellos were doing business with had already failed and the other three banks were on the brink. The final line read, "I have done what I can to avoid further depletion of your resources, but it is imperative that you be here to personally oversee our next steps. I look forward to meeting with you immediately upon your arrival."

James had his second cup of coffee and walked to his parents' house. Nancy answered the door. "James, I certainly did not expect to see you at such an early hour. Are you on your way to the mine?"

James stepped into the house, almost forcing his mother aside. "I need to talk to you and Father. Something is happening in Wisconsin," he said looking over Nancy's shoulder.

"Your father is still in his bed," Nancy said. "He had a bad night and I do not wish to disturb him."

"Let's go to him," James said. "He need not rise, but he needs to know about this turn of events."

With that said, James led the way to his father, who was awake and staring at the door as James and Nancy came in.

"What in Heaven's name is going on?" Michael sat up in bed with some difficulty as his raspy voice made the inquiry.

"I have just received and important summons from our lawyer in Wisconsin," James said as he approached the bed. He then read the letter in its entirety to his parents. As he placed the letter back into its envelope he said, "I will leave today. I ask you, Mother, to see to it that my house is looked after during my absence, but I have no idea what is happening, or what I will find when I get there. As you are already aware, Mr. Walton has expressed some concern in his earlier letters over the situation between the territorial governor and the Menominee and Ho-Chunk people, but he has never indicated the urgency he has expressed here."

Michael once again took a deep breath. "We knew going into this venture that there could well be some rough decisions, and I knew that you would prove yourself capable of dealing with whatever problems arose. Yes, you must go and do not worry about us here. We have good people working for us and your house will be kept well in your absence. Now go!"

Less than two full days later James was en-route to Wisconsin. The words in Walton's letter were swimming in his head. He tried to envision any scenario that would warrant such concern. The Wisconsin holdings represented a significant part of the Castello investments and James felt the burden of being the one who might well need to make decisions that could jeopardize those investments.

By the time James reached Mineral Point, the weather was beginning to cool. The daytime temperature was staying below 50 degrees and the nights were often nearly 30 degrees cooler. While Mineral Point was then one of the larger towns in Wisconsin, it offered few amenities. James secured a room at a small rooming house. He took advantage of an offer from the keeper of the house to have his coat brushed and a warm bath prepared before he went to the Walton office. A young woman took his clothes from the keeper. She and James exchanged pleasant smiles and she disappeared into a back room. He felt a noticeable disappointment when he retrieved the clothes an hour later and it was the keeper of the house, not the young woman, who handed them to him.

James arrived at the Walton office, which was merely a small wood structure across from the post office, late that afternoon. Robert Walton greeted James without rising from his desk chair. He merely held out his hand saying, "It is good to see you again, young James. I am certainly happy you have arrived."

James sat facing Walton over the top of a large desk, which was partially covered with various papers and a big grey cat. "Your letter sounded almost desperate," James said. "I actually managed to make the trip in a surprisingly short time thanks to a freight company owned by a friend of my father. Now what is the emergency?"

As I informed you in my letter, there are, or I should say were, four banks in this territory. One has failed outright and two more are destined to close their doors soon. I have managed to convert the funds held in those two banks into gold and silver coins, most of which were minted in Mexico, but the holdings of your companies have been substantially reduced by the failure of the first bank. I was a big supporter of President Van Buren. I have had the honor of meeting and talking to him on a couple of occasions and I had confidence in his financial beliefs, but the fact of the matter is that these problems seemed to manifest as soon as he was elected."

James took a moment to process what had been said and asked, "Do you have any ideas as to what course we should take?"

I have taken the initiative to take possession of all the treasury of the company. Up to now, the mine foreman has been in charge of paying the miners. We are paying them in silver and I thought it too risky to have him in possession of large sums for which he had very little security. He kept the payroll in a box in his desk drawer. I have a strong box here in my back room."

James replied, "That seems a good decision, but I detect a pause in your confidence."

"It is not so much my confidence as my second-guessing my decision," Walton explained. "My deciding to take control of the funds from the mine foreman resulted in a marked disagreement with him. As a result of our argument he quit his job. Because the company was providing him with a house, he moved out and was gone from the area in just a few days. The investors that are here held a short meeting and appointed one of the supervisors from a small mine to take over as foreman, overseeing all of the holdings. It was at that meeting that the group asked that I contact you. They are of the unanimous opinion that, because of your controlling interest in the holdings, you should be here to manage the overall operation. I will tell you that there was substantial conversation during that meeting about your youth. You will have your work cut out for you in obtaining their confidence."

James looked down at the floor and thought for a moment before addressing the information. "I had not planned to stay here for any length of time, and certainly not permanently. My father is not well. I was hoping that I could address whatever needs taken care of in a few days and return to Florissant. In addition to our involvement in the mining there, we also have a farm to take care of. I have procured a room at the rooming house not far from here and told the proprietor that I would be here for about one week. I will extend that time, at least until I can meet with the investors." James smiled and continued, "I must admit that an extended stay will be more tolerable if I can make the acquaintance of that young lady who works there."

"Ah, yes," Walton said. Her name is Catherine Hughes. She came here from Ohio. Her father, as I understand it, died when the girl was very young. Her mother re-married to a close friend of her dead husband's. He works at one of the mines. I think Miss Hughes is related in some way to the owner of the rooming house and she helps out there, but perhaps you should consider moving into the small house left vacant by our departing foreman. That would save on expenses during your time here. Meanwhile, I shall attempt to get the investors together as soon as possible. Because of the current events, I have had a lock installed on the house. Take a look at it and consider my advice."

After getting directions and the key to the vacant foreman's house, James left the office and walked for some time around the small, but obviously growing town, but he noticed several buildings that were only partially constructed with no indications of recent work on many of them. He assumed that the halt in construction might have something to do with the economic woes of the local banks.

James found the vacant foreman's house simple, but adequate. After a short inspection of the house, he returned to the rooming house. To his delight, Catherine Hughes was in the parlor area. He asked her if the matron of the house was present.

Catherine smiled. The smile had a way of making James almost dizzy. No woman had ever affected him in that manner. He simply smiled back. Catherine diverted eyes ever so slightly and said, "She is in the pantry. I will get her."

James informed the matron that he would be leaving early the next morning. He paid his bill and went to his room. After having breakfast at the rooming house the next morning, James gathered what little clothing he had and was leaving the house. Catherine was on the front porch. Again, she smiled. James thanked her for brushing his coat.

"I hope I shall see you again before my business is done here," he said.

"I would like that very much," Catherine replied.

CHAPTER TWENTY-FIVE

The weather was cooling rapidly by the time James settled into the house in Mineral Point. The year 1837 was quickly coming to an end. James knew that it was possible that he would be spending the rest of the year in Mineral Point; a fact he was reluctant to accept. He had mixed feelings about what was happening in the country. Governor Dodge had succeeded in making a treaty with the Menominee people. The treaty ceded nearly four million acres of land to the United States. Dodge was not well liked by the Ho-Chunk, the other indigenous people. They sent representatives to Washington D. C. to deal directly with the national government. The result was another treaty that resulted in their giving up all the Wisconsin land and leaving it behind.

James' meeting with the investors took place early in November. It was the first of several meetings, all of which included contentious topics, not the least of which was James' age. Some of the men voiced there concern that a 22-year-old man might not have the experience in life to enable him to lead them in their ventures. One of the investors decided to sell his share. In order to maintain his controlling interests, James arranged to buy him out. He had to draw a significant sum from the treasury, leaving enough to pay the miners, but continued success depended on the prompt payment of shipments made the previous month, but James felt confident that the financial situation would resolve itself in short order. His confidence stemmed from the fact that Mineral Point seemed to be holding its own. He was disappointed that the territorial governing body decided that Madison would become the capital. Madison, at the time was not even a town. It was planned and controlled by the very person who sold the land to the territory with an agreement that it would be developed soon and become the capital.

A sure sign that people in Mineral Point were planning ahead was the completion of its first hotel. The hotel was a modest one, but included an inn and a dining facility that rivaled those of much bigger towns. James was impressed with the hotel and decided that it offered him an opportunity to become better acquainted with Catherine Hughes. He invited her to dinner.

Catherine Hughes was not a strikingly attractive woman. In fact, in her everyday life she tended to blend in, rather than stand out, but she was almost instantly liked by nearly everyone she met. She did not always respond in kind. She tended to be wary of strangers and took her time in getting acquainted. She had very few friends. There was something different about James Castello. Catherine sensed that James was someone who could be trusted, but she could not explain why she thought that. They had only met briefly and no conversation had taken place between them until James asked her to accompany him to dinner at the hotel.

"I would be most honored to be your guest," she said. "But first you must understand something. I live with my mother. She is very protective and I cannot chance her being unhappy with my behavior, so before we go to dinner I must insist that you come to our home and meet my mother."

James responded without hesitation. "Of course. I understand. When would be convenient for me to do that?"

Catherine hoped her anxiousness was not showing. "This evening would be fine. Shall we say about six o'clock?"

That evening James went to Catherine's modest home, arriving precisely at six. Catherine answered and smiled, "Mr. Castello, please come in."

Catherine's mother, Sarah, was standing directly behind her. James noted at once where that unique smile came from. He took Sarah's hand gently as Catherine stepped aside and introduced her mother.

As they sat, Sarah wasted no time in her obvious vetting of the young man who had so suddenly taken a liking to her daughter. "So James," she began. "Do you have family here in Wisconsin?"

"No," James said. After an uncomfortable moment he realized that both Sarah and Catherine were awaiting more of an explanation. He continued, "My family is now in Missouri in a small community known as Florissant. We have a farm there and my father is involved in the mining operations nearby. He became interested a few years back in the mining here in Wisconsin and decided to invest here. That is why I am here now."

After several other questions, Sarah's posture relaxed and she sat back in her chair. She approved of James, but had reservations about him taking her daughter's heart and then running off back to Missouri, but she thought better of voicing her concerns at that time.

James knew it was time to do what he came to do. "I have asked Catherine to accompany me to dinner on an evening of her leisure. She has indicated to me that she would be willing, but only if you concurred. So, I guess I am asking, do you give me your blessing to take Catherine to dinner?"

Sarah smiled and reached out to touch Catherine. "I am flattered that you told this young man that he needed my blessing, but it is you that must decide. I assure you that I will honor your decision."

Catherine almost giggled and looked at James. "Well," she said with a teasing smile. "Let's see, I do believe that an evening of my leisure as you put it, happens to be tomorrow. You may call for me here at six."

As James left Catherine and her mother, he had an almost uncontrollable urge to skip down the street. He had just felt happiness unlike any other he had ever felt. He felt like shouting to the world but instead chose to walk upright and display only the steps of a man full of confidence.

The next evening James once again arrived at exactly six o'clock. Catherine greeted him at the door, took his arm and they walked to the hotel. Over dinner they exchanged family information and pleasantries of a various nature. When Catherine asked about James' plans for the future, he had to think carefully. He did not want to say anything that might be construed to be plans that could not involve the possibility that Catherine could be a part of the future.

"My father," James began slowly. "My father is convinced that this country is destined to grow, and grow fast. He is of the opinion that the concept of a nation that expands means opportunity for everyone who is part of that expansion. I have to say that someday I would like to travel west, but maybe that is just a dream. For now, I must concentrate on the holdings we have here and try to overcome the problems that have occurred as a result of the economic problems, which have caused all the banks to fail."

During the entire month of November hardly a day passed without James and Catherine spending time with each other. They dined at the hotel on at least six occasions during the month. They sat bundled up next to each other for carriage rides and sat for hours talking to each other when James visited Catherine. At other times Catherine and her mother would come to James' house. One evening after having dinner with Catherine and her mother, James stepped out onto the porch with Catherine as he was preparing to leave. They stood for several moments, hand in hand, and then they kissed. It was a kiss that sealed a good part of their future. They both knew at that time that they were destined to be together.

It was the middle of December when James received a letter from his mother. She wrote that, on December 11, 1837, Michael Castello died. Nancy assured James that things were under control in Missouri and that he should remain in Wisconsin and take care of business there for the time being. James immediately penned a letter to his mother. He expressed his regrets for not being with his father during the last days. He also described in detail the relationship that had developed between Catherine Hughes and him. He wrote that he intended to ask Catherine to marry him.

After posting his letter he followed through by meeting with Catherine and proposing marriage; she accepted.

CHAPTER TWENTY-SIX

James was almost constantly at odds with the other Wisconsin investors. He vowed that he would return to Missouri as soon as he could, but there were other vows to take care of first. He and Catherine were going to be married.

Almost every day a new problem with land and mining claims arose. Money was being spent on lawyers and the Wisconsin territorial government seemed to be in a constant state of chaos. The town of Madison was starting to grow and plans were made for the new town to be the capitol. The land offices in Mineral Point were adversely affected by all the confusion and land and claim owners were the ones that ultimately suffered.

December slipped away and it was not until Christmas that a date was set for the marriage. It was during the planning of the wedding that James felt compelled to tell Catherine as much as he could about what was happening. They sat in the warmth of James' company owned house and discussed their plans for the future.

"I am not satisfied with what is happening here now," James said. "If it were not for my deep love for you, I would probably throw up my hands and admit defeat in what I have been trying to accomplish here. I have tried to make decisions on my own, but I must admit that the occasional letters between my father and I were more often than not helpful. Now, with him gone, I am beginning to realize just how inexperienced I am."

"Now you listen to me," Catherine said. "I agreed to marry you, and now we know the exact date on which we are to become man and wife. When that happens, I assure you that I will be at your side and will support you just as a wife should. I hope you will always confide in me, but I trust in your decisions. You do yourself no justice by understating your abilities."

James seemed to relax just a little. "I know you will be the best wife a man can possibly have, but what happens if I do just give up what we have here and decide to return to Missouri and become a farmer?"

"Somehow," Catherine said. "I do not see you as settling into a farmer's life and being happy. Unless I have grossly overestimated your sense of adventure, I believe you will always be happiest when you have the pressure of major decisions pressing against your mind, and for that matter, your soul. If you truly desire to go back to Missouri, I will be at your side. When you become my husband, you become my life. Where you are is where I will be."

That night, James penned a letter to his mother:

December 27, 1837

My Dearest Mother,

Catherine and I are to be married on January 22nd. I love her more than I can say, and she has assured me that she loves me in return. I pray I can be a good husband. I do wish you could be here for the wedding, but the trip is difficult. I understand that.

I have confided in Catherine that I might at some point decide to return to Florissant. I, like Father, still believe that much of the westward expansion will continue. The United States, with the admission of Michigan to the Union, is officially doubled now and I am convinced that the St. Louis area will continue to be a starting point for those wishing to go west. It is of the utmost importance that we hold on to what we have there, regardless of what happens here in Wisconsin. The fledgling government of this territory is, in my humble opinion, in over their heads and their indecision is making things much more complicated than they should be.

The mining industry here is important, but we are seeing more and more that there is a new interest in the raising of cows, primarily dairy cows. We have had several of our best miners take on small dairy operations. I personally do not see how they will have much of a market for their product, but they seem persistent, at least for the time being.

Please keep me informed as to what is happening there. If you need anything, I will do my best to provide. Your assurance that you have adequate help, and that the other endeavors in which Father was involved in, are being well managed comforts me.

I know that you will come to love Catherine. I pray that I have the opportunity soon to introduce her to you.

Your Loving Son,
James M. Castello

James continued to work at the mine and he redoubled his efforts to become a more efficient manager. With the help and guidance of Robert Walton, one of the former bankers in Mineral Point was able to re-open a bank on a very limited basis and the bank became the official paymaster, but the company was still operating on a cash basis. It worried James that such large shipments of gold and silver were being transported with little or no protection. The need for reliable banks became more and more apparent as time went on, but James had a wedding to look forward to, and that made the everyday problems just a little easier to bear.

Finally, the wedding day came. The ceremony itself was not a large one, but the small church was nearly full, mostly of people who were associated with the mines and those who were sincere friends of Catherine and her mother. Some of those friends arranged to leave the church while a small reception was held. They had earlier coordinated with Catherine, and by the time the reception was over, they had moved all of Catherine's belongings into the small house where she and James would begin their married life.

Over the next year it seemed that James was dealing with one crisis after another. Miner's unions were formed and failed, one of the payroll shipments was hijacked and two more of the most experienced mine managers quit. To make matters even worse, the last letter that James received from his mother indicated that there were problems developing in Missouri, but she assured James that they were being handled.

As the Wisconsin winter settled in, James sat at the supper table with Catherine.

"It has been nearly one year since you and I became man and wife," James said as he reached for Catherine's hand. I feel as though I have neglected you. I do hope you understand."

Catherine stood, turned, and gently sat on James' lap. "I do not feel neglected. You are doing what must be done. My fear is that you are doing too much. You are often so tired that I expect your face to drop into your supper plate. I believe we have enough wood stored to last the winter and things will begin to slow down at the mines. You need to rest. Now, eat your supper, and then we will talk more."

James decided to take his wife's advice. He informed the necessary people that he would be unavailable for a few days. Winter was approaching. It seemed that so many important things in the past months, and James wanted the remainder of the year to be special, especially for Catherine. He had no idea how special it was going to be. On that early fall day of 1838, while again sitting on James' lap, she kissed him and smiled; a bigger smile than James had seen for quite some time.

She almost giggled. "I have been pretty sure for quite some time, but now I am certain that I am with child. By the spring of the year coming, you will be a father."

James felt a mixture of panic and elation. He had began recently to start preparing to leave Wisconsin; hopefully in the coming spring, but an infant would make that trip difficult to say the least. He tried to hide his concern.

"That is wonderful news," he said. "You will be a wonderful mother, and I promise that I will accept the responsibility of fatherhood with the sincerity it deserves."

"I have no doubt about your ability to be a fine father," Catherine said with a small frown. "But I detect a hesitation on your part. What causes this hesitancy?"

James thought for a moment and then said, "I will not try to mask things. The only thing I really like about the Wisconsin Territory is the fact that you are here with me. I have been contemplating ways in which I can get away from here without too much of a loss. My father had visions of this place. I fear that I do not have those same visions. We could not leave right now, and I likely will not be able to finalize any plans during the period of your pregnancy. That means that our child will be born here. It also means that, should we be ready to leave then, it would be a difficult trip with a newborn child. I do not mean to imply that I am disappointed that you are pregnant. I am elated, but we must plan carefully over the next months. I do not really own this house and we could find ourselves looking for another should I carry out my plans too quickly. Understand this, Catherine, I want you to be a significant part of my every decision."

"I thank you for that," said Catherine. "And I will, once more, say that I am here for you and I will, while not holding back my opinions, support you in whatever you decide. You take care of business and I will take care of this little one that grows within me."

CHAPTER TWENTY-SEVEN

Signs of spring were finally beginning to show. The trees around the growing town had that hint of green that reveals that the life within them would soon burst. The smooth Juneberry that Catherine loved so much was showing its white flowers, and another spring delight was about to be born. Catherine was entering her ninth month of pregnancy and was anticipating the birth with an excitement that she had not foreseen.

Notwithstanding the initial bouts of morning sickness and the early fears of being a mother, the pregnancy presented few problems. Catherine was healthy and the support she received from James was without fault. In fact, other women with whom she associated with expressed their impressions often, sometimes to the point of showing signs of jealousy. One of those women, Cara Beattie, was a well-qualified midwife. She claimed to have delivered half of the babies in the Mineral Point area in the past ten years and she assured Catherine that she would be there when the time came.

James was not much surprised when Cara's eldest daughter burst into the mine office shortly before noon and May 22, 1839. "You must come at once. Everything is going fine, but Mother says to tell you that it is also going quickly."

By the time James arrived at the house, a curtain had been tacked up around the bed in the bedroom and the unmistakable sounds of childbirth greeted him at the door, where he was instructed to sit at the kitchen table while Cara's daughter poured him some coffee, dropped a cold roll in front of him and disappeared behind the curtain. James could only stare at the open bedroom door and see the makeshift curtain flutter with movement. Five minutes later James heard a loud slap and the crying of a newborn. He rose quickly, but once again faced the young lady. "Mother says that you must wait just a little longer, but you are the father of a very healthy baby boy." With that, she grabbed a kettle of hot water and again went around the curtain.

When James was finally allowed into the bedroom, Cara removed the curtain to reveal a smiling Catherine holding a swaddled red-faced baby. James sat on the edge of the bed and pulled back some of the small blanket to expose more of the baby. He took Catherine's hand, squeezing it, and asked in an almost whisper, "So this is Charles?"

Catherine smiled first at James and then down at the newborn. "I think that is the name we decided on, should it be a boy."

James placed two fingers under the child's chin. "Welcome to the family, Charles."

Cara and her daughter said their goodbyes and left the house. While Catherine and the baby rested James sat at the table and penned a letter to his mother. It had been some time since he received a letter from her, but he knew she was anticipating the birth and he had an obligation to inform her as soon as possible.

May 22, 1839

My Dearest Mother,

It is with a great joy that I inform you that you are the grandmother of a healthy baby boy, born on this day, only about two hours ago. Both Catherine and the boy, which we have named Charles, are in good health and are resting comfortably as I write this.

In your last missive, you wrote that you were experiencing some difficult times and had resorted to taking in boarders to help with expenses. I pray that things are better. I assure you that I am still contemplating my actions here. There have been recurring problems with some of my associates and two of them have offered to buy my interests.

With the new responsibility of a child, I must now make decisions based on what is best for my family, including you. As soon as Catherine has recovered fully and young Charles has a strong foothold on life, Catherine and I will begin to discuss the future. As I have said before, I am not really happy with things here in Wisconsin.

At the present time I am truly only a part owner of the house in which we live. If I decide to liquidate my holdings, I would be faced with finding new living quarters. I want to avoid that for as long as is logically possible.

I am still working at the mine at least four days each week and attending to business matters another two days. I long for more time with Catherine, who has lately pointed out to me that I am missing the arrival of spring.

I will write to you regularly and ask that you do the same.

Your Loving Son, James (and family)

James posted the letter early the next day, but could not expel the thought that what he had divulged to his mother was true. He was overjoyed with the arrival of his son, but that happiness could not transfer to his overall existence. He was becoming more and more resentful of his life, and of Wisconsin. He was actively resisting the people that wanted him to become more involved in the politics of the area and he still maintained that the area in and around St. Louis promised to be more valuable, both monetarily and emotionally, than Wisconsin could ever be.

James and Catherine had discussions about the future nearly every day. While an exact time schedule for moving to Missouri was not discussed, Catherine knew it would not be long. She went so far as to have a local carpenter build a sturdy cradle for Charles. When James saw the cradle he knew that it was built to provide as much comfort as possible for a young child. He knew also that Catherine had resigned to the notion that a move was inevitable.

Nearly six weeks after James sent his letter to his mother he received one from her. The fact that his mother was now in her 55th year was something James had not thought about until receiving the letter. It was that letter that set things in motion. James read the letter over several times:

June 13, 1839

My Dear James,

I was so happy to receive your letter announcing the arrival of your son. I pray that you, Catherine and Charles are in good health and that I have the privilege of meeting that youngster before I join your father at heaven's gates. I know that day may be coming at any time.

The funds we used to expand the house I think were well spent, but the fact that it is now, at least in part, a boarding house, has taken its toll on me. The family that now maintains the farm and livestock live here with their children and we are presently providing room and board for one other couple that is planning to go west next spring. The father has taken employment at a livery and the mother and her 15-year-old daughter are sharing the domestic duties in return for a reduction in the family rent. That helps greatly.

I am now 55 years of age and cannot do the things I once could. I honestly do wish you were here. I fear that we could lose a true legacy should I pass before you return. I must also tell you that you are correct in your assumption that this area is a steppingstone for those whose paths are leading to the lands of the west. But that fact has also brought some problems. There are constant conflicts between those who own slaves and those of us who do not. In addition, we have experienced a significant influx of unsavory characters that are prone to steal whatever they can from whomever they can. Sadly, their victims are often left with little or nothing and many do not have much to begin with.

The milk cow gave birth to a bull calf yesterday morning. We were hoping for another female, as the heifers bring a better price, but then, the bull calf will provide us with much needed meat.

I anticipate any news you have and I pray daily for you and your family. Give my love to the young one.

Your loving Mother.

James showed the letter to Catherine. "I think that I must begin preparations to go back to Missouri as soon as is practical. I have an uneasy feeling that Mother cut her words short for some reason and I fear she is not well."

Catherine read the letter carefully and turned it face down on the table. "I have been anticipating this conversation for some time. You know that I will be with you no matter what happens. I have discussed this with my mother. She understandingly does not want to be separated from us, but she knows that we will ultimately go to Missouri. You do what must be done, but please inform me of your decisions as soon as you make them. I love you and I will always support you."

CHAPTER TWENTY-EIGHT

James was becoming increasingly frustrated with the postal service. He paid twenty cents to post a letter and his mother had to match that amount for a reply. Then, it was always more than a month before her reply reached him. So much could happen in that amount of time. He could opt for a private delivery, but the logistics of locating someone who would actually deliver a letter seemed daunting. James decided to be more proactive. He could travel to Florissant almost as quick as a letter.

In the last week of June James sat on the bed and watched as Catherine nursed their son. "I am going to start liquidating our holdings here. It is time we started making plans to go to Missouri. I cannot shake the feeling that Mother is declining in health. I think we could sell everything easily and re-invest it in the property in Florissant. It sounds as though a boarding facility and some sort of mercantile might be a timely investment and we can also liquidate the mining property in Missouri to further that goal."

Catherine raised her eyebrows and squinted as though she wanted to choose her word carefully. "This little one is strong and healthy, but he is just a baby. The trip will be difficult, but I agree that it must be made. I only ask that you put it off as much as possible, but not so much as to force us to travel in the winter. We must inform my mother of our plans and keep her informed as the decisions are made. The crazy thing is, I do not have any hesitation in trusting your decisions. Get started as soon as you can. I love you."

"I am so lucky to have you," James said, wiping the forming tears from his eyes. "And I am so lucky to have this little one too." He stroked Charles' head and stood up. He took a seat at his desk and penned another letter to his mother:

June 28, 1839

Mother,

As I write this, my mind is in turmoil, but I have decided that the time has arrived for me to return to Missouri and begin building a legacy for my family. I caution that you may be better off to not reply to this letter as the lack of efficiency in the postal service has manifested in very slow delivery of letters. Sometimes I truly believe that I might put the letter in a large box and ship it through our freight contacts more quickly, and probably without too much greater cost.

Catherine and young Charles are both well. The fact that Charles is just over one month old seems to be impossible when one sees how he is grown. Catherine is urging caution in our decision to travel with him, but I feel that he will endure the trip better than one would think.

I will begin meeting with the investors here tomorrow. I intend to offer them my share of the holdings at a bargain in order to divest myself as soon as possible. I do not wish to put off our travels fore such time as we might find ourselves dealing with the late fall or early winter. Travel is much improved since I first came to Wisconsin, and most of our return will be on the Mississippi River and will be downstream. I have very good contacts with freighters and I am confident I can secure passage with little effort.

Since I was first aware that Father and Mr. Riviere made their agreements, I have believed that it is in my destiny to pursue business in St. Louis and Florissant, and more importantly, I feel I must be there to assist you. Your health and wellbeing has been a constant concern of mine for some time now.

I will arrange for a private courier to inform you when we embark. Until then, please take care. If all goes well, we should be able to introduce you to your grandson before the autumnal equinox.

Your Loving Son and family

The next several days left James constantly worn out. His sleep was often interrupted with dreams that portrayed his colleagues as monsters that wanted to fight him to his death. The dreams, for the most part, had no basis in fact. The negotiations to sell his interests were going well. The one point of contention did not come as a surprise to James. The investors were of the opinion that a reliable mine manager would be much more likely to be found if they had the advantage of offering him a home to live in. While James personally paid for many of the improvements, he did not expect to be compensated, but asked that he be allowed to remain in the house until he could finalize his plans to leave the area.

When James informed Catherine of the problem she asked how long they likely would be able to stay in the house.

"I really do not know," said James. There are at least two of the men involved that do not wish to give us any leeway at all. It could be that we will have to find some temporary place to stay until we make final arrangements."

"Or," Catherine said. "We could just try to work our time schedule around theirs and leave sooner. I think we could be ready to go in one month's time, if you can settle your business by then."

James showed some surprise. "You really think that we can make the trip with an eight-week-old boy?"

Catherine shrugged. "I don't see why not, provided we can arrange for some rudimentary comforts. We need a comfortable cradle for Charles, one that can be moved easily. Maybe a small feather tick mattress for the cradle and a little larger one that could be rolled up for us. I have all the confidence that you will provide those simple comforts. Am I correct?"

James recognized the smile and hint of sarcasm in Catherine's voice and he once again admitted that her eyes could melt his soul. With a return sarcastic voice and a slight bow, he said, "I will see to your every comfort, my dear. Your wish is my command."

Just days later, James met with Sean O'Donnell, one of the freighters he knew well. He learned that O'Donnell was going to captain a barge down the Mississippi in late July or early August. He had a proposal for James.

"I have contracted to deliver two large trunks of personal belongings to St. Louis. I will provide a wagon and team if you would be willing to drive it to the dock. The wagon should have ample room for your necessities and you, the missus and baby. I need to be at the docks and it would help if I did not have to return for the wagon or pay someone to drive it."

A handshake settled the deal when O'Donnell also offered to build a small shelter on the barge for the convenience of James and his family.

Catherine agreed to the arrangements and a plan was almost finalized. The 50-mile trip to the banks of the Mississippi aboard a freight wagon promised to be one of the most difficult parts of the trip, but she sounded confident in saying that she would be ready to go.

All business arrangements were finalized by the third week of July and James, Catherine and Charles managed a reasonably uneventful trip to the dock on the Mississippi. They were aboard, settled into their little hut and en-route to Missouri on July 24, 1839.

CHAPTER TWENTY-NINE

Ending a long hard trip, James and his family arrived at the house in Florissant. To his dismay, his mother was in worse health than he had even imagined. The boarding house was, for all intents and purpose, being run by Theresa Gehring and her daughter, Hanna. The Gehrings were German immigrants. William Gehring worked at a St. Louis livery and wagon building business.

Theresa spoke very little English, but both Hanna and William possessed the ability to speak relatively good English and French. James was impressed with the young teenager's intelligence. She had evidently attended school in Germany during her early years. She was an avid reader and noticed James' copy of *De La Démocratie en Amérique*, written by Alexis de Tocqueville. The book was in French. James immediately granted her request to borrow the book.

Following Michael Castello's death in 1837, Nancy Castello, by necessity, became an efficient businesswoman. She oversaw the workings of the small farm and managed to convert a modest home into a popular rooming house. The main house was attached, but used only by Nancy and had adequate room for James, Catherine and the baby. Many of James' belongings were still in his bedroom, just as he left them when he traveled to Wisconsin.

Within days after James and his family moved into the house, there was a marked improvement in Nancy's health. Her heath problems were still obvious but she seemed to regain color in her face and become more animated whenever she was holding young Charles. James confided in Catherine that he believed Nancy's problems were more due to melancholy related to his father's death and James' absence than of her actual physical condition.

Catherine responded to James' assumption with, "My dear husband, I have been lucky enough to have been informed about, what one of my mentors called the facts of life, and your mother has likely entered into a time when she can no longer bear children and no longer has a husband even if she could. I will not explain further, but be patient with her. She needs patience and understanding more than anything right now."

James accepted Catherine's explanation and, the days and weeks that followed, he paid close attention to his mother's moods and activities and paid her close attention when she seemed to need it and left her to her own when that seemed to him a better plan.

As part of his assuming the position of head of the family and head of the family business interests, it became necessary for James to visit various men in St. Louis. On a day when James was in the main part of St. Louis to visit with a lawyer, he was impressed, and almost shocked, at the changes that had taken place since his departure, only two years prior. The streets were literally filled with people. Shops of nearly every kind were seemingly doing good business; especially those that featured travel supplies. The wagon works where William Gehring worked was teeming with activity as they built and repaired various types of wagons for families that were headed west. Everywhere people were talking about the Oregon Trail. His father's predictions were coming true before his eyes. He knew the west was almost without limits, but all these people were almost overwhelming. He wondered, sometimes out loud, where they would end up and what their stories would be.

The evidence of slavery was obvious and James feared for the native people of all of North America. Some of James' acquaintances gave him a horrid account of what was being called "The trail of tears" where an entire nation of Cherokees had been forced off their homelands in Georgia and other southern states to Indian Territory. Some accounts were that as much as 20 per cent of the Cherokee people died during the forced move.

One evening, as James was returning home after performing various farming chores he encountered the young Miss Gehring hanging out the wash. She smiled and, referring to the Alexis de Tocqueville book, said, "Mr. Castello, I want to thank you so much for your loan of the book, but I must confess that my French is mostly limited to speaking as opposed to reading, and I must apologize for keeping the book so long.

"Do not worry about such a trivial thing," James replied. "I too, took a long time to read the book. It is lengthy, and I fear that my reading of the French language is also below my ability to speak it, but I remain impressed with Mr. de Tocqueville's observations. I have enquired of a merchant in town as to the possibility of obtaining the new English version. Perhaps you and I might take turns reading it if I can get it."

"That would be wonderbar," she replied, inadvertently using the German word.

When Michael Castello moved to St. Louis in 1820, he became friends with William Carr Lane, who also came from Pennsylvania. Lane served as Mayor of St. Louis from 1823 to 1829. He was again elected mayor in 1837, and was ending that term when James returned to the area. Lane became a quick friend to James and often sat with him discussing local politics, and more often, local problems. The city was plagued with lawsuits stemming mostly from property ownership disputes and tax collection. When Lane left office John Daggett, who was a member of Board of Aldermen during the Lane administration, succeeded him.

During Lane's final days in office he was party to a court hearing in which several Frenchmen were disputing the ownership of a section of land, most of which was inside the boundaries of St. Louis. Lane asked James to accompany him to the hearing to help him better understand the French vernacular that was being used. James agreed, and was introduced to John Daggett during that proceeding.

The introduction to Daggett and the notoriety of the court proceedings resulted in James being summoned to court frequently to aid in the communications between the people involved. In the process, he also found himself sitting in on negotiations and arbitrations of various lawsuits. He often received some sort of payment for his help, but more often he was actually advocating for the underdogs in the cases. He became known for wearing one more hat. In addition to being a mine owner, a farmer and an innkeeper, he was now becoming a politician. He often referred to the documents and letters generated by his father and Antoine Riviere. Riviere was one of the earliest St. Louis founders and his ties to the Castello family proved to be valuable, if only by reference.

James' father, Michael, had influenced the growth and development of St. Louis and the village of Florissant and one of Michael's main focuses was the establishment of a formal educational basis for the people. James vowed to continue with that vision, which resulted in even more meetings and more involvement in the local political process.

James had always promised to keep Catherine informed as to what was happening. The updates routinely came in the form of conversation over a late supper. Charles, being just over two years old, was just beginning to learn the strict manners of the dinner table. He was talking and beginning to learn how to ask for things during meals. On one such evening in mid-August of 1840, Catherine gave Charles a little extra pudding, obviously to keep him quiet for a little longer.

"Well, Mr. Castello," she said as she sat up a little straighter in her chair. "What is going on? You seem to flit in and out so quickly that we have had little time to just sit and talk."

"Catherine," James said. "I have learned long ago to recognize when you have something on your mind. You are not interested in what I have been doing. In fact you have been rather aloof of late. So, you tell me, what is it that you want to know?"

"I want to know, dear husband, if you are ready to be a father once again," she said with a giggle.

The remaining months of 1840 seemed to James and Catherine to come and go more quickly than normal. By Christmas, they had once again expanded the boarding house. William and Theresa Gehring headed west with one of the many wagon trains, but Hanna, after a very emotional discussion with her parents, chose to stay behind and become a permanent employee of the Castellos. As Catherine's pregnancy progressed, Hanna became more of an asset. She was developing into a very attractive young woman and often turned the heads of the young men at the church she attended on a regular basis.

Through an arrangement made by her father, each week Hanna received a copy of four-page newspaper published in Fayette, a small town just a few miles west of the Castello's place. The newspaper was obviously a pro-slavery publication and routinely castigated President Van Buren for his assumptions of equality, but the reason Hanna's father arranged for her to get the paper was its practice of publishing short stories in serial form. Women authored some of the stories and he hoped to encourage Hanna to further her education.

The newspaper generated some lively discussions that usually included Hanna Gehring, and often included topics other than the stories; political debate among them. Several of James' acquaintances found fault with that fact alone and questioned the practice of having women, and especially such a young one, participate in political debate, but those discussions influenced James to become ever more active in local politics and increased his interest in politics on the national level.

By the time Lucy Ann Castello was born on February 24, 1841, James Castello was well recognized in both business and political circles. When the town of Florissant was formally established in 1829, James' father, Michael Castello was a member of the board of trustees. Michael had often told James that the town would distinguish itself, if only those who cared would always stand for what they believed. One of Michael's passions was education.

CHAPTER THIRTY

When the Missouri Constitution was adopted in 1820, it called for one or more schools in each congressional township, but the people in charge suspended that provision for an entire year because they thought it to be too expensive. Michael Castello fought hard and long to see that the mandate was upheld, and James found himself fighting time and again to keep the schools intact.

When one local school was on the brink of closing, largely because a teacher could not be found, James had a serious conversation with Hanna Gehring.

James started the conversation. "Hanna, I want to discuss something important with you, but first I must ask you if you have any plans, or for that matter any visions, of your future. If so, I ask that you confide in me and tell me what you want your future to be."

Hanna fidgeted in her seat and sat up very straight before replying, "Mr. Castello, I want to learn about everything. I want to read every book. I want to be a part of this growing nation. I want to understand God. I want to someday be a wife and a mother. I want...."

James held up his hand. "Okay, I think I understand. Now allow me, if you will to make some suggestions and some observations. Since we received our English copy of *Democracy in America*, I could not help but to notice that you literally devoured the words. I have noticed that it is not unusual for you to read two or three books at the same time. Nearly everyone I know has loaned you at least one book and it has come to my attention that you have borrowed copies of textbooks from the school. In the short time I have known you, you have succeeded in educating yourself beyond what I could have possibly believed."

"Your flattery is overwhelming," said Hanna. "But, one of my teachers in Germany precipitated my hunger to know things. She learned of my parents' plan to go to America. It is she that taught me the basics of reading and writing the English language. She did that on her own time because she too wanted to come to America. I only hope and pray that she also is here. It is somewhat of an irony that I have come to a place that seems to prefer French over English in many cases."

Hanna continued. "You mention Mr. de Tocqueville's book. Largely because of that book and my discussions with you and Mrs. Castello, I have come to realize that this nation is destined to greatness. I do not agree with all he has written in the book, but I sincerely believe that the form of government here is unique it that it is not truly a democracy, but rather a limited democracy based on a representative government. I also think Mr. de Tocqueville is most accurate when he writes that, in order for this form of government to succeed, its inhabitants must never lose their faith in God.

"That is exactly what I am talking about," James said. "Now, do you think you have the ability to put your knowledge to work by teaching others?"

"If I could instill others to want to learn as much as I want to learn, I would not hesitate one moment to do so, but I am still young. I am still learning. What exactly are you asking of me?"

James was trying to hide his excitement. "One of our schools, the one in fact you have borrowed books from, is likely to be closed down. The people that are in charge of keeping our schools operating have been woefully neglectful at times. This particular school, because of its location and the fact that the students are so diversified, has not been able to keep a teacher. I think you could be a wonderful teacher and I am prepared to present the idea if you can agree to try, first on a limited basis, and maybe a more permanent thing if you feel comfortable with the situation."

James paused for just a moment before reaching into a satchel next to his chair and retrieving a book. "Before you make your decision, I want you to read this." He handed her a brand new book, *A Treatise on Domestic Economy,* written by Catherine Beecher.

"I have not read it, and likely I will not," James said. "But I am told that this lady is a huge promoter of education and of women being directly involved in the education of our youth. I have a feeling that you are cut from the same cloth."

James left Hanna as she stroked the new book. As he stood up he noticed that Catherine was standing nearby. She obviously had listened to the entire conversation.

"So," Catherine said in a near whisper, "You are plotting to take one of our best employees and send her into a teaching job?"

James was somewhat taken back. "You do not agree that she would be a very good teacher?"

"I was teasing," Catherine said with a smile. "Of course she will be a good teacher. There are not many of that age that speak three languages and whom have the basic intelligence of that young lady."

A few days later, while James was discussing local politics with one of the men who oversaw the schools, James proposed that they consider Hanna as a teacher. After spending only a few days in the classroom of a long-time teacher, and respected man within the community, Hanna was offered the job. She began teaching in the fall of 1842.

The next three years were full of turmoil and James seemed to have some unexplained need to be involved. While not an active abolitionist, he frequently voiced his opinion that slavery and the concept of all men being created equal was a conundrum. The Supreme Court had overturned the case of Prigg v. Pennsylvania, stating that the Pennsylvania law prohibiting the capture and return of fugitive slaves was unconstitutional. The issue of slavery was dividing even the congregations in various churches. The Methodist Church divided into two sections, the northern section being anti-slavery, and those in the south, including Missouri, agreeing with slavery. The same issue resulted in the Baptists also splitting.

In October of 1845 the Castello family grew by one more, with the birth of James Joseph Castello. Charles, at six years old, became one of Hanna Ghering's youngest students. Later that same year Texas entered the United States as a slave state. The entry of Texas as a state proved to be one of the key issues that set off the Mexican-American War.

"I've a good notion to give up our mining interest entirely," James said one morning while having breakfast. Many of the young men who work at the mine have decided to join with Alexander Doniphan in the Mounted Volunteers. At present they are formed as Missouri regiment, but Doniphan has let it be known that he would eagerly take his men to the battlefields of Mexico. If that happens, we could lose a significant number of miners at a time when the mine products are most needed."

Late in the year of 1846, James' fears materialized when Doniphan and other supporters of the war took almost 1,400 Missouri men into battle in northern Mexico. At about the same time Catherine once more announced that she was pregnant. On March 25, 1847, Mary Julia Castello was welcomed to the family.

James began to remove himself from the mining operations, but he admitted openly that, while mining intrigued him, he was also concerned with other things. The Missouri legislators had recently passed an act that prohibited the education of any black person. James and Hanna had several conversations regarding the act, and James wrote several letters to members of the assembly.

French was still a predominant language in the St. Louis area. James continued to assist those non-French speaking people in understanding the political environment.

When some abolish promoting attorneys convinced Dred and Harriet Scott to sue for their freedom in the Missouri state court, James found himself routinely trying to explain to his friends and family what was taking place.

"I am being told that this case will not end here," he said during a meeting with several persons that were gathered to discuss the mining business. Slavery and human rights took over the conversation, but James took the final step to separate from the mining operations. He and Catherine focused on the boarding house and a subsequent mercantile business.

1849 brought still another child, John, into the family. By then things seemed to have settled down. Charles was now one of the older students at his school and was establishing himself as a leader. His friendships blossomed quickly. He was proving to be a great asset to the mercantile business, often assisting customers, especially the miners, who were anxious to tell their stories. He paid close attention to those who were gearing up for a trip to California, where recent discoveries of gold made stories, both true and greatly enhanced, were just what a ten-year-old dreamer wanted to hear. The Mexican War had ended and left a significant group of men who had experience one adventure ready to head to California on another.

Nancy was a big part of the mercantile business, but considering her age, she was openly grateful for Charles' involvement and often instructed him in the keeping of the business records and inventory.

The French citizens, with whom James routinely visited with, were divided almost evenly in their opinions when they learned that France had abolished slavery in the West Indies. James took the news as a positive indication that the world may well be headed toward putting the practice to an end. Zachary Taylor, who had just been elected as President of the United States, concerned James. It was common knowledge that Taylor was a slave owner, but he often said that he opposed the spread of slavery into U.S. territories and he seemed uncertain about whether he supported or opposed the Wilmot Proviso that prohibited slavery in any territory acquired from Mexico following the end of the war.

CHAPTER THIRTY-ONE

More and more the name James Castello was recognized in Missouri as being anti-slavery, but he was also known for his no-nonsense approach to criminal activity. James became a Freemason, largely because of a group of blacks who formed their own lodge under the Masonic banner.

Like so many other groups, James learned that the Masons as a whole were not always on the side of anti-slavery, but many of those who became close friends held to the same beliefs held by James.

On the last day of March, 1850 John Calhoun, one of the most ardent protectors of slave ownership died of tuberculosis. In July President Taylor died of a stroke, sending the self-made Vice President Millard Fillmore to the head of the nation. Rumor was that Fillmore was really not qualified, largely because Taylor did not trust him, but James and his associates accepted Fillmore as being more likely to side with the abolitionists. James cautioned his group about being too encouraged by Calhoun's death. "I agreed with Calhoun on one thing," he said during a meeting in early August. "He stated on several occasions that this issue of slavery might likely send this nation into a north and south split. I do not believe either side would win in that situation."

One member of the loosely organized group was Luther Kennett. Kennett worked in the mercantile and previously in the mine co-owned by the Castellos. He served as an alderman for St. Louis from 1843-1846. He showed interest in James' statement about the nation being divided.

"James", he asked, "could you tell us more about why you agree with Calhoun?"

"Luther, I did not say that I agree with Calhoun in his overall theories," James retorted. "What I said is that he may be right in saying that this slavery issue could be the end of a nation that is just starting to build."

As the meeting broke up, Kennett approached James. "Perhaps you and I could talk privately for a few minutes."

James stepped into an adjoining room and was followed by Kennett. "James, I have decided to run for mayor. I would greatly appreciate your support in my endeavor. While I know you and I do not agree on everything, I believe that you have established a trust among the people in this area. I have noted that you and Catherine are more that just a man and wife. You have a way with people. You are destined to be an important part of the forming of this nation. Might I depend on your support?"

"I will certainly support you," James said. "But please understand that I will continue to disagree with you in certain matters."

Kennett was successful in the election and became known more as a member of the Opposition Party, rather than the Whig Party under whose banner he ran for mayor.

James met frequently with Mayor Kennett. Although Florissant was becoming more and more of an entity separate from St. Louis, the politics of St. Louis directly affected those living in Florissant. The boarding house and mercantile flowed with the times and those times were often difficult. When almost every miner that dreamed of someday getting rich disappeared into the throng headed for California, the Castello business did well at first supplying the travelers, but as the years wore on the business often suffered. It was during one of the lean periods in 1855 when Kennett announced that he intended to run for Congress. This time he was openly a part of the Opposition Party and had James' support in every way except financially.

Charles had just turned 16, when he came to James one morning with a surprising proposal.

"Father,' Charles said. "One of my friends, Jason, has been working at the lead mine for nearly four months now. He makes good wages and told me that, now that I am of age to work there, he thinks I would be hired at once. Your former interests would of course be a benefit to my being hired."

James closed his eyes as though in deep thought and then said, "Son, there are many things to consider. I believe that your education has progressed much quicker than I imagined, and I must tell you that you have matured greatly in the past few years. You are no longer a little boy, but I also believe that you are aware that our finances have suffered lately. If you are considering going to the mine because of our recent money problems, then I say it is not necessary. If you think it is time to be your own man, I applaud you. If you are somehow planning to work and also continue with your studies, then I would ask how you propose doing that."

Charles displayed a grin of self-confidence. "You have responded exactly as I thought you would. All of your statements apply. I am a man now. You were working when you were my age and the works you did in the mines intrigues me. As for the financial health of this family, if I can contribute, I would consider it an honor to do so, but that is not an exclusive part of my desire. I want to have my own money and I want at some point to own my own property. As far as my studies are concerned, I love to learn new things and I think that involves being a productive person. I can read and write, with some degree of efficiency in both English and French. I can, to some degree communicate verbally with my German friends, and I know enough to curse with the best of them in a working environment."

James chuckled at the last words. "Sometimes using foul language is a substitute for knowing what to say or how to say it. I do not think you will have that problem and I hope you will not let the ruffians around the mine bring you down to their level."

Charles replied quickly. "Then you have no objection to my applying for the job?"

"On the contrary, I do object, but I know that it will do no good. You have decided to spread your wings, but do not forget the rules of this house and who is in charge here."

Charles rose and turned. "I will always be aware that Mother is in charge," he said.

The first few weeks of Charles' employment took its toll. He came home dirty, tired and humorless. After washing up and having dinner, he retired early and slept fitfully. He seemed to be rejuvenated each morning and often discussed his work for several minutes during breakfast. The family time came to an end just before Christmas, when Charles moved into the company boarding house. He explained to his parents that the move kept him close to his work, saving travel time to and from the mine. He also explained that the bosses preferred the men to stay in the boarding house.

At the Castello house, things were going smoothly. While the profits from the rooming house and mercantile were still low, they had increased enough to give some encouragement. Stagecoach stops and taverns were becoming more popular and became significant competition to the boarding house. Nancy was slowing down with age. Winter put her kitchen garden on hold, but she had an ample supply of dried herbs and often traded them for other commodities. Catherine displayed a phenomenal talent for making things work. She kept close tabs on the finances, supervised the cooking and took care of the children. The various peddlers and merchants considered her both a friend and a formidable business adversary.

Charles was the one person in the family that experienced and displayed the most noteworthy change. Almost from the first hour that he became a resident of the boarding house at the mine, he became friends with two men who had recently returned from California. They were both broke as a result of their escapades but they were rich in stories. Both vowed to return to California as soon as they could afford to do so. They were sure that they had been on the verge of discovering a mother lode and that they would become rich beyond their dreams if only they could find what they called a grubstake. One of the men, Melvin Potter, seemed to Charles to know what he was talking about. He truly believed that it was gold, not lead or iron, that would make an individual wealthy. Charles was so thoroughly impressed that he even breeched the subject to James and suggested that maybe he should consider investing in a California mining claim. James dismissed the idea instantly.

In late August of 1855, James was surprised by a visit from the latest priest of St. Ferdinand Catholic Church. The priest was accompanied by a freewoman, Agnes Printer. Miss Printer did not hide the fact that she was an activist and intended to help every black person become free. Father Santuis said he was introducing Agnes to James so that James might understand her frustration. Agnes told James of an incident the previous May when a fellow activist, Mary Meachum helped a small group of slaves cross the river to Illinois, where slavery was outlawed. She related that less than one dozen slaves were guided across the river and most of them had been arrested and returned. What she was upset about was the fact that several newspapers had kept the story alive by enhancing it. She showed a copy of one of the newspapers to James. The headline read, "Stampede of Slaves."

"Stampede!" Agnes exclaimed. "Them dumb newspaper men don't have any idea what a stampede is."

James was more than a little confused. "What do you want me to do about this?"

"Miss Printer thinks you may be one of the people that the blacks can trust," said Father Santuis. She is hoping to get you to run for public office and try to get some laws changed."

The short meeting broke up with James telling his visitors that he was empathetic but did not have any interest in joining the political scene as a candidate for anything.

CHAPTER THIRTY-TWO

For nearly a year, various residents in and around Florissant encouraged James to run for office. Some even suggested he could be elected to Congress and become President or Vice President.

For the most part, James dismissed the ideas and continued to assist those who needed his help as an interpreter or as an advisor. That changed on July 4, 1856. The old St. Ferdinand, now better known as Florissant went all out in an Independence Day celebration. Dignitaries from St. Louis and all the surrounding townships were recruited as speakers. The ladies of the community, especially the Catholic Church, displayed a myriad of garden vegetables, pies, cakes and preserves. Hogs were roasted and beer and ale flowed freely.

Once again, James was approached by Father Santuis. Santuis was accompanied by no other than Congressman Luther Kennett. They had a proposal.

"James, my friend," Kinnett began. "I understand that some of these fine townsfolk have been encouraging your running for office. Have you considered doing so?"

"It is good to see you again," James replied. "No I have not really even considered becoming a politician. My main concerns now are my businesses and my family, not necessarily in that order." One thing I would like to call your attention to, however, is this continuing practice of lessons in the St. Louis schools being taught in French. I think it is time to start instilling upon these young minds that they are part of a nation of English speaking people and that they should realize that English is quickly becoming the language of business.

"That is being addressed," Kinnett replied. "But what Father Santuis and I have to propose is not an actual political office, but rather an office whereby you could be directly involved in many of the problems now confronting the County of St. Louis. We suggest to you that you would be a fine sheriff. The sheriffs are becoming more and more enforcers of the law. While their primary duties still include the collection of taxes and other debts and the keepers of the jail, they are expanding their duties in gathering fugitives and prosecuting crimes."

James squinted. "Are you suggesting that I run for sheriff so I would be responsible for capturing fleeing slaves?"

Father Santuis interceded. "What we are proposing is that, by being involved, you could have input. Maybe you could be a louder voice. Maybe you could curtail some of the arrests of freed slaves. Maybe you could make a difference."

That evening James and Catherine were seated at the table. Charles, who really wanted to talk about gold and the fact that the California rush was slowing considerably, joined them. James mostly ignored Charles' attempts to start a conversation about mining. He directed his words to Catherine.

"I was confronted several times at the gathering today. Of those who approached me were Father Santuis and Luther Kinnett. They have asked that I consider running for election as Sheriff of St. Louis County. Some of the things they said make sense, but I need to know what you think."

"The ladies of the Catholic Church were very well represented in today's festivities," Catherine said. "It surprised me that almost all of those who approached me did so by offering an apology first, saying that, by expressing their political view, they knew they were going where women are not supposed to be going. Then they let me know in no uncertain terms that they wanted you to run for office. One of them, a widowed mother of six, told me that Father Santuis had already convinced you to become sheriff."

Nancy, who was seated in a nearby rocking chair discussing a book with Lucy Ann and Mary Julia, closed the book and turned to James. "I think it is a good idea. These two girls are quickly becoming young ladies and they are contributing a great deal to the business here.

We ladies can handle this. I think that, if Catherine can give you her blessing, you should do what you think is right."

"So much for women staying out of politics," James said with a grin.

Within weeks, James was actively seeking the office of Sheriff of St. Louis County. He traveled around the various small towns and spent a great deal of time in St. Louis, where he had developed both good friends and bad enemies within the court system. There were a number of families whose loved ones were not in jail, largely because of James' effort on their behalf. More schools were teaching in the English language and James was credited with promoting education of both men and women. The families that benefitted from the expanded education largely supported James, but he had his detractors, especially those who viewed him as an abolitionist.

The election was contentious to say the least, but James won and took over the office of sheriff in 1857. The next few months had him wondering if he had made the right decision. Things happened rapidly, with one surprise after another. The most important of those surprises was when Catherine informed him that the family was going to expand once again; she was pregnant.

"Woman," James said. "Maybe you should stop washing our underwear together." He then hugged her. "You know that I think you are at your happiest when you are growing with child. I hope you also know that I have bitten off a large amount of responsibility here of late and I will need to have your continued support if I am to succeed."

Catherine pulled away slightly and looked James straight in the eyes. "Now I suppose, husband, that you could start washing your own underwear or maybe, just maybe it is the fact that you take your underwear off for reasons other than washing that has us going forth to multiply."

They both laughed, but they both admitted that another baby would tend to complicate their life in one more way. The boarding house was full and provided a decent income, but the farm was in need of some serious management. The man who helped with the farm had recently begun to train oxen that were being used to pull wagons and carts for those heading west. The new enterprise promised to be profitable, but the initial investment was sizeable. James became mostly passive regarding the operation, but was impressed with the training process. As he and Catherine stood at one of the fences and watched two young oxen in training, James spoke softly to Catherine.

"It seems to me that this is a fine example of cooperation between two beings. I am told that, once the training begins, the animals are always placed next to each other the same way. The one on the left is always on the left. They learn to know their place, but they also learn that they cannot work alone. They depend on each other. I think that is much the same way we train ourselves. If we are successful, we each know our place, but we also know that our most important asset is the one that stands beside us, helping us to pull the load."

Catherine leaned into James and said, "My aren't you the philosopher, tossing up metaphors and analyzing life?"

James was almost immediately disappointed when he was sworn in. He had a small office in the courthouse, a building in which he had attended both hearings held there in the case of Dred and Harriet Scott. It was the building that also represented the treatment of slaves. James, as sheriff, was required by law to settle disputes in estate settlements. This often resulted in him participating in the auction of property. The auctions were held on the courthouse steps and the property quite often included slaves. Following each of these events, James was literally sick to his stomach.

It had been nearly ten years since the first Scott trial was held and there were numerous suits for freedom filed in the St. Louis court, but the Scott case became more and more complicated and ended up in the Supreme Court. A few months after becoming sheriff, James was told that the Supreme Court ruled against the Scotts and declared in the ruling that slaves were not citizens, but property, and as such had no standing to file a lawsuit. The suits for freedom came to a halt, but the property settlements went on.

On one particular day, less than one month after the birth of his son, Francis Ferdinand, James sat staring at the newspaper in which there were a total of nine legal notices bearing his name. He had carefully worded the notices, which ended in the words, "...on Monday, the 13th day of September 1858, between the hours of nine in the forenoon and five in the afternoon at the front door of the Court House, in the city of St. Louis, State of Missouri, I will sell at public auction, for cash, to the highest bidder, all the right, title, interest, claim, estate and property of the aforementioned William Jones, of and in the above described property to satisfy the writ of execution to me directed."

James had repeatedly refused to make an exact list of the properties involved because such a list would necessarily include the descriptions of slaves.

Talking only to himself he said out loud, "Is this really the world I want that little boy and his brothers and sisters to grow up in?"

It was the first time James was aware that he would willingly leave Missouri if he found promise somewhere else.

CHAPTER THIRTY-THREE

Charles was barely 20 years old when gold was discovered in Colorado. The preceding two years had taken its toll on James personally and on the business, especially the farm.

Charles came to James and Catherine with the news. "I have told you of my friend Jason. He is well versed in gold mining and tells me that his contacts tell him that the gold found in Cherry Creek in Colorado is but the leftovers of a probable mother lode west of Denver. He is seeking backing now and is going to Colorado as soon as he can put the finances together. I have managed to save a significant amount of money, largely thanks to you, but I believe I should not go to Colorado just depending on luck. I think that an investment in one or more claims in the area Jason talks of could prove to be very profitable."

James looked at Catherine, held out his hand to her and turned to Charles. "The mining business is a cruel bedfellow. I have watched people get rich and I have watched people lose everything. I have also watched people get rich and then squander their riches on other mining dreams. Your friend sounds as if he has good information, but I would want to know if it just sounds good or if it is credible. You get me proof that it has some merit, and I will discuss investing. I am not asking for guarantees, only good odds, and I must tell you that I will get involved only with the blessing of your mother." He squeezed Catherine's hand just a little tighter.

Just weeks later Charles once again met with his father, this time he was accompanied by Jason. Jason had with him an account written by a miner that described an area called Gregory Gulch after the man who discovered gold there earlier. According to the account, a town was already being developed and anyone thinking about cashing in on the developing rush needed to act quickly.

James read the missive, and then directed his questions to Jason. "The mining that I am familiar with is that of lead and iron. I have never witnessed this placer mining. Can you describe it to me?"

With that, Jason produced a drawing depicting a long wood box with a series of small pieces of wood arranged at intervals. "Here are the plans for a sluice box like the ones we used in California. Gold is much heavier than the other materials contained in the dirt and gravel. This sluice is placed near, or sometimes even in the creek and water is directed down its length. These cross pieces, called riffles, tend to slow the water and create a vortex, which causes the gold to settle behind the riffles. At various times, the riffles are cleaned and the gold is retrieved."

James looked closely at the drawings. "How is the water directed into these contraptions?"

"That," replied Jason, "is what makes these two claims in which I propose to invest more inviting. A friend of mine, Darrell Miller, has already staked the claims and he tells me that they are located in such a way that the water can be directed easily into the sluice from the upstream and flow nearly the whole distance of the claim. We just shovel the gravel and sand from the banks and streambed into the sluice and let the sluice do the rest of the work. We can thus work the entire length of the claim and take our pay dirt from both banks and the bottom of the creek. It is hard work, there is no denying that, but I am a hard worker and so is Charles. My friend tells me that his tests so far show a significant possibility that these claims could easily produce as much as ten dollars per day."

James leaned back slightly in his chair. "That sounds good, but I am skeptical. If I buy into this I need to know just what my money is going for. I assume that a certain part of it is going for travel, but what equipment is needed?"

Charles interceded at that point. "We have discussed this at length. Our travel costs to Colorado would be minimal, especially if we were to take a couple of those mules you have. We first talked of the oxen and that may come later, but for now a couple of mules and some provisions for resting and eating is about all we need. Once we get to Colorado we will have to purchase the lumber and tools necessary to build and operate the sluice and have ample funds for boarding until we can begin to retrieve the gold. The biggest cost is the purchase of the claims. You have those figures in front of you."

The next day James sought out Gabriel Blanchard, an old fur trapper and trader who had befriended James' father in the early 1820s. James knew that Blanchard was one of the bold men who ventured into the Rocky Mountains in search of beaver. He met with Blanchard at a local tavern. The grizzly old trapper was eager to accept a pint of ale and tell all he knew.

"Gold eh? There have been rumors for years that there may be some in those mountains. Some of those headed for California a few years back are said to have found a little gold somewhere on the Platte, but it wasn't enough to keep them from continuing on. I will tell you this: you better be tough as an old boot if you plan on heading into that country. It is rough. It is cold and it is a million miles away from everywhere. I spent one winter in a camp of Utes. I stayed relatively comfortable and made it back with a nice load of pelts, but I was the exception."

Blanchard took a long pull from his tankard and continued, "Yessir, I'll give you some advice if you are planning to head that direction. If you have to deal with the Utes, be honest and fair. They will not stand for deceit of any kind. Cheating them once will make them lifelong enemies. Treating them fairly and honestly will earn you their friendship forever."

James considered Gabriel's statement. "It is my twenty year-old-son that is planning to go," he said. "He is requesting my blessing and a substantial amount of my money. I will pass your wisdom on.

"Twenty eh? That is about what my age was when I went there. He's plenty old enough, but like I say, he has to be tough as hell, too."

James' next meeting was with one of the lawyers involved in his other business dealings. When he provided the figures and asked for advice, the lawyer responded by suggesting a very strict contract between Charles, Jason and James. Given the fact that James would be investing nearly half of the estimated amount, the lawyer had a contract drawn up giving James one half interest in the claims to be purchased. His investment would include two saddle horses, one mule and a reasonable amount of provisions, largely from the farm and mercantile.

He then sat with Catherine and discussed the proposal. Her response, after looking at the document was typical of how she had responded to most of James' ventures.

"Well, here we go," she said. "You know that you have my support if you think it is the right thing to do. I, of course, worry about Charles. He is young and has always had us to lean on. On the other hand, he has proven to be a responsible adult lately. I will not pretend that I was not happy with you getting away from mining. With your current responsibility as sheriff, you certainly could not have kept up anyway. So, in a way, I am a little apprehensive about you once again being part of a mining operation. This sounds to be much different, but it is still mining. But yes, I think you have made your decision and I will go along."

"Good," James said. "I will summon Charles and Jason to supper tonight. Meanwhile, I have to go to the courthouse and deal with some other problems."

With that, James left the house and arranged for one of the farm hands to go to the mine boarding house and leave a message for Charles.

It seemed to James that the St. Louis area was suffering one dispute after another and that people were refusing to get along. They were becoming more and more dependent upon the courts to intervene. One lawsuit after another was being filed. Street fights were not uncommon and the jail was at its capacity almost constantly.

When James picked up the latest writs of levy and seizure, he confided in a clerk with whom he had become friendly, "My son is heading off to the edge of the Rocky Mountains in the west. A day like this one almost makes me wish that I were accompanying him. Missouri has developed into a hotbed of crime and I truly believe this state will eventually be famous for its support of slavery and that it will not prove to be a good thing."

"Sheriff," the clerk said. "You know that I agree with you, but you also know that the law is the law and you cannot procrastinate with these writs. You are just going to make the judge mad, and that is never a good thing. Now, say hello to that wonderful wife of yours and wish your son good luck. I will take care of the proof of publication as soon as I see the notice."

That evening James met with Charles and Jason in a room separate from the rest of the house. He had three copies of the contact. All were written in the clear hand of the lawyer's secretary. He handed a copy to each of the young men. Charles was the first to speak.

"I guess I did not foresee this being so formal. I was hoping we could just agree on something and get on with our plans."

"Son," James said. "Perhaps if this just concerned the two of us, we could come to an agreement on less formal terms, but you have chosen to take on a partner, and he evidently is ready to trust you, so this contract will protect all of us. I would like to say there is room for negotiation, but I am afraid that is not the case. If there are things that concern you, I will explain, but unless it is something quite serious, I am going to be steadfast."

Charles studied the papers for a few minutes then asked, "Why the saddle horses instead of mules?"

James replied, "I am under the impression that you need to make as quick a trip as possible. If you take care of these horses, they will serve you well. The mule is one that has not been used for plowing. It is a mule we traded for and it is accustomed to packing rather heavy loads. Relieve it from its burden each day and provide as much water and grass as is possible and you will find that it will serve you well to take your provisions and likely will have some use after you start your mining. The horses will be little more than an asset once you start mining. You may well want to trade them for something more useful. We have most of the rudimentary tools here at the mercantile, so hammers, nails, shovels and the like will be much cheaper here than if you try to buy them in the middle of a mining boom."

"That is very true," Jason said. "When I was in California I witnessed people paying unbelievable amounts for basic things. We should take whatever is practical with us."

The discussion carried on for nearly an hour, but when things started happening they happened fast. The summer was over and the two adventurers wasted no time in getting ready for a trip that could change their lives forever.

CHAPTER THIRTY-FOUR

Following some surprisingly accurate maps and directions provided by Jason's friend, the two gold seekers' trip was fairly uneventful. The men each had one rifle and one revolver, and thanks much to Charles' training by his father; he was able to provide several meals on the trail.

When the duo was about halfway to their goal they entered into a farming community that proved to be a perfect place to spend a few extra days to give the animals a much-needed rest. A visit with some locals impressed Charles with just how right his father was about the slavery issue. According to the livery owner, the town was called Humboldt until recently, when the farmers in the area renamed it as Junction City. It was a bustling town, but the stable owner cautioned Charles and Jason about getting involved in any discussion involving slavery. There were a number of Free Staters who originally settled there after a failed attempt to bring a steamship up the Kansas River. They were steadfast in their beliefs and it was not uncommon that disagreements with those who were on the other side of the issue to become violent.

As far as Jason was concerned, the most important commodity they acquired in Junction City was a bag of pre-ground and roasted coffee. Jason had acquired a taste for strong coffee in California and said he actually preferred coffee to any sort of alcohol. In addition to the coffee a good supply of dried meat and even some dried apricots were added to their fodder. When they returned to the trail both men felt as though they could go forever, but before leaving Charles penned a letter to his parents.

August 4, 1859

My Dearest Mother and Father,

I am writing this while at rest in a small community at the junction of the Republican and Smoky Hill rivers as they come together to form the Kansas River. Known as Junction City. I am told that the posting of a letter here will result in a very quick delivery to you. The inhabitants here are mostly farmers and mostly friendly. We have been very successful in replenishing our provisions, even to the point of acquiring some ground coffee. That seemed, in itself, to have put new life into Jason. He is very fond of coffee.

We befriended a local liveryman, who warned us to avoid any political conversations. It seems that the controversies we left behind are not unique to Missouri. I was somewhat skeptical, Father, when you cautioned us that this was probably true, but sadly, the problem seems to have infiltrated nearly every settlement.

Today is our last day of rest here. Daylight has greeted us and we are almost ready to again look toward the western horizon. It appears that we are now more than halfway to our destination. The weather has been cooperative, but we have been cautioned by more than one not to dally. We feel urged on constantly. There seems to be a significant number of people, mostly men, who are doing exactly what we are doing. It is a rare day that we do not encounter other travelers. I pray that Jason's preliminary arrangements prove to give us an edge. I must say that I am anticipating our adventure more each day.

Mother, please give all the children an extra hug for me. I already miss them, especially Lucy and Mary. I have no one to tease.

I will write again as the opportunity arises. Until then, all my love,

Charles

On a clear morning, several days after leaving Junction City, Charles arose from his bedroll and began reviving the small fire. The sun was just coming up and the surrounding plains took on a golden hue. Looking to the west and just a little south of their current path Charles saw something different. He spent several minutes watching as it became more apparent that what he saw was a mountain. The sight thrilled him and he shouted at Jason.

"Jason look! I think I can see the Rocky Mountains."

Jason stood and looked to where Charles was pointing. He then took the map from the saddlebag of his saddle and smiled at Charles.

"That, my friend is Pike's Peak. That is the reason so many are beginning to call this the Pike's Peak Gold Rush. Our destination is about 100 miles to the north of that peak, but we are now within sight of our destiny to become very rich men."

Jason drank his coffee that morning when it so hot as to burn his lips. He rose and began loading the packs on the mule and removing the hobbles from the horses.

"Come on, man," he said to Charles. "Daylight is wasting."

Charles pitched the remainder of his coffee into the fire and poured the remaining coffee from the pot into the fire also. Normally, Jason would have protested such a thing, but not on this morning. He had his vision set on the west and nothing was going to stop them now. Within minutes the pair were in their saddles and once again on the trail. Later that day they could make out more of the mountains. It was almost dark when they finally stopped. They were tired and the horses had been pushed to their limit. They had walked several miles at intervals during the day to save the energy of the horses, but finally admitted that the day was over.

Two days later, as they were again settling into a quick campsite, Jason seemed a little out of sorts.

"You have been in a strange mood all day," Charles said. "Did your morning visit to the bushes not succeed in evacuating your gut this morning?"

Jason sneered. "I think the Lord is playing tricks on us. I think he has been moving those mountains farther away. We did not seem to gain on them even a little today. I just want this trip to be over. I saw two other fires last night and I am reminded once again that we are not the only ones headed for Gregory Gulch."

The next morning, an even greater mood changer occurred when the boys met another traveling group of four men. What was different was that these four were headed east, not west. They told Charles and Jason that the gold in Colorado was a hoax. They recounted that they had been panning for gold since early May and had little to show for their efforts. In fact, they said, they had two good gold pans that they no longer had any use for. They offered to trade the pans for enough coffee to make a couple of pots. They explained that they left Central City broke and had not had a cup of coffee in two days. Jason complied, saying he only hoped more coffee would be available.

One day later Charles and Jason arrived at their destination. They were met with both good and bad news. The good news was that Darrell Miller was still getting some gold from the claims. The bad news was that many of the other claims in the area were played out and one problem remained: Claim Jumpers.

Darrell explained to the boys: "These are good claims. I have not developed them to the extent possible and my offer to sell is still good. As you can see, I have built a small shack, mostly so I can guard the property. I propose that I will lower the selling price some if we can agree that I can stay here with you through the winter, or at least until I can find my way back east. I will gladly help where I can, but I have a bad leg and that limits my mobility. That is the biggest reason I want to sell in the first place."

Jason and Charles made a cursory inspection of the shack and the property. The shack was small, but Darrell did an acceptable job of constructing it and there was a good fireplace. They agreed that, if Darrell would help them build the sluice and do most of the cooking, he could stay. The next day they traded one of the saddle horses and its tack for some building supplies. The town was obviously constructed quickly, but it seemed to still be growing. The boys took that as proof that gold was still being produced. Before leaving town, Charles sat in a tent, which was called a tavern and penned a letter to his parents:

August 16, 1859

My Dear Parents,

Well, we made it. Things are not quite as rosy as I had hoped, but Darrell Miller assures us that the claims are producing gold, although in small amounts, largely because he has simply not been able to do some serious mining. We have procured the necessary lumber and nails to build the first segments of our sluice. We have also procured a wheelbarrow, which I will push back to the claim. The shovels that we brought from Missouri have so far only been used to dig shallow latrines and put out campfires. I am sure I am about to get much more familiar with them.

We noted that only a few of the placer projects are using long sluices. Most are either panning or using rocker tables. Both are inefficient, but the small claims prevent much larger operations.

Our claims have a significant incline from top to bottom. Jason is confident that we can divert enough water to make the sluice operative. The water will travel through our sluice and back into the creek, thereby not reducing the water in the creek by any appreciable amount.

Another sluice operation is in place about one fourth of a mile upstream from our claims. While Darrell and Jason get started on our sluice, I will go see what I can learn from these men.

One thing that concerns me is the number of men who have given up and left the area. Some of those whom we have talked to are still confident of the possibility of finding good gold, while others say that the placer gold is being depleted and some are talking of actually tunneling into the earth to find the sources. That seems to me to be a costly and dangerous approach.

The town is not really much of a town. It consists mainly of wood storefronts with tents attached. The tavern I now sit in has more wood inside for tables and benches than it does on the outside. In fact, it has only a small wall with a tent attached and a very large and very crude sign. The tavern owner serves a decent venison sandwich and a big helping of optimism. He says this town is growing and will continue to grow because it sits on one of the richest square miles in the nation. I certainly hope so.

I must conclude now. Jason is arranging to haul as much of the lumber as possible. The mule is about to become a big part of a mining operation.

As always, give my love to the children if I can still refer to all of them that way.

All my love,
Charles

The next day, the three men arose early and began constructing the sluice. Jason was in charge of that and once the basic structure was laid out, Charles set out upstream to meet the neighbors. He found that the neighboring claim did have a sluice system and the owners said it was working well. They showed Charles a section of the sluice in which a piece of sheep hide was pinned down below the riffles. They explained that this method greatly increased the catching of the finer particles of gold. One of the owners also showed Charles particles of quartz that were found near the edge of the claim. They explained that the quartz was the reason for speculation that a tunnel or shaft could be used to follow the quartz and retrieve what was being called lode gold.

While lode gold might be plentiful, the neighbors also said that the retrieving and processing the gold required much more equipment and would prove to be very costly. Charles returned to his claims and relayed all the information to Jason.

CHAPTER THIRTY-FIVE

After three days of hard work, the sluice was built and in place. The necessary ditch was dug into the bank of the creek and water was running through the sluice. Jason held his fingers into the cold water, feeling the action created by the riffles.

"It feels good," he said. When I was in California, I learned how the water creates a vortex. By holding your fingers between two of the riffles, you can actually feel the vortex. This sluice will catch gold."

Charles held his hand in the water. Jason was right. He could feel the water pulsing against his fingers. Jayson and Darrell pointed out a pile of "pay dirt" next to the new sluice.

"This is some of the best dirt and gravel we could get right here. It is time to see if the sluice will work," Jason said.

Both Jason and Charles began shoveling the dirt into the top of the sluice. The water turned muddy and they shoveled even more. At the end of three hours the pile was gone. It was time for the first test. They shoveled the tailings away from the bottom of the sluice so the wheelbarrow could be placed under the outlet and partially filled with water. Jason went upstream and placed a small dam into the diversion to stop the flow of water. Carefully the boys removed the riffles and shoveled the dirt that had settled into the bottom into the wheelbarrow. They then began the slow process of using gold pans to finally determine if they had recovered any of the precious metal. They had gold! After three hours of sluicing and another hour of panning and drying, the result was nearly one tenth of an ounce. Barring any problems the new miners calculated that 13-hour days could produce an ounce of gold per week.

Early the next morning Darrell announced that he had decided to leave. "You boys are set here. I think you can recover a goodly amount of gold now. I thought I might stay the winter, but that just adds to the expenses and, while I still have money in my pocket, I am going to head back east before the weather turns bad. I wish you luck."

Charles was disappointed in the fact that Darrell left. He knew that meant a little more work for Jason and him, but there was a bright side. The shack would be less crowded and less food would be needed.

The cleanout at the end of the next week was shy of the hoped for ounce, but it was close enough to spur the new miners on. They had developed a pattern whereby one would attend the sluice for three hours and the other would fill the wheelbarrow with pay dirt and bring it to the sluice. They traded off, working at least 12 hours each day. To avoid theft, which was a real problem in the area, they cleaned the sluice each day and piled the concentrates near the front door of the shack. At the end of the week they did the final processing.

After nearly a month, the gold was not increasing. There were good days and bad ones and the average hovered around one-ounce per week, but like so many others, the two hoped for more. Charles expressed some of his frustration in a letter to his parents.

Back in Missouri, James gathered the family in front of the fire and handed the letter to Catherine to read aloud. She perused the letter for a moment and then said, "This is addressed to the whole family."

September 28, 1859

My Dearest Parents and Family,

Lord, how I miss you. I do hope you are all doing well. It meant so much to me to have all of you sign the last letter I received. I know that Frank did not actually sign it, but his scribble was precious.

Things here are not going exactly as I had hoped for. We have found gold, and really it is a fair quantity, but we are not going to get rich quickly, that is for sure. We spent half of yesterday repairing the sluice and I had to take our wheelbarrow in to a blacksmith. I managed to tie the thing up on the back of the mule and the mule did not like it much. I think at times it would have been easier to turn the whole package over and haul the mule in the wheelbarrow.

Darrell had originally planned to stay and help us through the winter. He changed his mind and left. While he could not do much, we looked forward to having him cook for us. Jason is not a good cook and I just do not like doing it. Oh, Mother to have you here making your wonderful biscuits would mean so much.

Maybe it is just living in such close quarters, but Jason seems to be a little out-of-sorts lately. I hope he perks up. Then there is the matter of the criminal element hereabouts. There are those that would literally steal the shirt from your back. There is constant feuding over claim ownership. So far nobody has challenged our rights, but we are told that it can happen to anyone. There is really no law here right now. Disagreements must be settled among those who disagree, and that is not always a good thing. Father, you could provide some good advice to these people, were you here.

I am sorry for the short note, but I must get to work. There is much to do. The gold awaits me.

Lovingly,
Charles

Catherine laid the letter aside. "I know that boy well," she said. "There is something between his words. I sense that he is not happy. This adventure of his is not working out as he thought it would. He had some big dream of running off to the Rocky Mountains and picking up gold off the ground until he was rich."

"You are probably right," James replied. "But I think that sometimes the best path to the truth is the hardest one to take."

From that day on the letters from Charles were more frequent and the underlying sentiment seemed to be that he was less than happy, but he also indicated that he had no intention of giving up. Almost every letter had words that told of his belief that the big cleanout was coming at any time.

In mid-October, something happened that promised to change everything. As Charles was digging into the creek bank and filling the wheelbarrow, he encountered solid rock. Finding rock that could not be easily removed was not unusual, but this was different. The rock was obviously granite, but it had a streak of quartz nearly five inches wide. Charles managed to chisel out a big chuck of the quartz. That evening he sat in front of the shack and used a hammer to crush the quartz on top of a large rock. He then put the crushed rock into a gold pan. He confirmed what he thought in the first place when he observed a small amount of gold in the pan. It was such a small amount that he quickly decided that it was of no amount to be pursued, at least by the methods he was using.

Later that week, while visiting with the men on the neighboring claim, Charles mentioned his discovery. Two days later a man showed up on the claim and wanted to see the quartz outcropping. When Charles inquired as to the man's reason for wanting to see the quartz, the man simply stated that he was interested and that he and his associates might be interested in purchasing all, or part of the claims.

Jason was instantly interested in selling, but Charles held back, reminding Jason that he owned only one quarter of the claim and that any decision to sell rested with Charles' father. Besides, this man had not made an offer, he only expressed interest and the gold they were retrieving was consistent, if not overly impressive. Charles agreed to write his father and ask for his opinion.

When he received James' reply, it came by special courier and James minced no words. He told Charles that he was not ready to give up and that Charles should not be either. They had been mining for only a few months and they were making ends meet. James wrote that he would seek some advice, but admonished Charles to make no agreements, whether actual or implied with anyone. "When you are seeking to sell something, the buyer has the advantage. When someone is coming to you to buy something, you have the upper hand."

As the fall of the year was making its presence known, Charles upgraded the small corral where the mule and horse was kept and built a small shelter for them. Feed was expensive, but both Charles and Jason resisted selling the two animals. When they were needed, they were indispensible and Charles had become attached to the mule, which he chose to call "Egghead."

By early November the miners moved the sluice a little farther down the creek. Just one day after moving it they recovered a nugget that weighed nearly one quarter of an ounce. The next day it snowed. Nearly four inches of snow blanketed the area. The boys decided it was a good day to go to town and pick up some provisions. The tavern was now a real building. The boys decided to get a bowl of stew and a beer. No sooner had they arrived than the same man who asked to see the quartz approached their table.

"You greenhorns fixing to pack up and head back to Missouri?"

Charles was instantly defensive. "First of all, we are not greenhorns. We have learned our trade well and Jason has extensive experience in California as well as here. No, we have no intention of leaving."

With that, he pulled the nugget from his shirt pocket, slammed it on the table and said, "Not when we are getting gold like that."

The man did not seem impressed. "Those nuggets are few and far between, the real gold is in that mountain behind you and the only way to get it is to tunnel. I know a few things you boys do not, but if you decide to head east, look me up."

"Maybe we should think about this," Jason said. "You see that snow out there? That is just a sample of what is coming."

"My father is not interested in selling out," Charles said. "And our contract is such that if you decide to sell, my father and I have the first rights and the buy out price is exactly what you invested, plus any profits to date, and I will tell you now, that it isn't much."

Jason finished his stew, drank his beer and said he was headed back to the claim. Charles joined him but conversation was almost nonexistent.

CHAPTER THIRTY-SIX

The Castello home was relatively quiet. Catherine was preparing the evening meal and the scent of her signature biscuits filled the room. Lucy was concentrating on stitching a sampler, while 11-year-old Mary sat beside her and watched her every move. Francis, who was just beginning to master walking, was almost running around the table.

When James came through the front door, all the children greeted him and he had to force a smile. Catherine gave him a peck on the cheek and stood back a little, looking closely at his face.

"You look tired, and frankly, a little upset. Take a seat and supper will be ready in a few minutes."

James sat down and Francis crawled up onto his lap. He bounced the young man on his knee, but without much enthusiasm. It had been a tough day. He spent the entire day at the courthouse and at the jail. His duties as sheriff caused some personal strife when he was required to remove a man who was a life-long friend from the property of a new landowner who had erected a fence. The dispute over the boundary ended up in several physical altercations over a period of nearly nine hours. James had no alternative but to remove his friend from the property. A lawsuit would likely be the result.

To make things even worse, one of the jailors was attacked by an inmate and suffered some serious cuts and bruises. He resigned before the doctor had completed dressing the wounds.

Lucy Ann interrupted James' thoughts by presenting her sampler to him. "What do you think of my work?"

James looked at the neatly embroidered cloth. He certainly was not an expert in needlepoint, but the work was obviously very good. It suddenly dawned on him that Lucy was a young lady. The first stiches she did just a couple of years ago were rudimentary and consisted mostly of individual stitches applied as she learned each of them. This sampler was much more. The words, "GOD BLESS OUR HOME,' were intricate and precise. The pictured house, which was just beginning to take shape, already displayed an elaborate design of roof angles and windows.

Catherine, who was proficient in needlecraft and sewing, stepped up and placed her hand on James' shoulder. "This young lady, thanks to her fine teachers," she said as she stood up straight and mocked breathing on her fingernails and rubbing them on her apron, "has come a long way in her education, both in domestic skills and more academic ways."

James kissed Lucy on the cheek saying, "I am very proud of you, young lady."

During the supper that evening, James asked each of the children how their day had been. The replies were mostly in the "it was okay" category, but the reply from 13-year-old James Joseph came as a surprise.

"I got into a fight at school today," he said. "But I won, or at least he gave up before I did."

James pushed his plate toward the center of the table. "What were you fighting about?"

"Well, this kid, Larry, he called me a nigger lover because he saw me talking to Samuel's sister."

"And who is Samuel?"

"He is this black that I fish with sometimes. His folks work the fields over on the Moreau place. Nobody cares that I fish with Samuel, but it sure did bother some of them that I talked to his sister. I think it is because she is pretty, but she is also black, so I guess she can't be pretty. Anyway, it is over now and I know you don't like fighting."

James had never addressed the slavery problem in front of his children, and knew he had to be careful.

"Son," he said. "You are right. I don't want you getting into fights, but I understand why you did. I disagree with what is going on with the slaves, but I have also sworn to uphold the law, and the law here is such that slavery is legal, but there is no law that says you have to treat people like animals on a personal basis. Your friendships are important and it is important to always know who your friends are."

Nancy was listening carefully and decided to join the conversation. "Your grandfather and I came here a long time ago. He befriended the Indians and the blacks and did business with both. It always bothered me just a little that there were people that were more than willing to take advantage of everything the natives knew, but chose to turn against them when it was more convenient for them. You listen to your father, pay attention to your studies and concentrate, not on what others think, but on what you believe."

James put an end to the discussion by tickling young Francis under his chin and asking, "And how was your, day little one?" He received a little giggle as a reply and returned his attention to his dinner.

After the supper clean up was finished James and Catherine sat side-by- side in chairs in front of the fireplace.

Catherine held out her hand and James took hold of it. She asked, "Okay, now what is bothering you."

"Several things," James replied. "I have been worried about Charles. That latest letter from him seems to have a hidden message. I think the boy has doubts about himself at a time when he needs to be more confident, although, the same might well be said about me today. The day has been difficult and there are those who think I should no longer be sheriff. There is only one man they have to convince of that and I would throw up my hands and walk away."

"And who is that man?"

"C'est moi. It is I", James replied. "If they ever convince me that I am not doing the right thing, I will give up my position immediately. I am not sure I am making a difference anyway."

"You have consistently sided with the dog that is most likely to lose the fight," Catherine said. "You just advised your son to do what he thinks is right. You set a good example doing that, but I too think you might be fighting a losing battle. As for Charles, he is young and will bounce back. He sat and listened to the stories his friends told him. Running off in search of gold was an adventure he had to experience, but do not forget that you are part of that adventure. You decided to invest in it. You decided the idea was worth a shot, and ultimately it will be you who will make the decisions to make it all work or tuck your tail and call it quits."

Several days later, James had the opportunity to talk with a freight man, whom he became acquainted with through some of his dealing with those who were equipping themselves to head off to the west or northwest. George Barrett had worked in the mines, built freight wagons, guided groups on the Santa Fe Trail and managed to do it all at a relatively young age. Now, he was making plans to go to Colorado. When James learned of Barrett's plans, he met with him at the courthouse. Barrett was transferring a piece of property to a new settler and told James he was investing in some property in Colorado in order to open a freight hauling business there.

During the conversation Barrett told James of the push in the Nevada Gulch area in Colorado for lode mining. He explained that he was taking some equipment to Colorado and that some people there were going to modify it in order to retrieve gold from the underground veins.

"My son, Charles is in that exact area right now," James said. "I recently received word from him about this proposed underground mining. In fact we have two claims there that are supposedly well located for one of these underground mines. I am told that people are interested in buying us out for that exact reason."

"My advice to you is to hold on a little longer," Barrett said. "Right now they can dig the holes, tunnel into the earth, pick out the ore, but they have no efficient way to process it beyond that. The gold that is in the creeks and rivers is already processed for the most part by Mother Nature. It has already been extracted from the main lodes over the centuries. The future in Colorado likely lies in the more aggressive digging. If you like, I will check in with your son upon my arrival and put out a few feelers as to your claims."

"I would greatly appreciate that, George," James said. "When are you planning to leave?"

"My men are loading the equipment as we speak. With any luck we will be headed west at the end of this week. I probably will not return.

Frankly, I have had just about enough of what is happening around here. I have been to Colorado twice now and I think I might just like to become a permanent part of the Colorado of the future."

That afternoon James wrote a short letter to Charles and posted it before he went home for the evening.

November 14, 1859

Charles,

> *I want to post this today, so it will be brief.*
>
> *I talked to George Barrett today. You know who he is. He will be headed to Colorado before this week is out. I have asked him to contact you. He is an honest and intelligent man. Please trust him and what he has to say.*
>
> *He has re-enforced my thoughts that we should hold on to the claims there for the time being. If Jason wants out, I think we would be better to buy his share, rather than sell the whole thing. Keep that in mind. You should receive this well before Barrett gets there. He is likely going to have a slow trip. Please keep me informed.*

Your Loving Father.

When James returned home that evening, Catherine and Lucy had just returned also. Upon finding out that his wife and daughter had been within a block or two of him at least two times during the day, James wondered why they had not seen him.

"You should have looked for me, we maybe could have had a lunch," he said.

"We had things to do," said Catherine. "We came upon George Barrett and he informed us that you were very busy and that he was going to Colorado and was going to contact Charles at your request. I must admit that our encounter with Mr. Barrett took longer than I wanted it to. I think he may have eyes for Lucy and she was giggling like a little girl at his attentions."

"Oh, Mother," Lucy said while blushing slightly. "He is a nice man and he has a wonderful sense of humor. Besides, he is going to Colorado and says he will likely stay there."

"This is not a very good time to be headed west," James replied. "He will likely have a hard time of it. Winter will be upon him, but he told me that he is taking some equipment to some people that are planning to do some underground mining, and they need the equipment as soon as possible. They are paying George a premium to get it there quickly. He has also volunteered to contact Charles and give us an opinion as to how things are going. George is probably making a good move to Colorado. Things around here are at a boiling point. I have never seen the turmoil such as what is happening. There is even talk about Missouri seceding from the Union. I think, at least for the time being, Missouri will not fall into the secession movement but that cannot be said about other slave states where people hold the beliefs that the northern states are treating the southern states badly. I have said for a long time that this could happen. Even Father foresaw these problems years ago."

"We can only pray for the best," Catherine said.

CHAPTER THIRTY-SEVEN

George Barrett was a seasoned freighter. Having made two other trips to the base of the Rocky Mountains, he felt better prepared for this one, except for one thing: He was headed out at the wrong time of the year. He knew it would be an outright miracle if he did not get snowbound somewhere along the way.

Barrett had two large freight wagons with huge wheels on the back and smaller ones on the front. They were built of heavy planks. The sides of the wagons were equipped to carry spare wheels, one front and one back. Four sturdy mules pulled each wagon, which was loaded with several pieces of heavy iron and an assortment of gears and blocks that originated from all points. Barrett was contracted to a speculation company. All he knew of his cargo was that it was important to the mining activities in the Jefferson Territory that many were referring to as Colorado.

Barrett chose his route via the Oregon Trail. A more direct route was mapped, but Barrett was familiar with the northern trail, and more importantly, he had on previous trips had friendly encounters with the Indians in the Platte River basin.

For this trip, Barrett chose mules rather than oxen. The oxen were tougher in a lot of ways and required less food and water, but they were slow and George Barrett had no time to waste.

Each of the mule teams also had to have a horse and rider. For some reason mules were better behaved if they had a horse to follow. So, George rode the lead horse, followed by the first wagon, and then his top hand rode another horse in front of the second wagon. Two men managed each wagon and provided driving and maintenance services. The cook rode a separate mule and led a pack mule. Each day the cook would venture out ahead of the rest of the group and begin to set up a camp. He was called, simply, "Cook."

While cooks in these situations were often thought of as being the lesser of the men, Barrett's cook was considered an equal and Barrett made sure his other men understood that mistreatment of the cook in any fashion would be dealt with by dismissal from the entourage. Cook was also an excellent shot. He could use a small caliber rifle effectively for rabbits and other small game, or he could choose his .54 caliber Hawken rifle for an occasional deer. Cook was especially proud of his rifle. It was one of the originals; hand made by the Samuel Hawken, but had been converted from its original flintlock design to the more efficient cap lock.

One evening, as the sun was just beginning to fall behind the horizon of North Park, Cook came riding in from the west. Barrett noticed at once that Cook was not leading the pack mule. He rode up beside Barrett, who without waiting for any explanation, asked about the missing mule.

"The mule is okay," Cook said. "I left him with some friends of yours and we have been invited to their camp for the evening."

"And pray tell, what friends of mine could you have encountered?"

"They are Utes. At first I thought my days had come to an end. I had just shot a small deer and they rode up as I was preparing to dress it out. They started babbling on about something and I was only able to pick out a few of their words, which I think were Spanish. One of them asked if I was traveling with the wagons that were coming from the east. When I told them I was, they asked who you were. When I told them, one of them smiled and, using sign language, got across to me that I could share my deer with them because they knew who you are. They helped dress the deer and headed back to their camp. You can see the smoke now, if you look hard."

Barrett was somewhat confused and asked Cook for more information.

"Did they say which one of their tribe knew me?"

"Boss," Cook replied. "I was having one hell of a time convincing myself that they were not there to steal my deer and maybe my top knot along with it. They seemed friendly enough, but only because I mentioned your name. Now we better get moving or the only thing left of that deer is going to be that lead ball I put in it."

It took only a few minutes before Barrett had his group moving again. They arrived at the Ute camp about two hours later and he was surprised to find out that Ouray, the chief of the Tabeguache band of Utes, was in the camp. Ouray met Barrett with a handshake. The two met about two years prior when Barrett was transporting some freight on the Santa Fe Trail.

"Welcome George Barrett, I am happy that we meet again," Ouray said in clear English. "Come we will eat first, then we can talk."

Ouray instructed some of his men to assist the wagon drivers and to take care of the mules and wagons, and then he led Barrett to the center of the camp. The band consisted of only about a dozen braves and four women. As soon as the men took their seats around the main fire, the women began serving the food. It was evident that Cook's buck was not the only deer that had given its life for the sustenance of travelers. The roasted venison was served on flat bread made from flour ground from corn. Cook seemed to especially enjoy eating someone else's cooking for a change. He also became quick friends with one of the women, who spoke acceptable English and explained some of the nuances of Indian cooking.

After the meal Ouray invited Barrett to his lodge. They sat in squatted positions and Ouray explained that he was in the final planning stages of trying to unite several tribes so they could deal with the impending influx of white men. He planned a more extensive trip in the coming year. Barrett discussed the situation honestly with Ouray, telling him how the tribes of the lower Missouri and Mississippi had suffered, but that he believed that the future of his kind probably rested in the United States expanding to the west. His accounts did not seem to surprise Ouray. In fact, Ouray said that he also thought the whites would increase their interest in the lands of the west, largely because of the discovery of gold, but also because they would soon realize that they could take advantage of the succulent grasses of the north and south parks, which for centuries had kept the bison well-fed.

After a long discussion, Ouray told Barrett that, while he considered the white man an enemy, he also believed that it would become necessary for him and other chiefs to sit with their enemies and work together for the good of all. He then told Barrett that the wagon drivers had been shown where to set up camp and where to allow their animals to go graze for the night. Barrett left the lodge with another firm handshake from the chief.

After assuring his men that they would not be scalped during the night, Barrett curled up into his bedroll, but sleep did not come easy. The powwow caused a lot of conflict in his thoughts. He knew the chief was right, but he also knew that his very livelihood depended on more and more white men traveling the trails. The loaded wagons, one of which was now serving as his shelter were evidence that more were going to come.

Early the next morning both camps were dismantled. Barrett prepared to continue west while the Indians were going to take a more southern route that would take them over the Rockies and down into their homes in the Tabeguache valley. With some departing words, Ouray told Barrett that he prayed the weather would remain cooperative and that Barrett would arrive at his destination in good health. Barrett wished the same for Ouray and his small band and the groups separated.

The remainder of the trip was uneventful. The weather had indeed cooperated and Jesse Whittington, the mine speculator with whom he had contracted with to haul the machinery, met Barrett in a timely fashion. When Barrett inquired if the man knew Charles Castello, Whittington's demeanor became obviously serious.

"Yeah, I know him," he replied. "If I have my way, I will own those two claims he has before the year is out. I have his partner convinced to sell, but Castello has some sort of a stranglehold on the man and I haven't been able to come to an agreement, but I will."

Barrett assumed quickly that the Castello property must have some significant value. He planned to keep his promise to James Castello and amass as much information as possible.

If it was Ouray's prayers that kept the weather in check, they evidently had an expiration date. The first day of December brought with it a heavy snow that seemed to have no ending. It was also the day Barrett first met Charles Castello and Jason Roth. The pair was in town obtaining some supplies and they were at a small tavern. Barrett had previously asked the tavern owner about Castello and pointed out the miners to Barrett.

Barrett determined quickly that Charles and Jason were at a point in their business relationship where they were just tolerating each other and not really cooperating with each other. He learned that Jason wanted to sell out, but could only sell to George and George's father, James Castello. George was awaiting word from his father as to whether they should buy Jason's part of the company. Barrett explained his arrangement with James and told the pair that he was obligated to send as much information as possible back to James.

The mining was almost at a standstill owing to the weather but Barrett determined quickly why Jesse Whittington was interested in the property. Everyone in the area was talking about the possibility of converting to lode mining, where tunnels and shafts are dug, following the source of the gold. The one big problem was in processing the ore containing all that gold. Barrett learned that he had been transporting part of the solution to that problem. All that heavy material in his wagons was intended to become a stamp mill for crushing the ore so the gold could be recovered.

Barrett decided he would remain in the Central City area. His crew intended on returning to Missouri, which gave Barrett an opportunity to send his newly acquired information back to James Castello via his trusted cook. Because the men could make use of the rivers for a good portion of the trip they were back in Florissant in the early days of 1860. Cook arranged to meet with James Castello as soon as he arrived in St. Louis.

CHAPTER THIRTY-EIGHT

The turmoil caused by the slavery issues continued to grow. Missouri was still trying to play both sides, but everyone assumed that they would eventually throw their lot into those seeking to secede from the Union. It was a given that, should Abraham Lincoln prevail in the 1860 election, the advocates of secession would redouble their efforts. The Nebraska Act of 1854 helped somewhat and Lincoln's supporters reminded everyone that Lincoln did not want to end slavery; he wanted only to prevent the practice from becoming commonplace as the nation expanded to the west.

By the time Cook met with James in January of 1860, James had given up his position as sheriff, but found himself continually trying to mitigate the unrest and violence of St. Louis and the surrounding communities.

The meeting with Cook was brief. He explained that his only order from Barrett was to deliver a handwritten missive, which consisted of six pages written on the larger stationary commonly used by businessmen. It was sealed in an envelope of paper similar to that of the letter. Cook handed the envelope to James, explaining that Barrett had instructed him that his only duty was to deliver and that he was not expected to return to Central City with a reply. James read the letter:

Central City, Jefferson Territory
Monday, December 12, 1859

James, my dear friend,

I hope this letter finds you in a timely manner. I chose to send it via my trusted cook rather than to rely on other forms of delivery.

As you requested, I have had contact with your son Charles. You are correct in your assumptions that his partner, Jason Roth, is anxious to sell his interest. Judging by my instincts, and assuming that you would ask for my advice, I would say that my impression of Mr. Roth is that he does not have an instinct for working hard and waiting for results. I am of the opinion that, if he were a partner in my business, I would send him packing.

As for Charles, he is somewhat discouraged right now. The mining operation is slow, largely due to the time of year and I think that Mr. Roth is at least partly responsible for Charles' mood.

I have also come into possession of some very interesting information regarding your claims. Jesse Whittington ordered the freight I delivered here. Mr. Whittington is a mining speculator who is involved with a group of people who plan to establish some underground mines in this area. He informed me that he is especially interested in the claims you own. He has also indicated that he will continue to apply pressure on both Charles and Jason until he convinces them to sell. I have informed Charles that he should avoid Whittington until such time as you and he can discuss the options. Knowing that I was arranging to send this letter to you, Charles agreed to wait. He has also confided in me that he has sufficient funds available to buy out Jason's interest. He did not divulge the particulars.

It may also interest you that the talk here in the most popular tavern is that there is a move underway to carve out a significant part of the Jefferson Territory and establish a new

Territory of Colorado. Largely because of this information, I have decided to stay in the area and establish a freighting business. I look forward to more contact with you.

Also, please relay my regards to your daughter Lucy Ann. I so enjoyed her humor when we last met.

If I can be of further assistance, I am surely available.

Your Friend,
Geo. Barrett

After reading the letter, James read it again. This time he read it out loud to Catherine, pausing several times to seek a response from her. They discussed at length the probability that James would ultimately decide to join Charles, but the most direct response from Catherine came when James read the reference to Lucy.

"What did I tell you? I knew he had a yearning to know Lucy better, and I think the feeling might well be mutual. She has asked three or four times if we have heard anything from Mr. Barrett."

James then asked Lucy to come into the room.

"As you have probably figured out by now, we have received a letter from George Barrett regarding your brother. Would you care to read it?"

"How is George?" Her hand was visibly shaking as she reached for the letter.

Almost teasingly, James said, "Read it for yourself. I will be sending a letter of my own to George. If you want to say anything to George let me know." He made a point to add just a little emphasis when he said "George."

Lucy took the letter and stood by the table as she read it. Both James and Catherine were closely studying her face. Catherine's suspicions were confirmed when a slight blush spread over Lucy's face as she finished the final lines of the letter. She handed the letter back to her father.

"You may tell George that I am well," she said, putting that same emphasis on Barrett's first name. "Oh, and tell him to inform my brother of that fact too, just in case he cares."

The same blush was accompanied by a very obvious smile. She almost skipped out of the room. A minute later James and Catherine heard the distinct giggle of 13-year-old Mary.

"Well," Catherine said. "I think we know what that is all about. It might well be a good thing that Mr. Barrett is not here right now."

"I am not sure that is a good thing," replied James. "I am afraid that our eldest daughter might start pining for a romance that has yet to develop. Now, I must prepare a letter to Charles. I only hope that he has already decided to buy out Jason Roth, but I want my lawyer to prepare the proper documents for the transaction. If George is right, we need to resolve this as quickly as possible. It sounds as if we can realize a significant profit from those claims if the situation is handled correctly. I will also write and inform George (again the emphasis) that Lucy is well."

The next day James met with his lawyer and explained the situation. The lawyer prepared a contract whereby Jason Roth would sell his one-quarter interest in the mining claims to James and Charles. A separate partnership agreement to be signed by Charles provided that the claims would be owned in common between James and Charles Castello and that each partner had the right of first refusal should the other decide to sell.

After showing the contracts to Catherine, James penned letters to both Charles and to George Barrett. That evening he told Catherine that the letters and the contract had been posted, but it would likely take some time before they heard from Charles.

"I am considering some other options also," James told Catherine.

"And I suspect that one of those options is for you to saddle up and head to the Rocky Mountains," she replied. "Am I correct?"

"It is," James said. "If, in fact, there is a future in underground mining, and if we truly have such desirable claims, I think we might think about developing the claims ourselves rather than to provide them to someone else at this point. Of course I will do nothing without your input."

"Husband," Catherine said shaking her head slightly. "I cannot count the number of times I have told you this, but I say it again. You will always find that I support you, even if I do not totally agree with you. I can also see that you are not happy with the way things are right now. I only ask that, should you decide that those mountains are drawing you to them, you wait and take the journey at a more favorable time."

"I will promise you that," James replied. "I have no desire to brave the elements more than necessary. I have been on this earth for nearly one half of a century and I would like to say that it is time to take it easy, but I will tell you now that going to Central City is quickly becoming more sensible to me all the time. Our family has endured much over the years and we have largely survived because of the ventures my father and I took in mining. I believe that the Good Lord has provided this earth with what we need to manufacture and grow everything we need, but we have to have the will to go after it. The railroad is being built into Kansas as we speak and Kansas will likely be a state in the very near future. Travel up the river by ferryboat is becoming commonplace and will mean that I can head west much easier than ever before. I also think there will be a day when we see the railroad expand beyond our wildest dreams. I want to be a part of all those dreams and I want to leave this turmoil of slavery behind. I have had enough of the constant fighting and political posturing. Maybe the people who have started to settle the west have done so with more reasonable expectations."

James realized that his discussion with his wife had served to convince him to go west as soon as possible. For the next several weeks he prepared for the inevitable trip. Part of his preparation included talking to other businessmen and procuring newspapers, which often times were reporting on the westward movement, although many of the articles were romanticized to a point that they were unbelievable. One thing was sure: George Barrett was not the only one who recently delivered equipment designed to mill ore. One company was bragging that their mill would be up and operating in six months or less. The newspapers also reported a marked interest in forming an official Colorado Territory.

As the early hints of spring began showing James declared himself ready to leave the slavery issue behind and head to Colorado. He assured Catherine that he would be very diligent in his assessment of their future. Before the spring had fully taken hold James Castello was standing on the bank of a partially frozen stream looking at some bare rock with obvious veins of quartz running in several vertical streaks. The contract with Jason had been accomplished. Charles and James were now partners and James was a gold miner.

CHAPTER THIRTY-NINE

The first few weeks of the newly reorganized mining adventure was difficult. Parts of the creek were still frozen and the only way to clean the sluice was to bring the concentrates into the cabin where James and Charles could work in the relative warmth of the fire.

The gold they recovered was significant, but not overwhelming. Each day they processed just a little more than the previous day, owing mostly to favorable temperatures, but the other miners cautioned that things would change quickly when the spring runoff began and it began a few days before the miners were prepared. They worked well into the night to get their sluice moved to higher ground, wasting a full day of sluicing.

Within a few days the diggings that had produced the best gold were filling with rock and mud washed down from above. The diversion ditch required constant attention. Charles went into town and hired a 17-year-old boy to help and they managed to stay ahead of the runoff, but gold recovery was not paying the bills.

One day, as Charles and James could only sit and watch the high water, Jesse Whittington visited them. Whittington walked directly up to James and introduced himself. Initially he ignored Charles, as though James was the primary owner of the two claims.

"The name is Whittington, Jesse Whittington," he said as he shook James' hand. "Mr. Castello, I presume? You are the owner of these two claims?"

James took Whittington's hand. "My son and I own the claims. This is Charles Castello, my son and my partner."

"Of course," Whittington said almost apologetically. "I do recall seeing both names on the documents that were filed recently, showing that a third owner, Jason Roth, is no longer part of the picture. I felt that Mr. Roth and I were close to an agreement. I was disappointed that he did not choose to sell his interest to me."

"Well," James said. "He really had no choice. Under our agreement with him, he could not sell his interest to a third party without the consent of Charles and me. I have been made aware of your desire to purchase the claims, but I am afraid that I cannot consider selling until I have fully evaluated the entire situation. I understand that you are interested in chasing those quartz veins underground. Would you mind explaining that process to me?"

Whittington went into a lengthy verbal dissertation, describing the geology of the area and the glaciers, forming of creeks and rivers and the theory that the good gold was locked within the veins of quartz and other materials. He explained that recovering the best gold would require the creation of drifts, shafts and other access methods to follow the gangue, or the rock that contains the gold. In the case of the Castello property, that gangue is quartz. He went on to explain that, once the gangue is separated from other rock it becomes ore. The ore must then be crushed to release the gold. Various chemicals, floatation devices and other means accomplish the process at that point.

"It is a complicated and very expensive process," Whittington said. "Most small miners with limited resources cannot pursue this type of mining. You should think carefully about your future here. Lode mining is coming and it is coming quickly. We have already acquired several claims that were available simply because the owners went broke. I have a stamp mill being constructed as we speak. I will keep in touch, but I will make only one offer should you decide to sell. After that, I will simply wait."

As the water slowed and summer approached, James and Charles, along with their hired man spent most of their time cleaning out the depression from which most of their pay dirt was found. The hole was nearly eight feet deep and more than 50 feet long. It had filled completely with rock and debris. The only option was to clean it out a wheelbarrow load at a time. The pay dirt was uncovered after several days of hard work. As they dug deeper and closer to the granite face, the pay became better. They were finally able to pay as they went and buy the necessary supplies to keep working.

In the middle of August of 1860 James met with George Barrett. Barrett was taking some freight down into the Tarryall area of South Park. He needed one more wagon driver that was familiar with oxen and asked James if he would be interested. He also explained that the movement to make Colorado a territory was progressing well and that James may well be interested in the land around Tarryall.

Barrett explained that one month earlier a group of men from Gregory Gulch stirred up a fight with some Ute Indians. The result was that five of the miners were killed. A vigilante group of sorts was organized and traveled into the Tarryall area to seek revenge. They were severely outnumbered by the Utes and returned to Central City, leaving their supply wagons and several mules behind. A friend of Barrett's recovered the wagons. The mules became property of the Utes. Barrett intended to retrieve the wagons and make amends, at least as much as possible with the Utes, whom he considered to be his friends. He intended to take two teams of oxen and return with the wagons in just a few days.

There had long been rumors of good gold being found in Tarryall and James became interested. He agreed to accompany Barrett. The subsequent trip provided James with several opportunities, not the least of which was becoming acquainted with George Barrett. He considered Barrett to be a man of integrity and spending a few days with him solidified his assumption. They discussed the probability that the area in which they were establishing themselves would soon be an official territory and that the name would likely be Colorado, a reference to the red rock formations and the color of the water that flowed through them. Barrett described a trip he took a few years ago that found him on the western side of the Rocky Mountains.

"I hauled several wagonloads of freight down the Santa Fe Trail for a Mexican group and ended up meeting the chief of the Tabeguache Utes, a man called Ouray. I never did get a good handle on all the various bands of the Utes, but I learned that Ouray was considered a man who could bring about peace between the whites and his various tribes. I ended up traveling with them for a distance on my return trip and I was impressed with the beauty of the lands they occupied. The term, Colorado, is much more applicable to that area than it is here. There are great cliffs of red rock and the Grand River flows with a constant reddish color. I again met Ouray while en-route here with Whittington's equipment and I look forward to seeing him again."

"Why would this chief be near the Tarryall diggings?" James asked.

"He is probably on another of his peace missions, and when those sluice worms decided to take on more than they could handle, he was probably the one that directed the Utes in the area to spank them like children and send them home. I lost some mules in the process, but I have to consider that the price of doing business. The two wagons are another matter. The Utes had no use for them and would simply had burned them had not my friend retrieved them and sent word to me."

Barrett and James headed to the Tarryall area of an early morning. The four oxen, having been well seasoned and trained, simply followed the two horses. By the end of the day the pair arrived at the placer diggings of George's friend, Russell Watson. As they sat around a small fire that evening, Watson described the turmoil that was present between various miners and with the Indians.

"Unlike, where your diggings are in the gulch," Watson told James, "The men that staked claims in this area literally grabbed everything they could. Now with the impending adoption of the Territory of Colorado, many of these miners will have to prove that their claims are productive. Otherwise they will probably lose them. Meanwhile there are those who are supportive of the southern states and they throw those disagreements into the pot, stir in a good helping of Indian hatred, and we end up with nobody getting along with anyone else. If these miners are not fighting with the Indians, they are fighting with each other. I hold that the men and women who have developed this nation so far will succeed beyond our wildest dreams, but it will not be accomplished without conflict."

"I know full well of the conflicts, having just spent time as the Sheriff of St. Louis County, but I have learned that, while some would say the conflict is all about one thing, that is not true at all. Some will make it sound as if the one and only issue is slavery, but there is much more. The founders of this nation were not perfect, but I believe in my heart that they did the right thing and that the true believers in a nation of government by representation will ultimately become our leaders. Those in the south that are at odds with the government want more than anything to be free. Their ideas of freedom may differ from some of ours and might well end up in a major conflict, but the time will come when we are the better for our mistakes. We cannot reinvent what brought us to where we are at, nor can we expect to correct all wrongs by simply vilifying each other."

"I think I have seen a spark in your pan," Watson said. "As long as we have hard-working freedom loving people like you sitting around our fires and in our homes, I think we will become a better nation. We are already a great nation, but each generation must hold their ground to secure it and always strive to make it better."

The next day, as George Barrett and James Castello sat in the lodge of Chief Ouray and Chief Colorow, the conversation with Russell Watson was still fresh in James' mind. He was impressed with both Ouray and Colorow and in their ability to discuss matters in a give-and-take debate. So many times during the past few years James had intervened in arguments that became shouting matches where nobody was willing to listen to the other side of the issue. In those cases the arguments often became physical altercations with neither side really winning.

Ouray expressed his regret that the influx of white men was just starting. He admitted that, while the tribes he represented were strong and willing to fight for what is theirs, they too would come to realize that some costly compromises would be required.

CHAPTER FORTY

By the end of August the Castello claims were yielding good gold. James and Charles had amassed a significant nest egg, but Charles was not happy. He suggested several times that they should sell the claim and go back to Missouri. James was noticing that there were more and more disputes among the miners and the businessmen in Central City.

One morning in early September three of the neighboring miners came to see James. They told him that there were two claims not far from him that were being disputed. They said they were sitting up all night at times to prevent claim jumpers and had finally come to an agreement among several of the miners to meet in a neutral venue and work out their differences. The problem was that they could not agree on who would pick the meeting place and who would act as moderator during the meeting. One of the miners knew that James had been a sheriff in Missouri and asked if he would consider being the moderator.

James reminded the miners that the sheriff, William Cozens, was a fearless man, whom he visited with several times. He asked if they had talked to him about the problem.

"We have talked to the sheriff and he has settled several disputes, but he upholds the law and usually ends up arresting someone," said one of the miners. "We want to try to settle some of these things among ourselves and, by the way, it was Sheriff Cozens that recommended we seek out your assistance."

The next day James arranged to use the facility of the Sons of Malta, which boasted a large meeting room, and more importantly, did not allow the use of alcohol. He also arranged a meeting with Sheriff Cozens.

"Sheriff," James said. "I must tell you that I am somewhat uncomfortable with my agreement to moderate a dispute with some of the local miners. I understand you told them to contact me and that prompted me to say yes, but I really do not understand just what my role will be."

"James," Cozens replied. "You know that I have long respected your level-headed way of dealing with things. These men need someone to keep them calm. My direct involvement seems to cause more problems than are solved. What we really need is a judge, but as it stands now, I only have justices of peace and all of them are miners and sometimes they are good friends of those who are involved. I think you can set your mining interest aside for the purposes of acting as a moderator during a meeting. Your recent sit-down with the Utes has become common knowledge and that has gained you a lot of respect. I will be nearby during the meeting just in case, but I am limited in what I can actually do. We have a jail of sorts in Central, but it is neither official nor adequate, so I try to avoid actually arresting anyone."

Following the meeting with Cozens, James visited with the four miners who were directly involved in the current dispute. He asked each of them to provide him with a bill of particulars, telling them that, while this was not a formal lawsuit, he had found while serving as the sheriff in St. Louis, that such a list of complaints, witnesses and evidence was helpful in reaching decisions, and in this case, hopefully some compromises. Each of the parties agreed to provide the information at least one day prior to the meeting.

The meeting was considered by most to be a success. Disputes were settled and there were no physical altercations or gunplay. Over the next two months, in addition to helping with the claims, James was called on several more times to moderate similar disputes.

After trading several letters with Catherine, James decided to make a trip back to Missouri. The aspen were just beginning to show their fall colors, but no snow had yet fallen. James decided to make the trip by himself and travel as quickly as possible. He arrived at the Castello farm in Missouri in the third week of October. The children had grown significantly. In fact, Lucy Ann could not be called a child and Mary would soon be 14 years old. The biggest change was young Francis. He was walking around and exploring everything. James' mother, Nancy, was showing her age and was getting feeble, but still managed to move around the house and sit with the family for dinner.

After settling in, having a short conversation with his mother and teasing the children at length, James and Catherine sat on the front porch. Each of the children went about their chores and studies and Lucy took charge of Francis. It was time to discuss the future.

"I am not going to mince words," James said. "I think this family has a future in Colorado. Based on my information the area will soon be designated as a territory and will become a very important part of the United States. I also believe that, in less than a month, Abraham Lincoln will be successful in becoming the president. When that happens a number of things are going to change, not the least of which is that the southern states are going to become even more unsettled than they are now, and Missouri is going to be part of that turmoil."

Catherine thought for a moment before responding. "Have you noticed how your mother's health has deteriorated? There is absolutely no way she could survive the type of move you are suggesting. And, what do you propose to do with the land and boarding house?"

"I know there are many things to consider, and yes, I have noticed that Mother is really showing her age. I am not saying that we need to pick up and leave in a fortnight. I am considering the possibility of selling our mining claims in the gulch. There seems to be some promising developments in the South Park and I intend on looking at those before I consider moving you and the family. I think Charles is at the point where he would sell out at the drop of a hat, but I do not think we necessarily need to invest in another mine. We succeeded fairly well here by providing food and lodging rather than me working in the mine. I think that is something we should look at in Colorado."

Catherine took James' hand. "Since the very day we found each other, I have returned to the Book of Ruth and I will once again quote: 'Entreat me not to leave thee, or to return from following after thee, for whither thou goest, I will go; and where thou lodgest I will lodge.' But I must tell you, husband, that I am weary of lodging here without you, so if we are to go, we should start planning as soon as possible."

"The trip is much easier now than it was when I first ventured west," James said. In fact, it is now possible to take a train to Atchison, thereby shortening the trip at least a little. I will look into some ways to make things as simple as possible, but we also have to consider what will be happening among the states, after this upcoming presidential election. I will be returning to the mine in a few days and I will write you as soon as I get there and have a few answers to our questions. Now, I should go in and talk to Mother."

After a short conversation with Nancy, James knew that she would not likely survive a trip to Colorado even if she wanted to go and she did not want to even consider it. She told James she would be staying right where she was.

James was back in the Nevada Gulch where the mining was once again slowing down for the winter when he heard the news that Abraham Lincoln had succeeded in winning the election of November 6, 1860. According to several newspapers, the turmoil among the Democrat Party members resulted in their not being able to put forth a candidate that could win. Because of the big split of votes, Lincoln only received less than 40 percent of the popular vote and did not have a plurality in even one of the southern states, but he succeeded in getting the majority of the Electoral College, with 180 electoral votes. The news also noted that, immediately after receiving word of the electoral votes, rumors flourished about states seceding from the Union.

In mid-December of 1860 George Barrett once again contacted James. Barrett was staying very busy with his freighting business, but while transporting some mining equipment to Fairplay, he invested in some property in the growing town. He explained to James that gold diggings around Fairplay were proving to be more substantial than those in Fairplay itself, but because the new town was so centralized to the mining district, it was becoming a significant supply center. Barrett had transported several large loads of equipment into Fairplay. He told James he intended on building a house there and making it the headquarters of his business.

"You should think seriously about selling your claims and heading that way. I think your background would qualify you to run a very profitable rooming house or hotel and you may want to look into why the place is named Fairplay," George said before departing.

About two weeks after his conversation with Barrett, James received one of his regular newspapers and learned that South Carolina had seceded from the Union. Others were expected to follow in the near future.

George Barrett's reference to why Fairplay was called Fairplay spurred some interest, and James started looking into the matter. He discovered that some of the miners in the South Park were doing exactly what those in the Central City area were trying to do. They were trying to settle their differences in a formal and dignified manner. The big difference was that the organizers in South Park seemed to be succeeding. The people in the area knew what had happened in the Tarryall area, where greed overwhelmed fairness and they set out to make things different. They vowed that their holdings near the confluence of the South Platte River and Beaver Creek would offer a "fair play" for anyone settling in the area. They organized a tribunal to oversee all disputes and encouraged everyone to abide by the decisions of the tribunal. When, shortly after the New Year, Barrett was once again hauling equipment from the Gregory diggings to Fairplay, James agreed to help. This visit left a lasting impression on James. In the first days of March James was ready to again change his plans. The official establishment of the Territory of Colorado was the determining factor.

CHAPTER FORTY-ONE

On February 28, 1861 the establishment of the Territory of Colorado was made official. County lines were drawn and Park County became one of the largest, with the Town of Tarryall named as the county seat.

As soon as James received word of the new territory being official, he discussed some of his plans with Charles.

"I have looked seriously at the possibility of pursuing a different line of business and doing so in the new Park County," he said to Charles. "I really think this place has merit and could be the beginning of our removing ourselves from the actual mining and concentrating on what those miners and others who are following the miners need. I do not think Tarryall is deserving of being the county seat and that may change. What will not change is the fact that there are new mining methods being used around Fairplay and the influx of miners and those headed farther west can be a great opportunity."

Charles smiled and asked, "Are you talking about selling?"

"I am, but not right now. I think we should wait, improve our claims as much as possible and even work them through this next season. That way we can maximize the value and realize a better profit. I propose that we start an underground operation with the sole purpose of having it there to entice possible buyers into taking over a working mine with the first drift already started. I have conversed with some people that would be willing to assist us for a small percentage of the final price."

By the first of April the spring weather was allowing some of the mining activities to begin and James wasted no time in contacting three of the miners with whom he had previously discussed the possibility of starting a drift to follow one of the quartz outcroppings, but on April 12, 1861, just one month into the Lincoln presidency, troops formed by the states that were seceding from the Union changed things. On that date the Confederate troops attacked Fort Sumter with canon fire and the Union forces surrendered. A civil war was inevitable.

One of the three miners left the gulch immediately to join the Union army. Several other miners followed him in the next weeks, but James was determined to go ahead with his plans. Within hours of the first round of blasting that created a portal to a future drift along the quartz vein, some of the claim holders close to the Castello claims contacted James. Once again, offers were made to buy his claim, and once again Charles wanted to sell immediately. James calmed him and encouraged the continued use of the sluices.

As was his ongoing commitment to keep Catherine up-to-date, James penned her a letter in late April:

April 20, 1861

My Dearest Wife,

We are once again sluicing gold. The yields are not great, but there is sufficient gold to keep us going. We have now established a drift or tunnel into the side of the granite face on our property. This type of mining is the way of the future, but it is very hard and dangerous work and I do not intend to become an underground miner. I have pursued it thus far only to add value to our claim.

Charles has become increasingly argumentative and has almost lost interest in our endeavors here. I struggle every day to keep him motivated and looking to the future.

Another problem is that the nation has now split for sure and a civil war has begun. Several miners have left the area, some to join up with the Union and others to go back to their southern homes to join with the Confederacy. We have already started seeing flyers posted asking men to join up. I find it somewhat concerning that some of these flyers do not promote fighting among the states, but rather fighting against the Indians. I fear that Chief Ouray and his bands and many more are going to suffer, much as they have in Missouri.

George Barrett has established a successful freighting business in Fairplay. I have asked him to keep me informed and to let me know of any property that would provide a good location for a hotel and rooming house and which is available for a fair amount.

As I previously wrote you, the new Park County is destined to grow. It is encouraging that the original designation of Tarryall as the county seat has been abandoned and the town of Buckskin Joe now has that honor, but it will not become official until next January. The town has attracted some significant speculators and is close enough to Fairplay to become important in my plans.

I dream every night of being able to get you and the children here, but I must first be able to provide you a home to come to. Please be patient with me and give my love to the children. Also, George asked how Lucy Ann is doing.

Until next time.

Your Loving Husband

As the year wore on the war was escalating. Colorado was not as affected as many other states and territories, but the turmoil was evident. The mine was doing well and the men who were working the drift encountered some gold bearing quartz almost immediately. After separating the ore from the other rock, the ore was sold to one of the men who had expressed interest in buying the claims. James allowed the miners to keep 60 percent of what they sold and he was impressed by the quality of the ore. The quartz was fairly easy to separate from gangue and the assays were impressive.

James received two letters from Catherine since his April missive. In both letters she expressed her concern over the war. Many of the anti-slavery people had left the Florissant and St. Louis area to go north and fight with Lincoln's army. Those men that remained and were not part of the military tended to be staunchly in favor of slavery and were very vocal in their opinions. Catherine indicated the idea of leaving Missouri behind was looking better all the time. She expressed one other concern, namely George Barrett. In one of her letters she wrote: "What is it with that man's interest in our daughter? He has only met her that one time."

James smiled as he read the question because he knew that Lucy had also asked about George. In late September James once again accompanied George on a return trip to Fairplay. James learned that, unbeknownst to him, George and Lucy had exchanged letters and that George had informed Lucy of the possibility of her father becoming a resident of Fairplay.

James was surprised by the revelation and asked George, "Why have I not been told of these letters? Do you not think a father should be aware that a friend has an interest in his daughter?"

"Now James," George replied. "Don't be getting your union suit all knotted up. Lucy is a 20-year-old woman, not a little girl and it was her that did not want to tell anyone we were corresponding. Quite frankly, most of what she wrote was about you and her mother and the miles that separated the family. At your request I have looked closely at a piece of property in Fairplay. I think, if you are serious about going into the hotel business, I think this is a good location. It is not far from a billiard hall that I own. I have two top-of-the-line billiard tables that were shipped all the way from Boston. Billiards has been a game of the French nobility for years and it is becoming very popular in the mining camps. Men play for hours on end."

"I have actually played billiards," James replied. One of the taverns in St. Louis had a very nice table and one of my French friends taught me to play, although I must admit that I did not play enough to really master the game, but I think you are trying to change the subject. What prompted your letters to Lucy?"

"It was she that wrote first," George said. "She made it clear that her mother and you would look upon that as very un-ladylike and insisted that I not tell you about the letter. She was inquisitive and did not think she was getting all the answers she wanted. She said that during your last trip to Missouri, she understood that you wanted to move the family to Colorado and she assumed that I would have some influence as to when that might happen."

As soon as Barrett finished his business with the men who contracted him to deliver their equipment, he took James to the billiard hall, where they sat at a table to discuss other matters. Then, late that evening they walked down one of the rudimentary streets where George pointed out two pieces of property.

"If you are serious about becoming part of this growing town, you should act as soon as possible," he said. "This piece of land and that smaller area across the way are both for sale. I have convinced the owner to hold off letting anyone else know until I could talk to you. The owner is ready to pack up and head north and he is motivated to sell."

James thought for a moment, and then replied. "From the looks of the wagon and horse tracks, it appears that this is a very busy road. I think a hotel could be built upon this piece, and perhaps even a house across the way. I think I would like to meet the owner as soon as possible."

"I anticipated that. We are scheduled to dine with him at seven o'clock," George said with a smile.

After meeting with the owner, James agreed to purchase both properties. Early the next morning he signed a promise and left to make the eighty-mile trip back to the gulch, where he would arrange to transfer the money.

At first Charles was not happy with what his father was planning, but he finally agreed. James cautioned him that it would take time to get things started, but assured him that he would be pleased with the end results. He then penned another letter to Catherine.

October 22, 1861

My Dearest Wife,

I have now taken steps to procure some property in Fairplay and have been in contact with a man who will look at the site and prepare plans for a small hotel to be built. It is my intention to start with a smaller building and expand, much as we have done with the Florissant property. This will take some time and I want to get as much value as I can from our present mining operation. Soon the winter will begin to slow our working and there are some improvements to make before we can sell.

Charles has indicated that he might want to return to Missouri when we complete the move to Fairplay. I will not discourage him from doing so, as it may well be an answer to what we are able to do with that property. I will keep you informed as to the progress. It is a significant distance from here to Fairplay, but George Barrett and his men are making the trip on a regular basis and I can go along at any time or send things with him as needed. Charles will be accompanying him in about two weeks time. I want him to see the area and share any ideas he may have

George has been a great asset and we have developed a rewarding friendship. He is running a small business in Fairplay that is managed by a well-known miner who was injured and can no longer tolerate the hard work that mining requires. The clientele of his billiard hall might also become sources of worthwhile information.

I look forward to receiving a reply with your opinions.

Forever,
Your Loving Husband

CHAPTER FORTY-TWO

For nearly two years James and Charles continued as much as possible to improve the property they controlled near Central City. The Fairplay property was paid for and James continued to use George Barrett as a go-between with people in Fairplay. The little town was continuing to grow. James remained involved in the various disputes in the Central City area and was gaining a reputation of being a very good arbitrator. Early in the year of 1862 James made his decision. He agreed to sell the claims for much more than he had anticipated.

He and Charles went to Fairplay where they immediately began erecting a two-story log building, designed to be a small hotel. As the hotel was being finished, they began construction on a house located close by. The time was approaching when James needed to get his family moved.

At about that time James became acquainted with brothers, John and Aaron Ripley. The Ripley brothers had made several trips from Missouri to the Territory of Colorado. They had a well-known reputation as guides. James met with them and formed a plan to move his family to Colorado. He and Catherine exchanged letters concerning the matter, but could not formulate a plan in which they could either dispose of the Missouri property or find some way to have it managed by someone. There was also the problem of James' mother. Her health had declined significantly and Catherine was of the opinion that she could not endure a complicated trip to Colorado. Charles saw an opportunity. He had long wanted to leave Colorado and return to Missouri. He offered to return and take over the operation of the business there. He could then look after his grandmother, but he wanted full control. He wanted James to give him the Missouri property.

James, having finally felt comfortable with a plan, wrote a letter to Catherine:

December 12, 1862

My Dearest Wife,

I am writing from a partially finished house in Fairplay. I will not complete the interior work on the house until you join me and can make it a home for us. I think we can finally plan on that happening. I know the decisions I have made will burden you, but I think you are capable and will once again rise to the occasion.

Charles desires to return to Missouri. The winter thus far has been mild and he is of the opinion that he can make the trip even before spring arrives. He wants to take over the rooming house and trading business and I have no doubt he is capable of doing so. He and I have agreed that the entire property and business will be his as soon as arrangements can be made. I have already sent instructions to our lawyer in St. Louis.

I, too, have been concerned about Mother and Charles has also agreed to oversee her welfare and keep the status quo as far as she is concerned. I have arranged with the Ripley brothers, John and Aaron to act as guides for your trip, but there is much preparation to be done. One of the brothers will travel to Florissant and meet with you as soon as he can. Charles will be there by then to assist you. The other brother will be in Atchison. When you meet the Ripley brother (I do not know at this time which one), you can select the necessary items you wish to bring to Colorado. I caution you that bringing large pieces of furniture will be nearly impossible. Those items you choose will be sent ahead to the other brother in Atchison. He will arrange for a suitable wagon and oxen team and provide room for you and the children in that wagon. I know that

Lucy and Mary are both accomplished riders. As you know, it is beneficial to have a horse leading the oxen. If they are of a mind to, they could ride horseback for at least some of the trip. You can then take the children by railway to Atchison and meet up with your other guide, at which time a true adventure will begin. I pray that those words from Ruth will keep you strong.

Along with building the house and the hotel I have also taken on another challenge. I guess my reputation as an arbitrary followed me to Fairplay. The miners here have formed a close-knit committee to review most of the conflicts. For the most part, they have agreed to abide by the decisions of the committee. They have asked me to be a part of this unique group, and I have agreed to do so.

The hotel will be ready for occupancy soon and I will be living there until you arrive and begin making the house into a home.

Please give the children and Mother my love.

Your Loving Husband

After posting the letter, James and Charles met at the hotel.

"I have made some decisions," James began. "I think you will be in concurrence, but if not, we can discuss any problems you might have. We have things well under control here and we can start renting rooms in a few days. I have contracted with the Ripley brothers to guide your mother and the children to Colorado, I know that your heart is not into the work we are doing here, and you have not shown a lot of interest for several months. You told me awhile back that your desire is to return to Missouri. You have indicated that you would take over the operation of the farm and boarding house in Florissant if you had full control of what was done. Am I stating your desire accurately?"

"You have," replied Charles. "I am not happy here. Perhaps I will not be happy in Missouri either, but I want to try. God willing, this war will not last long and maybe, just maybe, some common ground might be found. So, what is the plan?"

"Oh, yes, the plan," James took a moment, then responded, "I have already contacted the lawyers in St. Louis and they will arrange for you to accept ownership of the Florissant property. I caution you that there may well be a few snags caused by the original purchase of the property by my father, but I think we have dealt with most of the problems. So, I think you should make the arrangements to leave for Missouri as soon as possible. I will provide you with adequate funding for your trip. There is one caveat. Your grandmother is not well and will not be making the trip with the rest of the family."

"Rest assured that Grandmother's well-being will be a priority," Charles said. "I should be ready to leave in a couple of days.'

As James and Charles were rising to leave, a large burly gentleman approached. As the hotel was not yet ready to accept guests, James inquired as to what the gentleman wanted.

Rather than answer James' inquiry, the man asked, "Are you James Castello?"

"I am, and who might you be?"

The man extended his hand. "I am Quincy Taylor. My friends call be QT," he said while shaking James' hand. I have a claim about six miles north of here. I am among a group of miners who have decided that, barring out and out war among ourselves over claim borders and such, we are forming a committee to hear any grievances that may arise. Getting a territorial court involved takes too much time and often seems to make things worse. We have been told that you have a gift of making men talk out compromises and I have been sent to ask you to join our committee in an advisory capacity. We would also like to use this fine building as a meeting place. Is this something you will consider?"

James promised to think the proposal over and the man took his leave. He had only cleared the door by the time James had decided to become involved. First of all, he liked the idea of men settling their own disputes without resorting to violence. Secondly, he saw the idea of using the hotel as a meeting place could be a positive business decision.

Two days later James said goodbye to Charles. He had no idea when, or if, he would see his eldest son again. The emotions came on suddenly when he realized the possibility that this may be the last time he would ever see Charles again. The tears welled up in his eyes as he hugged

Charles and sent him on his way. He was to meet with Quincy Taylor that morning, but he first needed to be alone. He walked down through the developing town to the outskirts and sat on a big rock. His emotions were mixed. He was excited by the fact that he would see his wife and children and that they could once again become a family, but it was to be a family minus its firstborn. After nearly an hour of recalling all the things that resulted in him sitting on a rock at nearly ten thousand feet above sea level, he slowly walked back to the hotel. Taylor was waiting for him and he smiled at the idea of calling this huge man "QT." To his surprise, George Barrett was also waiting.

"Hello QT," he said, holding back a little smile. "And George, I did not expect to see you this morning. Please let us go in and get some fresh coffee. With that, James turned another page in his life.

CHAPTER FORTY-THREE

When Charles arrived in Florissant, he was greeted with a deluge of hugs, tears and confusion. His younger siblings did not even know what he looked like. Their only knowledge of him was what had been told to them by his mother. His grandmother had become a frail old woman and Catherine was showing her age as well. He was deluged with questions about the mine and about Fairplay.

"The mining camps are rudimentary at their best," he told the little gathering. "I think they have promise, but this civil war that has erupted had a negative effect on many of the miners. Like me, they all came from various places and many held deep opinions about what is going on. Consequently, several of the men we knew left the area and returned to their homes to join one side or the other. During my trip here I encountered several camps of men headed south and east, depending on their loyalties. They all wanted to know whether I was a Yank or a Confederate, and frankly I could not honestly answer, so I just went along with them and made no firm statements. It was hard for me and my only base of knowledge is my time here in Missouri, seeing the travesty of slavery and listening to the thoughts of my friends, and of course, Father, who has definitely sided with the North on this issue, but at the same time holds that not enough compromise was accomplished on either side before the roar of canon fire intervened."

Questions were asked of Charles about each of his descriptions, but Lucy Ann changed the tone of the conversation when she moved her chair closer to Charles as if she could make it more private.

"How is George Barrett?"

There was no privacy. The children giggled and Catherine gasped.

"Mr. Barrett in doing well. He has established a very successful freighting business and owns a billiard hall not far from where we built the hotel," Charles said, purposely leaving Lucy waiting for more.

"Have you talked to him recently?"

"Oh yes," Charles answered, obviously enjoying the anxiety that was building up.

Catherine intervened. "That's enough. Your brother needs to get settled in. We can talk more later."

"But have you talked to him?" Lucy was insistent.

"Yes, I talked to him on the day I left," Charles said, still playing with Lucy's inquiries.

"And...?"

"And, he sends his regards," Charles said, raising his eyebrows and smiling. "Oh, and he asked me to give you this." With that, Charles retrieved an envelope from his inner pocket and handed it to Lucy.

Lucy, ignoring her mother, took the envelope and ran into the bedroom, closing the door behind her. Less than a minute later Mary followed her sister. She sat on the bed opposite Lucy and folded her hands patiently. Lucy read and re-read the letter. Mary began almost bouncing on the bed. She cleared her throat a couple of times, but remained unnoticed. Finally, she could wait no longer.

"Well? What did he say? Did he say he longed for your presence?" Mary wrapped her arms around herself and closed her eyes, swaying back and forth.

"It is none of your business what he said," Lucy retorted. "I think George Barrett is a very interesting man and I hope to get to know him better once we get to Colorado. Meanwhile we have much to do. Mr. Ripley will be here tomorrow to look at what we can send with him and what we will take on the train to Atchison. Can you believe it? We are actually going to ride a train."

"I have heard they go very fast," Mary said. "And I have heard that there will be lots of young soldiers on board. Do you think we will be able to talk to any of them?

Lucy placed the letter in a box, which she placed in a small valise, warning Mary not to touch it, then replied, "I think you should pack some comfortable dresses and try to just enjoy the train ride because Mother tells me that you and I may be horseback for a good portion of the trip after we leave Atchison."

When the girls returned to the main room, they took charge of the younger children, giving their mother time to converse with Charles and start deciding on what to take.

Aaron Ripley had informed them that he and his brothers had arranged for two wagons and two ox teams. One wagon would be used primarily for transporting Catherine and the children and their personal belongings. The other wagon would carry provisions and serve as shelter, should the brothers need it for sleeping. The only furniture that Ripley agreed to transport was the dinner table and chairs, which he limited to four, and Catherine's rocking chair. She was adamant that she could not do right by her children without that rocking chair. Ripley was taking the furniture and some other items to the train station the next day. The items would be shipped ahead to Atchison where his brother would start loading the wagons and getting ready for the long trip.

Two days later Catherine and five of her children were at the train station. The surroundings seemed to be total chaos with soldiers, hand trucks and carriages going every which way. Lucy Ann and Mary, aged 22 and 16, respectively, took charge of young Francis, who was now nearly 6 years old. John, being now 14 helped with the baggage and tried to act much older. They were all almost shaking with anxiety. As they boarded the train, Aaron Ripley stood in front of them and explained that the train would be traveling around 15 to 20 miles per hour, and that they would have some short stops, but only for a few minutes at a time. It would likely take from 12 to 13 hours to get to Columbia, Missouri, where they would spend the night. A similar timeframe could be expected for the trip from Columbia to Atchison.

"I realize that the seats are not very comfortable and that it helps to stand up once in awhile," he said. "But, I caution you to do that carefully. Moving around on a surface that is moving under you can be challenging. I will check on you from time to time, but I have made arrangements to ride in the baggage car where I can keep an eye on your belongings. I will be with you when we disembark in Columbia.

With that, enjoy your trip. It is just the beginning of an adventure that will be part of your memories for a lifetime."

The bench seats were just big enough for the family to sit. Catherine had a small picnic basket full of various snacks and sandwiches. Lucy had a small valise, as did John. Those stored under the seats.

As the train began to move, John and Francis, who had claimed the window seats, sat eagerly and waited for the promised speed. Both had gripped the edge of the seat. They watched as the train passed each building. Francis waved at other children on the walkway. As the train gained speed, Francis' eyes seemed to open wider with each passing second.

"Faster! Faster!" Francis said, jumping up and down.

When the train reached full speed, Lucy seemed to relax. "This is amazing," she said to her mother.

Catherine showed a nervous smile, and replied, "I really do not think humans were meant to be speeding along at this rate. I do hope the engineer is watching for any animals."

As the day wore on, the gentle rocking of the train put both John and Francis to sleep. Mary changed places with Francis so she could let him lean against her. She leaned her head against the window.

"Mother, it looks as though we are chasing the sun. We seem to be getting closer to the horizon as the sun settles down."

Catherine turned in her seat and looked to the west. "I am told that we will see a lot of the sun setting on our trail as we continue west. Our lives are going to change every day. I pray your father is doing the right thing by summoning us to this place so far away."

"I will do anything I can to help us along," Lucy replied. She put her hand in the small purse she carried and, without anyone knowing, she gripped the last letter from George Barrett. She knew every word by heart and just touching it made her feel good.

The sun was setting when the first leg of the trip came to an end in Columbia. Aaron Ripley helped with the handbags and walked with them to a nearby hotel, where earlier arrangements had been made for two adjoining rooms. That evening they dined in the hotel restaurant. Catherine commented, telling the children to enjoy their meal and being treated special. They would have one more opportunity to have people wait on them and eat on fine china when they reached Atchison, but after that the going was going to prove much more difficult.

Mary put her fork aside and asked, "Is Father's hotel like this one?'

"As I understand it," Catherine replied, "The Fairplay hotel is just a basic rooming house now, but your father has plans to make it better as time goes on. He has also built a house, which he says will be adequate for the family, but will require a lot of work on our part to get the interior shaped up. We are going to arrive there with a table, four chairs and my rocking chair. I know that you are all getting too old to sit on my lap and rock, but I just could not leave that chair behind. At any rate our furnishings are likely to be pretty scarce for awhile."

The following day was basically the same thing. The train seemed to have smoothed out and the family settled into their seats a little sooner. Again, the train seemed to be trying to catch the sun most of the day.

Atchison was a surprise to Catherine. It seemed nearly as busy as St. Louis. The city boasted one of the most popular riverboat docks on the Missouri River. The Ripley's wagon at the train station was just one of many. The wagon road from Atchison west had become one of the most traveled in the country. Catherine was relieved to see her scant pieces of furniture loaded into the wagon. Aaron Ripley informed the family that they had accommodations for that night and one more. They would then be headed for Colorado. He encouraged them to take advantage of all the amenities at the hotel, because it would be a long time before they would have any similar comfort.

It was late spring of 1863 when the two wagons pulled by oxen faced the trail west and turned the page on the future of the Castello family. For much of the trip, they were not lonely on the road. Several other families were headed west. While the war raged on, there seemed to be little acknowledgment of it by the travelers. They were chasing the sun, or maybe a rainbow.

The family made very good progress. It was nearly 700 miles to Fairplay and they made the trip in just less than 80 days. They arrived in Fairplay on August 1, 1863.

CHAPTER FORTY-FOUR

For nearly three months James anticipated the arrival of his family, but he had little time to think about it. With the hotel finally opened and his involvement in the miners dispute committee, he concentrated on the final touches to the house. He promised Catherine that he would leave most of the inside of the house for her to transform it into a home, but there were other things that needed done before the snow began to fly.

The committee became so successful that several of the members, some of whom were adversaries whose grievances were settled in the committee forum, suggested that James become a real judge. The state was growing. Fairplay was becoming more and more the dominant town in the area, but had less than 200 official residents. Many of the residents, James included, frequently suggested that the name of the town be changed to South Park City, but the fact remained that the town, which already had a post office, was not even an official town as of yet. It was still known to many by its two-word name, "Fair Play."

When the family arrived on August 1, 1863, James was at the house. The two wagons pulled into the yard and the Ripley brothers immediately began to unload their cargo. Lucy and Mary were the first to run to their father and give him hugs. Catherine walked up to James slowly. The trip had been hard and she showed the results of a very long time on the trail.

As she kissed her husband and saw the smile on his face, she seemed to regain some vitality and it showed as she finally spoke.

"James Castello," she said, pointing her finger at him. "You have no idea how many times in the last three months I have opened my Bible to pray with the children, only to have it fall open to the passage in Ruth that I have many times repeated to you: 'Entreat me not to leave thee, or to return from following after thee, for whither thou goest, I will go; and where thou lodgest I will lodge.' I promised to remain committed to that passage and told you that I would follow you anywhere, but this has been the hardest thing that I have ever done and I vow it will remain the hardest thing I will ever do. The next time I see a glint in your eye that even implies that you want to take off on some sort of adventure, you may well have to do it alone. Now, you say you have a house that needs a woman's touch. Let us get in there and see what needs done."

James took Catherine's hand and led her onto the porch and held the front door open for her.

"Thanks to George Barrett, I have only recently acquired beds, which we shipped in while furnishing the hotel. The stove and the fireplace are both functional, but beyond that, I have not paid much attention to the interior of this place."

Lucy, who was standing behind her father as they started to enter the house, heard him mention George Barrett.

"Is George here now?"

James turned. "So it is 'George' is it? He is no longer 'Mr. Barrett?'"

Lucy displayed what had become her signature blush when Barrett's name was mentioned.

"Well, his name is George."

"I am well aware of your exchange of letters over the past months," James said, putting an arm around Lucy's shoulders. "He has told me of the letters, but not of the content. I will just have to guess as to what words have been exchanged. No, George is not in the area right now. I believe he has gone to Denver and probably will not return for at least another two weeks."

The Ripleys had already placed the table and chairs into the dining area when the family entered the house. Each of them took a whirlwind tour of the bedrooms and kitchen. The rocking chair had been placed in front of the fireplace. Catherine literally collapsed into it and looked around. James took one of the chairs and sat facing her. Francis sat on the hearth and the rest of the family started helping unload the wagons, placing the bedding in each of the rooms and carefully taking Catherine's baggage into the largest room. She just smiled.

"As you can tell these offspring of yours have been a great help. Each of them has gone above and beyond what I have expected and we have many times discussed what belongings we brought with us. This will be a home before the sun sets this evening," she said, while reaching out to hold James' hand.

Two days later, James took Catherine across the way to the hotel. She was impressed and immediately started to inspect the kitchen facility.

"It appears that you are not yet serving food," she observed.

"Not as of yet," James replied. We have only two guests at the moment and neither will be staying long." He pointed to two men engaged in a billiard match. "They are awaiting a group from the east and are headed farther west."

"You might have another guest or two if they were treated to some adequate table fare, "Catherine said. "I think Lucy, Mary and I can get this looking like a business in short order."

Two days later everyone in town knew that the Castello hotel was offering morning and evening meals to its guests. Another day passed and two more rooms were rented. Catherine and Lucy served four guests that evening. Catherine was back into the boarding house business and showed a distinct bounce in her step. To reduce the burden at home, the family started taking their evening meals at the hotel. Catherine and the girls started taking care of the hotel housekeeping and a portion of the income was saved for the girls.

Just before the end of the month, Lucy was sweeping up at the hotel when the light from the door was suddenly blocked. There stood George Barrett.

He grinned broadly, removed his hat and said, "Now Miss Lucy, aren't you a sight for these tired eyes. It appears you survived the trip in good order."

Lucy could not control her blush. "Hello Geo.., I mean Mr. Barrett. Thank you for the compliment. It is good to see you again. Please have a seat. I have a teapot on. Would you care for some?"

Barrett's lip curled slightly. "Tea huh? Don't suppose you have some coffee hiding there somewhere?"

"I can easily brew a pot. Please sit."

Lucy went into the kitchen. Just minutes later George could smell the unmistakable scent of brewing coffee. Lucy did not return to the room until the coffee was finished perking. She placed a steaming cup in front of George and put her teacup on the table before sitting. She took her time lowering herself into the chair, making sure her back was straight. She sat with her eyes down on her cup, afraid to look at George, lest the blush came on too strong.

George broke the ice. "The place looks good. When I last saw it it was just being built. Your father has a knack of getting things done once he sets his mind to it."

"Mother also has that quality," she said. "There is no doubt in anyone's mind that this is Catherine Castello's hotel. This morning we had four additional men at the breakfast table. They were just going to their claims and heard about Mother's biscuits and gravy. It was as if she just moved the Missouri business into a new home."

"Well," George said. "I wish your parents the best of luck. I must say also that I have truly enjoyed your letters. I am not sure your father thinks much of our correspondence and I have purposely kept him in the dark. It has proven to be entertaining to listen to him try to elicit the contents of our letters from me."

Lucy had relaxed and was enjoying the conversation.

She poured George another cup of coffee and said, "In your last letter you said that you were establishing another base of operations in Denver. Does that mean you will be living there?"

"No," he replied. "Although I will be spending a lot of time there. My freighting business is expanding rapidly. More trails are turning into roads and more settlements are being established almost daily. All those people need supplies and Denver is proving to be a hub in the wheel of the freight business. There is also this stupid war. A significant part of my business is the transporting of various supplies for the Union Army. I have just received another two wagons built by the Studebaker brothers. By combining my need of wagons with that of the military, I confess I have taken advantage and it has proven to be quite profitable for me."

The conversation carried on for several more minutes before Catherine came in and, after exchanging some pleasantries with Barrett, reminded Lucy that they must begin preparing for the evening meal. She asked George to join them, explaining that James was meeting with some Indians in Buckskin Joe, and would not be home until much later.

"James' meetings with the leaders of the various tribes have been beneficial to everyone," Barrett said. "I fear it will not be enough though. These new settlers are determined to run the Indians off and the government is going to help them to get that done. I assume that the treaty being addressed in Congress right now is the subject of James' current parley."

"You are probably right," said Catherine.

The evening meal included three hotel guests, along with two other men. The conversation at the table centered on mining and Barrett was asked numerous questions, especially about the war. Two of the men who were walk-ins said they were on their way to Denver to join the army. They expressed their opinions that the North would ultimately win the conflict and they could return to their mines. George promised to visit again before leaving the area. He made it a point to take Lucy's hand and lightly kiss it as he walked to the door. Lucy stood for a moment looking at the door before turning to see her mother's smile.

"Take it easy, young lady," Catherine said.

At that point Mary spoke up. "I thought you were going to fall at his feet and make him drag you out the door," she said with a giggle.

CHAPTER FORTY-FIVE

The second week of October 1863, James received a letter from Charles. He had had no communication with his son since the family arrived in August. James anticipated bad news even before opening the letter. Catherine sat nearby and watched as he read it. Sadness swept over his face and tears welled up in his eyes.

"What is wrong?'

James handed the letter to Catherine. She too felt tears coming as she read:

Florissant, Missouri
October 8, 1863

Dear Mother and Father,

I write this while grieving. Please forgive me if some of it does not make sense. I had started an earlier letter, but had not finished by the time it became necessary to compose this one.

I am sorry to say that Grandmother passed away yesterday. She had been feeling badly for several days, but we did not think it critical. The doctor visited with her on Monday, last and gave her some syrup for her cough, but saw no signs of concern beyond that. She died peacefully in her sleep. I wish you both could be here, but that is not possible. Her body has been taken to the mortuary just minutes ago. I will arrange for her burial today. She will be laid to rest next to Grandfather in the cemetery here in Florissant.

I know you will regret not being here, but Grandmother understood why we ventured off to Colorado. She and I had discussed it many times in the past months. She told me that there was something about mining that seemed to course through the veins of our family, but the fact is that I am much happier here than I was during my last year in Colorado.

The boarding house and trading post are doing well, although we are dealing with people that are aligned with the Confederacy and I have a difficult time keeping my thoughts to myself. Doing otherwise could well mean an end to our business, and possibly my life. The Confederates have taken what little crop we realized from the farm. They provided us with a stack of papers and promised compensation later, but I know that will never happen.

Thanks to your foresight, and the thoughtfulness of Grandmother, there appears to be no problem with my carrying on with the business. At the last meeting with the solicitor I learned that all the property and assets were transferred to my name, per your instructions to them, and Grandmother had also signed her ownership rights to me. I will be forever grateful for that, but it takes very little away from my feelings of sorrow upon our loss. I think I became closer to her in the last few months than I had ever been as a young child.

I pray that things are going well for you. The people of Florissant are treating me well and have asked me to become involved in the board of directors. Given the fact that this town would not be a town were it not for our family, I may take them up on their offer. There are things that are being neglected and I will not hesitate to call their attention to those things.

I know my brothers and sisters will be as saddened as I with the passing of Grandmother. Please let them know that she did not suffer.

I will write again soon.

Charles

Catherine put the letter aside. She and James held each other for several minutes before she summoned the children into the room and gave them the sad news. They all sat at the table while Catherine said a prayer and opened her bible to the familiar 23rd Psalm.

On October 8, 1863 Nancy Castello was laid to rest next to her husband, Michael, in the St. Ferdinand Cemetery. Charles stood with those attending the service and listened as the priest recalled that Michael and Nancy Castello, along with Michael's father, Juame, and Antoine Riviere could be considered the fathers of Florissant, Missouri.

"While this valley and this village existed long before these men came to the area, it was them who befriended the native people here and befriended the French settlers. I understand now that Nancy's son, James, is doing the same thing in the wilderness of the Territory of Colorado. May the Lord bless and keep the soul of Nancy Castello and look over those who survive her on this earth. I would now ask that you listen to the words of Victor Hugo."

Switching to French, the priest quoted,

"Demain, dès l'aube, à l'heure où blanchit la campagne,
Je partirai. Vois-tu, je sais que tu m'attends.
J'irai par la forêt, j'irai par la montagne.
Je ne puis demeurer loin de toi plus longtemps.

In English he said,

"Tomorrow, at dawn, when the countryside brightens,
I will depart. You see, I know that you wait for me.
I will go through the wood, I will go past the mountains.
I cannot remain far from you any longer."

He completed the service saying; "I know that Nancy will be with her family forever." With a standard benediction, the service ended.

In November of 1863, just weeks following his mother's death, James was elected to the position of Park County Judge. The county seat remained in Buckskin Joe and a small log courthouse was built there. Primarily, the courthouse was a place for maintaining records.

Few trials were held, but James made the two-mile trip at least once per week, usually to make some document official, sign a warrant or marry some young couple. A year prior, the town was almost left without people when a smallpox epidemic spread through the area. Those who survived continued to pull the gold from the creek. They, like the miners near Central City, also learned the art of going after the lode gold.

The few civil disputes were handled quickly when the litigants realized they were going in front of Judge Castello. His reputation followed him to the bench. Many of the men in and around Buckskin Joe were of the same mind of those in the Tarryall area who had claimed land, not because it was of any mining value, but because they wanted the land in anticipation of the Utes giving up any claim to it. One man in particular, J. P. Stansell, somehow avoided the sickness. He claimed he did it by working hard and refusing to give in.

In July of 1864 James attended several meetings in Denver and was present during the Colorado Constitutional Convention. There was a decided effort to make the Territory of Colorado a state. He spent the remainder of the summer trying to convince himself and others that he would be a good candidate to represent Park County in the territorial government.

James started using a small buggy and one horse to make the short trips to the county seat. He found the trip much less stressful than sitting in a saddle. On one particular day James was entering the courthouse when he saw one of the miners from Central City posting a handbill in a framed area meant for public notices. James approached the man.

"Kirk, what brings you to this area?"

"Well James, or I guess I should say, Judge," Kirk responded. "I have been appointed to place these recruitment notices at all the post offices. We are forming a Colorado volunteer unit that will serve for one hundred days." He handed the bill to James.

James was shocked at what the handbill advertised: **ATTENTION! INDIAN FIGHTERS. Having been authorized by the Governor to raise a Company of 100 day U. S. VOL. CAVALRY! For immediate service against hostile Indians. I call upon all who**

wish to engage in such service to call at my office and enroll their names immediately.

The bill went on to give instructions to go to the office in Central City to join.

James felt his temper swell. "What the hell is this? This country is divided by a civil war and Governor Evans wants to use our resources to kill Indians?"

Kirk stepped back. "Hey, Judge, don't shoot the messenger here. I am just doing a job."

James grabbed the bill from Kirk, "Consider your job finished here," he said.

Having had earlier received information that Chief Ouray and a small band of his tribe were camped about 30 miles south, James decided it was time to visit his friend one more time. Early the next morning he arrived at Ouray's camp. He was greeted warmly and invited into the lodge. He showed the handbill to Ouray.

"What do you make of this?"

Ouray sat quietly for a moment and then responded, "I know of this. I am told that the hostiles referred to are among the Arapaho and Cheyenne who are located many miles to the south and east of us, but I think that the real intention is to dislocate all of my people as well. I have been involved in recent treaty talks and we have compromised much. Some of my people are not pleased with what I have given up, but I believe that the alternative is total wiping out of our people from, not just our lands, but from the very earth we inhabit."

Ouray went on to explain that the south park and the small valley in which he was now camped is an important part of the survival of his people.

"The grass that grows here is like no other I have ever seen," he said. "The buffalo that come here to graze in the season before the winter comes get fat quickly. They are our very survival. We use much from these animals. It is not just their meat, but their hides that help us survive the winter."

"This news makes me angry," James said. "I do not know what I can do, but I will do something."

James and Ouray shook hands and James got into his buggy and headed back home. As he rode, he took notice of the grasses Ouray had mentioned earlier. The grass waved in the wind, giving the impression that it was not just grass, but an ocean, sending wave after wave into the foothills in the distance. At the base of one of the foothills James could make out a large herd of buffalo. He could see exactly what Ouray had described.

In the election of 1864, James surprised a number of people, including himself. He met the necessary qualifications to run for election to the House of Representatives for the Territory of Colorado. Park County was entitled to two representatives. James was elected with only nine votes separating him from Wilbur F. Stone, who was running for re-election, but almost 40 votes more than the next man. He and Stone became the representatives. The election was bittersweet. On November 21, 1864, the 100-day Colorado Cavalry unit attacked the villages of Cheyenne and Arapaho Indians in Sand Creek in the southern part of the territory.

CHAPTER FORTY-SIX

For all intents and purposes, James' first experience with the territorial legislature was a complete failure. The efforts to become a state failed miserably, the civil war was still going strong and the divided country had no desire to listen to the voices of the west.

James expressed his frustration to Catherine.

"The only thing I have accomplished as a representative is to wear several sets of shoes off a good horse, replace the wheels on my buggy and try to complain about the political situation to anyone who will listen. I have neglected my duties as a judge and I fear I have not paid enough attention to my family."

"Well," Catherine replied, "Your family has not felt neglected, especially your oldest daughter. Mr. Barrett has called here every time he passes through. He has asked that he be allowed to formally court Lucy, as if he isn't already, but I have informed him that he must ask you."

James was not surprised. "Considering her age, I am not sure we have any say in the matter. I like George, and he is a hardworking, and I believe, an honest man. Has Lucy talked with you about this?"

"She has, but in a somewhat passive way. She has asked me what I think of him and I have been honest with her. I also like George and I know that Lucy is beginning to think she is getting old, after all, she is almost 24," Catherine said.

She then added with some sarcasm, "Why she might get all wrinkled up any time now."

Getting serious again, she added, "I have cautioned her about getting married for the wrong reasons. She assures me that her feelings for George are genuine. I will say this: The man is persistent and I see no indication that he has eyes for anyone else. I have invited him to join us for Christmas dinner and suggested that it would be a good time for you and him to talk. Meanwhile, you need to talk to Lucy and it might be a good idea to also talk to Mary. She is the one that might well get married for all the wrong reasons. She has said several times that she is not going to wait as long as her sister has waited to betroth herself."

"Frankly," James said. "It surprises me that some man has not ran in and swooped Lucy from here long before now. She is well educated, and certainly will make any man a good wife. Now, as for this 17-year-old, up and coming spinster, Mary, I haven't seen any particular boy hanging around her. Have you?"

Catherine replied that she had not observed anyone paying much attention to Mary, with the exception of some flirtatious smiles now and again. Charles agreed to talk to her.

Christmas dinner was one to be remembered. George Barrett became an official suitor of Lucy Ann Castello. Although he and Lucy both agreed to take things slowly, their energy level was apparent and became even more evident when Catherine and Mary made sure that the couple was seated together at the table. There was a noticeable disappointment on Lucy's face when George told everyone that he would be going to Denver right after the first of the year to attend to business there.

"I hate the idea of traveling at this time of year," he said. "But there are things I must take care of, and while going is not an option, my next visit here in Fairplay will depend on the weather conditions. One of my contracts involves sending two wagonloads of supplies to the northern territories. Those supplies have been stored in Denver for nearly four months now and I must make sure everything is in order for my people to join a group traveling that way as soon as spring arrives."

"I, too, must go to Denver as soon as possible", James said. "It is imperative that I meet face to face with Governor Evans and with Alexander Cummings, who will be replacing Evans this next year. Perhaps we could travel together."

Catherine interrupted the flow of conversation. "Now, your food is getting cold and deserves your attention. The preparation of this feast, which I might add was largely accomplished by Lucy, needs to be appreciated."

Everyone took notice and the only sound for the next several minutes was the scraping of silverware across the china plates.

Two weeks later James and George left for Denver. They took a wagon loaded with some supplies for George's operation in Denver. James' saddle horse was tied behind. Not long after they were underway, George started the first of several short conversations.

"So, you are to meet with Governor Evans?" George asked.

"Yes, I sent him a message last week. I want him to know that I was extremely upset with his decision to send that 100-day Colorado Cavalry into the camps of the Arapaho and Cheyenne people. The government has just signed a treaty with the Utes, and Ouray tells me that he has little confidence in the United States keeping their word. He thinks the ultimate goal is for all his people to be systematically removed from their lands."

George thought for only a moment. "I have not talked to Ouray for some time. I did see Colorow on one of my recent trips. He, too, is concerned. I find it confusing that, since Lincoln declared all the slaves to be free, and this civil war still rages on, that there seems to be all too much attention paid to the Indians."

A few days later James met with both Governor Evans and Alexander Cummings. He expressed his concern, but Evans seemed to disregard James' concern and even placed any responsibility for bad action at Sand Creek upon the shoulders of Major Chivington. Cummings, for his part, simply said he would look into the matter. James wrote a formal complaint and filed it at the governor's office. He returned home both disappointed and tired. He was not looking forward to returning to Denver in early April for meetings with the judicial officials. He assumed his appointment to the bench was coming to an end, especially owing to his position in the House or Representatives, which he would also be paying attention to in April and a request that he represent the government in some capacity after the Treaty of 1864 became official.

In mid-March he was at the courthouse doing some paperwork. Lucy had asked to accompany him and he gladly agreed to have her along for company. He sensed that her presence had an ulterior motive. She busied herself wandering around the building and looking at the volumes of law books on the shelves. When James finally put his pen down and leaned back in his chair, she sat near him.

"Father," she said. "When do you plan to leave for Denver?"

James referred to some notes on his desk and replied, "I must be there on the 10th, so I will leave a few days prior to that to give myself plenty of time. Why do you ask?"

"I would love to go with you," she said. "It has been too long since I have seen and talked to George and I would appreciate the opportunity to do that. With you being there, you could be my official chaperone and prevent any unsavory rumors."

James recognized the sarcasm in Lucy's last comment.

"So, it is unsavory rumors that worry you, and not the fact that your mother would have a cow if she thought you were doing anything improper? I do not have a problem with you going, but your mother must agree. Your contribution to the everyday function of the hotel has become very valuable of late, and she will miss you. She was not really pleased that you took this little time to be with me now."

On April 10 the meeting of men associated with the Territorial Legislature took on a whole new focus. Thanks to the modern miracle of communication, the telegraph, the group received welcome news that General Lee had formally surrendered his troops to Ulysses Grant. The group discussed the news at length. While Lee's surrender only brought the war to an end in Virginia, it was almost everyone's opinion that this event would mean the end of the Civil War. It also meant that Colorado might be much closer to becoming a state.

On January 25, just as James' last meeting was ready for adjournment, a courier interrupted the meeting with another telegram, which he handed to the man chairing the meeting. The chairman read the telegram silently. His head bowed for a moment and then he read the message aloud:

"President Lincoln is Dead. Shot last night at Ford's theater."

The room went silent. The chairman then asked one of the members, a church deacon, to lead the group in prayer before the meeting was formally adjourned.

James met Lucy and George at a livery where James' buggy was readied for the trip back home. He was surprised that the news had already swept through the population of Denver. More information had been disseminated and George filled James in on the details of the assassination. George and Lucy took a few minutes alone to say goodbye before James and Lucy climbed into the buggy and began the 80-mile trip home. Thanks to George Barrett and men like him, the road was very much improved, but the trip would still take at least three days.

The people of Fairplay were aware of the assassination and of who did it. Some of the lodgers at the hotel were actively engaged in a billiards match accompanied by a lively conversation about Lincoln. The fact that the Civil War might be coming to an end was overshadowed by Lincoln's death. Even the one billiard player that disagreed with Lincoln's policies admitted that he would be remembered as a great man.

Lucy had been relatively quiet during the trip home, but that ended when she sat with her mother and younger sister and recounted nearly every minute she spent with George Barrett during her Denver visit.

CHAPTER FORTY-SEVEN

Shortly before James and Lucy went to Denver, Mary turned 18. Catherine thought it would be appropriate to put off such an important celebration until James returned. Mary did not agree. On the day of her birthday, March 25th, there had been a nice party at the hotel. Several of Mary's friends attended. One was a young man named Billy. Billy was only known by a few at the party, and those were guests at the hotel. Billy was a teamster and dropped the name George Barrett as a way of introduction.

While in Denver, James had an opportunity to speak with George alone. He asked about Billy.

"I assume you are talking about Billy Beery," George said.

"I have yet to hear his surname, but I was not real comfortable with the way he was paying attention to Mary," James replied.

George thought for a moment, obviously choosing his words carefully. "Well, Billy is a damn good teamster and I have used him a couple of times. He is one of the few that has tackled the Ute Trail with an oxcart, but somehow I just never got to really like the guy. I understand that he was part of that 100-day bunch that raided the villages at Sand Creek."

James felt his anger rising. "And that son of a bitch was in my house? I will find out who invited him. I am not sure that I want any of my family to associate with someone who joined the militia to kill Indians."

As soon as James had the opportunity after arriving back home he took Catherine aside.

"What," he asked, "do you know about this Billy Beery that was at Mary's party last month? Who invited him to that party in the first place?"

"Mary invited Josh Webster, who as you know, is one of our long-term boarders. He knows Billy and asked if it would be okay for him to tag along. I do know that he was in the military and got out just after Christmas of last year. Why are you asking?"

James looked as though he was in deep thought and responded. "I just noticed that he seemed to be paying a lot of attention to Mary and I thought it odd that he, nor anyone else thought it necessary for him to be introduced to me. I also noticed that he was somewhat older than any of Mary's friends, and I now know more about him. I intend to meet him eye-to-eye and ask him some serious questions."

With that, James went into the common area where Mary and Lucy were preparing the table for the evening meal.

"Mary," he said, "come walk with me."

He walked to the front door and held it open for Mary.

"Is something wrong father? You look like you are angry with me. Did I do something wrong"

She grabbed a shawl from a hook by the door and walked out. James followed her and began walking away from the hotel toward their home.

After a minute he said, "You asked if I am mad at you. The answer is no, but I want to talk to you about one of the guests at your birthday party. I noticed that one of the men seemed to be paying a lot of attention to you. Do you know anything about Billy Beery?"

Mary slowed her steps and replied, "I only met him that night. He is a friend of Mr. Webster's and has visited at the hotel several times. He usually plays a game or two of billiards. I have served Mr. Webster and him some refreshments, and he came to dinner at the hotel twice while you and Lucy were gone. I will admit that he might have flirted with me just a little. Why are you so concerned?"

"First of all, he is obviously somewhat older than you."

Mary interrupted, "Father, he is not someone I am keeping company with. He seems to be a nice man with a great sense of humor and I don't mind being around him, but I assure you, my time around him has been very short. You have nothing to worry about."

James decided that his daughter deserved an explanation.

"Do you remember my concern when I found out that the territory was organizing a short-term militia to fight Indians?"

"I do."

"Well, Governor Evans and Colonel Chivington led people to believe that this bunch of soldiers were organized to fight aggressive Indians, and then Evans told the Indians to go to Ft. Lyons where, under the treaty, they would get supplies. But that was in direct conflict of what the military mission was. The Colorado Cavalry went down into the southern part of the territory and attacked two encampments of Cheyenne and Arapaho people. At the time most of the men from those camps were out hunting. The cavalry killed many, many Indians, but most were women and children. They called it The Battle at Sand Creek, but there was not much battle to it. That affair is one of the reasons I went to Denver. I talked to Governor Evans about it, and I think he regrets what happened, but he falls short of saying it was a mistake. He simply says that Chivington was to blame for any mistakes because he was never authorized to leave Denver. William Beery - Billy - was a member of those volunteers. I want you to be aware of that."

Mary did not hesitate to answer. "I am happy that you told me. Now I should get back to the hotel. We have a full house and Mother and Lucy need my help."

Mary turned back to the hotel and James continued to the house.

"Tell your mother that I have some paperwork to do and tell her I would like her to bring the boys and you home as soon as possible. Lucy can clean up and join us. I will have something to eat at the house."

Mary turned her head and said, "I am not sure what provisions are at the house. I will see to it that Mother brings you something. I will suggest that she take the boys back after dinner and I will help Lucy clean up."

When Catherine returned to the house with the boys James filled her in on the concerns he had with Beery. Catherine acknowledged that she and James should keep abreast of the situation, but she did not think there really was a situation.

"I do not see any indication that there is anything going on, but I will keep an eye on things, meanwhile, you should read this. It arrived in today's post. She handed James a letter from Charles:

April 30, 1865
Florissant, Missouri

Dear Mother and Father,

I pray that this letter finds you in good health and that things are going well for you. We have not communicated for some time and I felt it necessary to bring you up to date on a few things. Father, the enclosed clipping is from the Missouri Democrat newspaper. I cut it out soon after your election and set it aside. I should have sent it sooner. I think it tells well of the respect you have here.

First of all, things are going well here. I have expanded the cattle herd and the boarding house is thriving. Most of our current lodgers are long term. I have learned of Lee's surrender and Lincoln's untimely murder. I hope and pray that this means an end to the whole mess. I say this only to you, but it is my belief that this nation will be better served as one united nation.

I avoid national politics, but the local Democrats have asked me to run for mayor. I think I will take them up on the offer. I meet with them this week to launch a campaign. I have been involved with the local political scene for some time now and I think I can represent the township fairly, after all our family has played a major role here.

How does Mary feel, now that she is an old maid? Please give her my love. I do hope that she celebrated in a dignified manner. It seems almost unreal that so much has happened since we last visited. I am quickly approaching the ripe old age of 26. It does not seem possible that it was six years ago that I went to Colorado.

Mother, please write to me as soon as possible and bring me up to date on what is going on. I know only what I read in the newspapers and some of that is on the dark side.

All My Love,
Charles

James put the letter on the table, smiled and said, "A Democrat? The son of the first Republican Sheriff in St. Louis County is a Democrat. I wish him luck in his pursuit of the mayor's office and I am glad I am not there where I might be forced to vote for a Democrat. Lord have mercy."

James then picked up the clipping. It read: *We are pleased to find that our old time friend and fellow citizen, James Castello, Esq., formally among the best known residents of our city, and at one period Sheriff of St. Louis County, is a member of the Senate of the incipient State of Colorado. Mr. Castello some years since migrated to the Territory, bearing with him the kind wishes of a host of warm friends, by whom this information will be received with lively interest. Mr. Castello will both ably and honestly discharge his duties as a representative of the Republican sentiment of his district.*

"Your pride is showing," Catherine said as she put the letter back into the envelope. "Democrat or not, you are proud of your son and rightfully so. You know he was never happy here in Colorado. He has deep roots in Missouri and I think he has a promising future. Now let us retire for the night. Tomorrow promises to be a busy day."

James found that, indeed, the next day was a busy one, and the one after that, and many more to follow. He made two more trips to Denver before the fall leaves began to show their color. The trips were somewhat easier due to the increased use of stagecoaches in the area, but it was still an inconvenience

George Barrett was in Fairplay more often and had finally arranged for James to meet with William Beery, who always seemed to be in Fairplay while James was either in Denver or at the county seat. According to Catherine, Beery was indeed flirting with Mary whenever he had the opportunity. The meeting was to take place in Buckskin Joe, which worked well for James, allowing that he always had things that needed attention there. He also learned that Ouray would once again be camped not far from there.

CHAPTER FORTY-EIGHT

After completing the necessary tasks and paperwork at the courthouse, James traveled to Ouray's camp, which was at the base of Mt. Pisgah, almost 40 miles away. He spent the night, feasted on roast elk and discussed several topics with Ouray. He noted that Ouray looked tired and inquired as to his health. Ouray said only that the constant traveling and worry about the fate of his people was taking its toll, but that he intended to take advantage of the winter by staying in one place for a while.

Leaving early the next morning, as he was traveling back to Buckskin Joe, much to his surprise, he met a small entourage of ox-drawn wagons led by none other than William Beery. Beery immediately recognized James, telling him that he had just come over the Ute trail and was going to camp next to Twin Creek, which flowed not far from their meeting place. He suggested that James join them for the night.

"Perhaps fate has intervened," Beery said. "I was looking forward to meeting with you at Buckskin Joe. Of course a camp with smelly teamsters and even smellier oxen will not be as comfortable as your office in the courthouse, but at least we can get to know one another."

James agreed to stay at the camp. "The fact that we have never formally met is the biggest reason I wanted to meet with you. I will follow you to your camp."

An hour later, Beery had his camp set up. The oxen were turned loose in a large patch of tall grass. James unhitched his buggy and turned the horse loose in the same patch. Beery had an impressive store of provisions and began tending the fire and preparing a meal.

"Now this will not compare to the table fare your wife has presented to me at your hotel, but it will fill your stomach," he said while stirring some beans into a pot. "I put the beans into water on the other side of the pass. They are well soaked and will not take much time to cook."

James was impressed with the way Beery handled the food. The two men that were with him took care of the animals and prepared their bedrolls and then everyone filled their plates and sat down.

Everyone ate, and then one of the other teamsters took the plates to the creek and washed them up. Beery poured a cup of coffee for James, one for himself, and then sat facing James next to the fire.

"So," he asked, "what brings you this far south?"

"Two things," James replied. "First, I met with Ouray, chief of the Utes. He is camped about 40 miles from here, and I planned on meeting with you on the return trip. This worked out well. I will not mince words. I was set back on the night of my daughter's party, when I noted your presence. I was left with the impression that you had no desire to actually meet me and shake my hand. I know that you were a guest of one of the hotel guests, but the fact is that the gathering was to celebrate Mary's birthday and, being her father, I thought it proper that you be introduced to me. That bothered me and that is one of the reasons that I requested a meeting with you."

Beery smoothed his moustache. "Judge, I apologize for giving you the impression that I snubbed you, but I felt very out of place that night, and quite frankly, I am a little intimidated by you. It seemed that every time our eyes met I could see something that gave me the impression that you did not like me being at that party. I admit that I avoided you. I feel that I know you already. You have a long reputation, which you have built over the past years, and well, I don't easily take to judges and sheriffs and politicians in general."

"I really do not consider myself to be a politician," James replied. "As for being a sheriff, that seems a lifetime ago, and I will be a judge for a little longer, but that too, will become part of my past. There is something else that bothers me and I wish to ask you about it."

James pulled the handbill from his inside pocket. He had saved it from the time he took it from the young man who was posting the bills at various locations. He unfolded it and held it out to Beery. As soon as

Beery saw the large print: **ATTENTION! INDIAN FIGHTERS** he knew what was coming. Beery took the handbill and held it low in his lap.

"I know you have befriended a number of the Utes. George Barrett has also told me that you and your family have the longstanding respect of the Indian people, dating back to your days in Missouri. I want you to understand that I signed up with these people to ward off Indian attacks, not to attack the Indians."

James interrupted, "But you were a part of the Colorado Cavalry that attacked the villages of the Arapaho and Cheyenne at Sand Creek."

"That is true," Beery said. "I was part of Company K, but I did not go with them to Sand Creek. A group of Union soldiers from the Signal Service were sent to Camp Evans to train several of us in the various special services performed by them. It was my understanding that this training would mean we could go on after the Colorado unit was disbanded and become part of the Signal Service. I was one of the ones left behind to continue my training when the others went south and engaged the Indians at Sand Creek."

"Engaged them? That is an interesting way of using the word suggested by Colonel Chivington and Captain Soule," James said. "Do you know what happened on the banks of the Big Sandy?"

"I have heard both sides of the story," replied Beery. "And, just so you know how I felt about it, I mustered out along with the others from the Colorado Cavalry at the end of our 100 day commitment. Some of the others I trained with went on to join the regular army. I was really interested in becoming part of the Signal Service, but I was fearful that I would not be able to accept the authority of commanding officers. I took my pay and decided to return to looking at the asses of my oxen instead."

Beery rose and went to his pack. He returned with a brass telescope and handed it to James. Retracted, the telescope was one foot long, but James removed the lens cap, extended it to its full three feet, noting the U. S. Signal Service engraving on the first section and looked through it at the peak looming in the faded light above the Ute Trail.

"That is all I have to recall my days with the Cavalry and, believe me, it is enough," Beery said.

"I can see the peak much more clearly," James said. "And I think I see some other things more clearly too. Thank you for your honesty, now I must get some sleep. My wife expects me home tomorrow.'

The next morning James left while Beery and his helpers were just getting the yokes placed. He and Beery agreed to meet again in Fairplay.

That evening when he arrived home, John came out to meet him. "Mother told me to take care of the horse and carriage. She said to send you right in. She needs to talk to you."

"Is anything wrong?"

"I don't ask a lot of questions," John said with a smile. "It is much safer that way, but no, I don't think anything is wrong."

James walked into the house with some trepidation. Catherine was seated in her easy chair. She stood up, kissed James and sat back down. James did not wait for her to explain.

"John said you wanted to see me right away. Is anything wrong?"

"No, not really," Catherine said. "How was your trip?"

"Well I met and talked to Billy Beery, but we can get to that later. What is on your mind?"

Catherine almost chuckled. "I do not know why I was surprised, but Lucy told me this morning that George has finally asked her to marry him."

"That is good news, is it not?"

"Oh, it is wonderful news, but you might not be quite so elated when I tell you what their plans are."

James stroked his beard as though he was milking a cow. "Don't tell me they are going to run off to Oregon or something."

"No, it is not that bad, but they want to get married in Denver. Lucy is up at the hotel right now, but she will be here in a few minutes. I will let her explain the whole plan. Meanwhile I saved you some biscuits and gravy. I will warm it up and you can eat while we wait."

"Biscuits is it? That is funny. When I met with Chief Ouray he asked as to your health and told me how much he liked your biscuits. It seems you made quite an impression on him and those with him when they last visited here."

James was just finishing his meal when Lucy came through the door.

"Father, welcome home. Did you have a good trip?"

James pushed his plate aside and replied, "My trip was fine, but I understand that you have some news for me."

"I know that Mother has already told you what is going to happen, but I wanted her to save the details for me. George and I want to get married in Denver. Do you remember Father Machebeuf?"

James had not heard the name in some time. "Of course I remember him. He was one of the first priests to come into the area when I was in Nevada Gulch with your brother. Sheriff Cozens was a good friend and arranged for Father Machebeuf to acquire a house in Central City to use as a church. In fact, I attended his first wedding there and it was when Cozens got married. Why do you ask?"

Well, George has become a very good friend of Father Machebeuf, who now heads a parish in Denver. George has asked him to marry us in the church there."

James stood up and hugged Lucy. "That is good news. I will be proud to have my daughter marry George Barrett and I will be especially honored to have Father Machebeuf perform the ceremony. When is all this to take place?"

"December 13th," Lucy said, almost whispering.

"Travel to Denver in December? Well, that gives me another reason to go. I have to be with the General Assembly in December and I must be there to vote on several proposals. I will likely have to stay there until the end of the month, which means your mother will be coming back alone, but we can work that out later."

Over the next several weeks everything revolved around wedding preparations. Lucy and George revealed that the plan was for them to remain in Denver after the wedding and wrap up George's business there. He had entered into a partnership and would be turning the every day business over to his new partner. The couple would then return to Fairplay and occupy the house that George had built one year earlier. He planned on taking some short freight trips and managing his billiard hall. George had already gone back to Denver to start things in motion.

In early December, during a fortunate break in the weather, Lucy, Catherine and James boarded a stagecoach headed for Denver. Reluctantly, they left the management of the hotel to John and Mary.

CHAPTER FORTY-NINE

The marriage of George Barrett and Lucy Ann Castello was not a big affair. Only a few friends and business associates of George's were in attendance, and a few friends and acquaintances from in and around Central City came. The timing was not good for a large wedding, but the ceremony was a memorable one.

Father Machebeuf gave a wonderful sermon based on the importance of a family and the responsibilities of a man to his wife and visa versa. He related his personal story of arriving in the territory shortly after gold was discovered in Nevada Gulch. He told how his first mass had been held in the Sons of Malta meeting house and that his first wedding was that of William and Mary Cozens, both of whom were present.

James spent nearly an hour visiting with Cozens following the wedding. Cozens was still considered to be one of the most honest lawmen in the west. Catherine visited with Mary and determined that Mary was not happy with the life they were living. She said they were considering leaving the Central City area, but William was procrastinating at every turn. She said he had expressed an interest to venture into some sort of enterprise similar to what James and Catherine were involved in.

Two days after the wedding Catherine was once again boarding a stagecoach. James, Lucy and George stood by as she boarded. James assured her that he would be back home as soon as the session ended. Lucy told her mother that she and George would try to be back in Fairplay as soon after the first of the year if possible.

The trip home took one day longer because of a short snowstorm and Catherine was forced to spend the night in a way station that offered few comforts other than a warm fire. She sat in front of the fire for nearly two hours before falling asleep in her chair. The stationmaster chose not to wake her. He simply covered her with the two quilts she had and went to bed.

The remainder of the trip was uneventful, but their arrival back home was not.

Evidently, John and Mary had disagreed on almost everything, and the cook that was hired before James and Catherine went to Denver had proven to be, according to Mary, some sort of tyrant that slammed things around when she was told by young Mary to do something.

"I had to constantly remind her who was boss," Mary said.

John interrupted, "You might be her boss, but you are not mine!"

After nearly an hour of listening to the back and forth between John and Mary, Catherine had both of them and the cook, Mrs. Bradley, seated at a table in the hotel.

"Now, let us get a few thing straight," she said. "I will not tolerate this bickering to go on. John, you and Mary have to get along. This is a business and it will not thrive if there is a constant turmoil among the people involved in its purpose, so let us discuss the problems now and find solutions. We are all going to miss Lucy. She was a major part of getting things done, but she has taken a new path in life and we must do that, too. Mrs. Bradley, I know you have only limited knowledge of this hotel, having done only intermittent duties up until now, but I am proposing that you take a permanent position as of today. I will caution you that I have some considerable experience in the fact that the Irish people have quick tempers, and I will suggest that you take a deep breath whenever you feel that Irish rising to the point where it allows your mouth to override your brain. Is that clear?"

"I am more than happy to accept your offer to be employed permanently," Mrs. Bradley said. "Aye, that I know to be true of the Irish, and I am no exception. Me husband reminds me frequently, he does. I will try my best to serve you well."

Mary let a tear roll down her face. "I really do miss Lucy already, but I know that we must forge ahead, in spite of the fact that she has abandoned us."

Catherine smiled and took Mary's hand. "She has not abandoned us. She is now a wife, and that must be her first priority. She and George will be moving into George's house here as soon as they can. I am sure she will be there for you. She is still your sister."

John was still being somewhat stubborn. He pointed at Mary. "Just so she knows that she is not my boss. I have some chores that need done. This place is going to be real cold if I do not get some firewood in here soon."

After John left, the three women discussed their plans for a few more minutes. Catherine returned to the house. As she walked through the door, the loneliness seemed to engulf her. She sat at the table and let the tears flow freely. It was not just that Lucy was not there. She thought about all the time she spent without her husband at her side. He seemed to think he could make things better for everyone. She admitted to herself that he was a benevolent man, but she wanted deep down for him to back off a little and spend some time with her.

James sat in a hotel room in Denver. Many of the same thoughts were going through his head. Once again the General Assembly had accomplished much less than he had hoped for. The vote to make Denver the capitol did not make it to the floor. About the only important thing that was accomplished was that the assembly voted to carve out parts of Lake and Costilla counties and create Saguache County.

Two months earlier President Johnson had appointed Alexander Cummings of Pennsylvania to be the third governor of the territory. Cummings proved to be just as passive at the assembly as he was when James met him before his appointment. As for President Johnson, he seemed to take very little notice of Colorado beyond the acquisition of the Ute lands. He had not even certified the few actions taken by the assembly. James was starting to think his time was being wasted. He had now missed another Christmas with his family and had little to show for it. On the stage ride home, he began thinking about other options in his life. He was approaching 52 years of age and, upon reflection, had been quite successful, but he was beginning to think there was more.

The next assembly, to be held in February, would consider some other county lines. James was considering making that his last assembly

Upon arrival back home, James found his family at the house. Mrs. Bradley was handling things at the hotel. As he walked through the door, six-year-old Francis was the first to greet him.

"Daddy, wait until you see!"

Francis was the only one of the children that called James Daddy. He thought about how his mother would have reacted to that. She did not like the monikers of Mommy and Daddy, and had been adamant about that in James' early years.

"See what, young man?"

Francis took James' hand and led him to the fireplace where a young puppy was curled up on a piece of a quilt. James shot a questionable glance at Catherine. She stood up and took his other hand while they looked down at the sleeping puppy.

"His mother was run down by a horse and cart that spooked when a man dropped a large board into the back of the cart," she said. "The dog's owner came to the hotel and explained that he now had six puppies that were yet to be weaned. Mrs. Bradley somehow convinced me she could care for the puppies. She went home and came back with several milk bottles at about the same time the man came back with the puppies. We managed to spread the word and by the next day we had found homes for all but this one, the runt of the litter. Francis sat with that puppy for hours, feeding it a little at a time and taking it out back so it could relieve itself. He informed me that this was his puppy and that he would take care of it forever. So, there you have it. It is up to you to tell that little boy that he cannot have a dog."

As the family sat down for dinner James realized how rare an event this was. So often they had dinner at the hotel and Catherine and the girls were paying attention to the guests.

"I like the idea of us having a meal here at the house," he said. "Let's set at least one day a week when this happens."

Catherine agreed that it was a good idea. Mary said that it would be good to have a day away from the hotel.

"I think we should make it a whole day," she said. "We could all do something together. My schooling and the hotel seem to take up all my time. The only socializing I get is with the billiard players and a rare visit with school friends. I think we should make every Saturday a family day – all day, not just for dinner."

"I just spent a good amount of time riding alone in a stagecoach and thinking about this very thing," James said. "I think it is a grand idea and I also think that I am going to back away from some of my other involvements and enjoy spending time with loved ones and watching this young man train a dog."

He rubbed Francis' head and then settled into his meal.

"I received a short letter from Charles," Catherine said.

James paused only briefly with his fork in his hand. "What did he have to say?"

"As I said, it was a short note, mostly to inform us that he was seeing a woman on a regular basis. Her name is Dora. She is about six years his junior and about the only other thing he wrote about her is that she is well educated. He also mentioned that he had acquired a new bull last fall."

"He gets a bull and we get a dog," James said with a slight chuckle.

CHAPTER FIFTY

James hoped against hope that 1866 would be a better year. Fairplay had nearly doubled in size and was finally being considered to replace Buckskin Joe as the county seat. At 52 years of age, he was one of the oldest, if not the oldest resident of the town, which many considered a small city rather than a town. James was one of many that advocated for the formal designation and they proposed that the name be changed to South Park City. The idea did not take hold, but Fairplay did become the county seat.

Of the utmost importance for James was building another home. For this project Francis sought the help of two of his school friends. The new home was not an extravagant multi-room mansion. It was to be a simple one room with a pitched roof and a large front opening with no door. The construction took place just outside the back door and the sole occupant was to be a young dog, now named Avorton, which was the French word for "runt." James had no input in the dog's name, it was chosen by Francis.

While building the doghouse, another name cropped up. Francis' friends had taken to calling him Frank. At first, James did not like the informality of the nickname, but as the day wore on, he became accustomed to it, and found himself using it. When Catherine heard the name being used she passively informed everyone that his name was Francis and that she was his mother, not his mommy. Her comments resulted in some giggling and then Frank and his friends went back to work. The finished product, complete with homemade shingles, was a work to behold to everyone except Avorton. He refused to stay inside unless Frank was right there with him and, having not yet been weaned from the bottle, Avorton would be spending most of his time curled up on the quilt in front of the fireplace.

Mr. and Mrs. George Barrett returned to Fairplay in the spring. Lucy wasted no time in getting their house ready to be a home. The house was not far from her parents' home and Lucy made frequent trips to visit with her mother. After she had the house fixed up to her standards, she invited her mother and father to dinner one evening. The table was set to perfection and Lucy presented a large roast beef with vegetables from a friend's garden. George had obviously received his instructions. After a prayer, he rose and carved the meat, placing a generous slice on each plate as it was presented to him. Following the meal the four of them retired to the living room with hot coffee for everyone. George began the conversation:

"I have decided to use the building now being used for the billiard hall as a business office. I hate to lose the billiard hall. It is a profitable enterprise, but it is a little small. The two tables are too close together and players also get into each other's way. Some have encouraged me to turn it into a full-fledged saloon, but I did not want the headaches. Occasionally I bring in a keg of beer from Denver, but it goes bad quickly and is usually not profitable."

James interrupted:

"Let me think about this. We have talked about adding some rooms to the hotel. The plan is to build a two-story addition, with rooms on the second floor and then move our billiard table into the ground floor of the addition and thereby expand the use of the existing structure. Would you be interested in renting the ground floor? We would include my table, giving you three tables with plenty of room?"

George agreed to consider the idea and he discussed it with Lucy later that night. She thought the idea had some merit, but cautioned that doing business with family can be risky.

"I have been doing business with your father for years," George said. "Do you know that I hauled that billiard table of his all the way from St. Louis? I also brought those two I have in the parlor on other trips I made. I never thought there would be so many miners that could learn to play real carom billiards. I think we could do well."

James and Catherine had a similar conversation that same night. Catherine had agreed for some time that the hotel needed to expand, especially in the kitchen and dining area. By adding on in the manner James was proposing, they could have the extra room and some extra income if George agreed to rent the ground floor of the addition.

The subject then changed.

"I noticed that you and Lucy were very engaged in some sort of serious conversation while George and I were talking. Did she tell you how things are going?

Catherine reached for James' hand. "She seems to be very happy. I think she was glad to get out of Denver. She said it is changing fast, but then so is Fairplay. I am constantly amazed at the rate at which this town, and the whole state for that matter, is growing in population. Has there been any more discussion about Colorado becoming a state? I see that Nebraska is being considered. I would have thought that Colorado would receive that distinction before Nebraska."

James replied, "I do not think we will get statehood for a while. There is still too much animosity between the Indians and the government, and every time the eggheads in Washington D. C. sign a treaty, they do not even let the ink dry before they violate at least one of the provisions and some of the Indians have the same problem. I pray that the latest changes will make a difference for the good, but I am not holding my breath."

The next day James met with George at his billiard hall. After a few more terms were worked out, James agreed to the proposed expansion of the hotel. The first load of lumber was delivered two weeks later. James attended to all his other obligations and George took on the supervision of the addition to the hotel. By the time of the first snow, which was late in September, earlier than most years, the new building was enclosed and the roof completed. Before Thanksgiving, there was a new business in Fairplay. The family decided to celebrate Thanksgiving Day at the Castello house. At Mary's request, the meal at the hotel would be limited to guests only and served early, giving the help some extra time for their own families. Mary had another request. She wanted to invite William Beery to the family dinner. James and Catherine were both set back at the notion and questioned Mary at length.

James was first to ask, "Why in the world would you want to invite him? Your mother and I need an explanation, and it better be a good one."

Mary sat quietly, obviously thinking about her answer when Catherine spoke up.

"Young lady, answer you father, and see to it that you tell us the truth. Have you been keeping company with Billy Beery without our knowledge?'

"Not really keeping company," Mary said. "He has been a frequent customer for dinner at the hotel. He has a new job at the Wells Fargo office and, being alone, it is easier for him to come to the hotel for his meals. We have sat and talked several times and he has walked me part way home when I have to come home after dark. I really like him. No, it is not that I like him; it is that I have fallen in love with him. He is so charming and has a great sense of humor."

Catherine gasped. "What do you mean you have fallen in love with him? What can you possibly know about falling in love?"

"Mother," Mary replied. "Did you know when you fell in love? Did someone have to tutor you on the feelings you would have? Did you read a book? Did you tell Lucy how she would feel when she fell in love with George? Tell me Mother, if I do not know what it feels like, who does? Am I to sit around waiting for someone to tell me that I am in love?"

James then spoke. "Wait just a minute. First of all, I do not like your tone right now. You have always respected your mother, and I want you to be very careful about pushing your remarks to the point of rudeness. Now, I will tell you what I think. I do not know William Beery except through what others have said and with my few encounters with him. I do not dislike the man, but I have some mixed feeling about him. Sometimes I have a feeling that he is not entirely honest. I will agree that he is humorous. The few conversations I have had with him have proven that. You say he is charming. Well, that can be both good and bad. If he has simply charmed his way into your life I might well have a problem with that."

"Father," Mary said, "he has not just charmed me. He has informed me that he loves me. I am nearly 20 years old. You and Mother have guided me through the past years with knowledge, and respect. Both of you have trusted me to make decisions and I want you to respect me now. It is important to me that Billy comes to our Thanksgiving dinner. I truly want you to welcome him and give him a chance to show you that he also respects me. He has said many times that you are a special man. He admires what you have accomplished in your life and he feels much the same about Mother. Please do not disappoint me."

James turned to Catherine and said, "Well, Wife, I think our daughter has asked a fair question and she makes a good point."

Catherine sighed, "Of course you can ask him to dine with us. We are only thinking of your wellbeing. Have you discussed this with Lucy?"

"I have," Mary said. "She is tickled pink and she has also cautioned me, but she can truly see that Billy makes me very happy."

On Thanksgiving Day James sat nervously in the living room with George Barrett. Catherine and Lucy were busy preparing the food and Mary had gone to walk back with Beery.

"This whole thing with Billy Beery has me on edge," he said to George. "I still do not know how this all happened. I just have a bad feeling about that young man."

"James, there is probably nothing you can do at this point without completely alienating Mary. Just let the chips fall where they may. She is a level headed young lady and you must trust her to make the right decisions," George said.

Just as George finished his encouragement, the front door opened and the couple walked in holding hands Billy wore a dark brown jacket and vest with a tie. His pants were recently pressed and his beard and moustache trimmed. He sported an almost boyish smile and walked immediately to James who stood and shook hands. George then did the same.

"Thank you so much for accepting me today, Judge," he said.

He then turned and walked to Catherine. "And thank you for bringing me into your home. You have no idea how important this is to me."

Everyone sat for dinner and there was a plethora of chatter for some time. As the meal came to an end and the last of an apple pie was devoured, Billy looked at Mary and she nodded with a smile.

"Judge," he said. "I have something very important to ask you and I beg an affirmative answer. I ask here and now for your daughter's hand in marriage."

The room fell completely silent until James dropped his fork onto his plate.

"What?"

"Sir," Beery said. "Mary Julia has already agreed to marry me, but will not make it official without the blessing of her parents, and that is only right. I assure you that my intentions are of an honorable nature and I assure you also that I will be a good and faithful husband."

Catherine stepped up behind James and whispered into his ear. He listened and then addressed Mary.

"Is this true? Do you want to marry this man?"

"Father, I told you before that I love this man and I tell you now that I want more than anything else to spend the rest of my days with him."

"Well," James said. "Your mother says she will bless this if I do and I cannot give a real good reason why I should not. So, yes, I guess you have our blessings."

A cheer went up, Mary kissed Billy, Lucy kissed George and Catherine kissed James.

CHAPTER FIFTY-ONE

While James and Catherine chose not to object to Mary Julia's marriage to William Beery, they still harbored some reservations. The Thanksgiving event had been a big surprise but the couple had more surprises coming, the first just one week later when William Beery and his fiancé announced that their engagement would not be a long one. In fact, it would be only one month. They had set a wedding date of December 22.

The next weeks saw an abundance of activity, not just in the Castello family, but also in the town, the county, the state and the nation. Once again, there was a movement to make Fairplay the county seat and this time it seemed to have a lot of support. Rumor had it that, effective the first of the year, there would be a new governor. The movement to get the change in the county seat was encouraged by the possibility that a new governor would stand behind their efforts.

On the national level a new proclamation declaring Nebraska as a state was prepared, but Andrew Johnson had not yet been convinced to sign it.

The real issue at hand for Catherine and James Castello was the fact that soon both of their daughters would be married women.

Catherine was on the verge of tears when Mary told her about the wedding date. Mary was still four months from her twentieth birthday. She and Mary sat at the table one evening.

"You are going to make me grey before my time," Catherine said. "But I can see that you are happy and I only want to help. What do you want done?"

Mary displayed a big smile. "Mother, I am not asking for much. I ask only that you and Father accept this decision just as you accepted my plan in the first place. We do not want a big affair. We will be happy with a simple wedding attended by family and close friends. Billy has no family in the area, but has several friends with whom he has worked and associated with, so the number will be small and the ceremony will be simple."

And so it was. The couple was united in marriage on December 22, 1866 and set up housekeeping in a small house, which Billy rented from a local businessman. James displayed happiness at the wedding and at a small gathering at the hotel, but the reservations still lingered. Three days later the family was together for a Christmas dinner. All of the women pitched in to make the dinner, while the men lounged in the living room talking about politics, business and plans. Billy told them that he would be very busy for the next several months. He was, among other things, still working at the Wells Fargo office and was also taking on the responsibility of delivery of the mail. His exact route was not yet known. George told Billy that he had an interesting contract that could be better accomplished with a freight path that Billy was familiar with, namely the Ute Trail. The two agreed to talk over the plans in the near future.

Upon hearing about the Ute Trail, James became very interested. Some of his Ute friends had recently visited him in Fairplay. They had concerns about the trail being used more frequently, but told him that the Ute Chiefs seemed to be accepting the fact that they were being forced to cooperate with the whites.

George had some interesting information.

"James," he asked, "do you remember us talking about the problem of bringing beer from Denver?

"I do," James replied. "I know that there is always an interest in serving it in the billiard room and I have been of the opinion that serving beer may be a good alternative to whiskey. I would just as soon not take that step. Men seem to get invincible and stupid when they have too much whiskey."

"I may have a solution," George continued. "Neither Lucy nor Catherine are much in favor, but Leonard and Charles Summer built a small log building at the edge of town. They started up a small brewery and they are turning out some respectable tasting lager. I will meet with them in a couple of weeks and maybe work out something whereby they could provide me with some of their product. As long as we can keep the barrels cold, the beer will maintain its taste. Keeping it cold right now is certainly no problem and Leonard has suggested that he may have a plan to harvest some ice and keep his beer cold for a good part of the summer. I have promised Lucy that I would only serve it during the day and never on Sunday. As you know I have an experienced saloonkeeper running the billiard hall. He is not only experienced, he is very big and doesn't take any guff from anyone."

"I can attest to that," Billy said. "He took no time and very little effort to escort me out of the last saloon he worked in, and I will tell you here and now that saying he escorted me out is the kind way of saying what happened. Nobody in his right mind would stand up to Jack Bandon."

The next day an absolute blizzard literally buried the town. The wind blew drifts that met with the eaves of houses. For two days nobody went outside. The guests at the hotel tried to shovel out the front entrance, but gave up after admitting that the wind was blowing the snow in faster than they could shovel it out. To make matters worse, they only had one shovel to work with. One of the men had the foresight to bring the shovel into the back porch before the storm intensified. James determined that the problem would not repeat itself. He planned to have several shovels stored permanently on the back porch.

It was another two weeks before things in Fairplay and all of South Park began moving again. The storm reminded everyone how difficult it was for the majority of the population of Park County to travel to Buckskin Joe, and while Fairplay was growing constantly, Buckskin Joe was experiencing a decline in population. Finally, as one of his last official acts, Governor Cummings declared Fairplay to be the county seat. Once again, James and some of his associates attempted to have the new county seat renamed South Park City; once again, their efforts failed.

Yet another territorial governor was appointed early in the year. Alexander C. Hunt was a devout Republican and tried to compare himself to Abe Lincoln. He even resembled Lincoln, but he had his enemies. He came to the territory with the other gold seekers and was appointed judge of the Vigilante Committee in 1861. He subsequently took the appointment of U. S. Marshal for the Territory of Colorado. In that capacity, he and James met a few times and James was encouraged that Hunt might succeed in quelling some of the conflicts with the various tribes, but he remained silent when some of the men in Central City formed a group and offered a bounty for Indian scalps. James was quick to remind Hunt during a meeting in Denver that the bounty was unacceptable and, as governor, Hunt should ostracize those responsible.

"Governor," James said, "I have become well acquainted with several of the Indian tribes of Colorado, most notably the Utes. I have learned that men who would rather avoid conflict lead them, but those leaders must also look to the welfare of their people. I have, also befriended and had business associates among the men in Central City. I have dealt with a significant number of the miners and businessmen relating to legal issues. It is my belief that there are relatively few of them who actually support this barbaric assault on Indians, yet there are those who are in desperate positions and may well take advantage of the bounty that is being offered. I beseech you to publicly denounce the bounty and what it represents."

"Judge," Hunt responded. I have always had the utmost respect for you and have found that you are a very honest and respected man. As you know, I have had some significant interactions with the Utes as the Ex-Officio of the Office of Indian Affairs. I promise you now that I will look into this matter."

"Thank you for that," James said. "I must also tell you that, largely because of the conflicts that seem to be ongoing in places like Park County, I have learned that the Utes are seriously considering forming alliances with some of the plains tribes. Should that happen the result could well be that the tribes will become more aggressive, and that spells trouble for those who are settling in the whole territory."

When James returned from his trip and the meeting with the governor, Catherine informed him that another family dinner was being planned. This one hosted by George and Lucy at their home.

"I have been instructed that the only obligation that you and I have is to show up," Catherine said. "I am not expected to cook or help in any way, and you are requested to leave all political and business behind and just enjoy the evening. Lucy and Mary will prepare the meal. Mary told Billy about the set of dominoes you have and suggested that you engage George and Billy in a game."

It had been a long time since James had even looked at his domino tiles, which he acquired from a French trapper friend of his father's. The tiles were of the best ivory and had a distinctive clicking sound when dropped on a table. He readily agreed to bring the set out.

"I would enjoy playing a game or two. I do not think I have played a game since the girls were just little ones and I don't think the boys have ever played. I look forward to the evening."

Following the family dinner, James and Catherine returned home and were sitting in front of the fire. The boys went to bed and Catherine asked if James had enjoyed the evening.

"For once we were not presented with problems and, other than Billy's attempt to turn the domino game into a gambling game, there were not conflicts and no big surprises. Yes, I did enjoy the evening."

"I really expected a little more," Catherine said. "Did you happen to notice that Lucy wore her apron the entire evening?"

"I did not think it unusual," James said thoughtfully. "I assume that she put it on in preparation for the evening and just did not take it off. Now, why should I have noticed?"

"Do you not remember the many times that I wore an apron for extended periods of time?'

"I do," James said, and then a sudden realization appeared on his face.

"Are you trying to tell me that Lucy is pregnant?"

"I am, but Lucy wanted to make sure you knew before she told everyone else. She strutted around in front of you several times, but you failed to notice, so she asked that I break the news to you as soon as we returned home."

James let loose with a laugh, and realized that it had been a long time since he had experienced the euphoric happiness that he felt at that moment. He pulled Catherine up from her chair and danced her around in a circle.

Before the year came to an end James and Catherine were the proud grandparents of a new baby. The boy was given the name Charles in honor of his uncle, who was still in Florissant, Missouri and was still the mayor. Upon getting the news, Uncle Charles immediately penned letters to George and Lucy and to his parents. Reading the letter, James could almost feel the pride his eldest son displayed. In part, he wrote: "I thought being sworn in as mayor was the epitome of good things that have happened, but having this young boy named after me eclipses all of that."

CHAPTER FIFTY-TWO

Early in 1868, James acquired another appointment. President Johnson, after conferring with some of the Ute representatives, appointed James to the position of Receiver for the new United States Land Office in Fairplay. His friendship with Chief Ouray became more intense. He considered Ouray a friend and the feeling was mutual, but no matter what happened, it seemed the Utes were always getting the short end of the stick.

At one meeting with both Ouray and Colorow, James told them of his background, saying that, if the truth was known, he sometimes wished that he had returned to Missouri. He told his friends that he had always liked the idea of raising cattle and was sometimes jealous of his son's success in Missouri. He was somewhat surprised when Ouray informed him that he should consider getting some cattle and raising them on the grasses of Twin Creek near the western base of the Ute Trail. Several years before, when James visited Ouray in a camp near Mt. Pisgah, Ouray told him of the great grass that grew in the area.

As the year wore on, James was spending more and more time in his duties as the receiver. Lands were being transferred, claimed and settled at a rate not anticipated by anyone. Catherine was handling the business at the hotel and she was getting tired. Now that Lucy had a family, she was unable to lend a hand most of the time and hiring help was a constant trial.

James was relaxing in the land office when Vincent Albus came in. Albus had been in the area for some time, but James had only brief conversations with him.

He greeted the man, "Mr. Albus, what can I do for you?

James expected that Albus had some questions about a claim or a homestead, but Albus' reason for coming to the office surprised James.

"I am not a man to mince words, Mr. Castello. I am a businessman with a significant amount of money at my disposal. I came to this area with the intention of starting a profitable business. After considerable research I have determined that the business I would like to have is already established. I am here to ask you if you would consider selling me your hotel. I do not expect a decision right now. I know that you will need to discuss the proposal with your wife and your business associates, namely George Barrett, whom I understand is your son-in-law.

"Well," James said, "This comes as a surprise. I suppose that selling the hotel is a possibility, provided a good price is offered. I, frankly, have been neglecting the hotel of late and that has placed an extra burden on my wife. Evidently, you are aware that George Barrett and I have an agreement as it relates to his operating the billiard hall in the hotel. If I were to consider selling it would have to be with a full understanding of that arrangement and could very well depend on his wants and needs."

"I understand completely," Albus said. "I should like your permission to discuss some options with Mr. Barrett."

"I have no problem with you talking to George. In fact, I would insist on it, but I ask that you give me time to discuss this matter with him and Catherine before you do that."

Albus took his leave and left James sitting at his desk with his head in his hands. After a few moments, he left the office and walked to the hotel, where Catherine was supervising the work of a new employee as they prepared for the evening meal. Four men were in the billiard room. Each had a mug of beer resting on shelves that had been installed recently for just that purpose. Noting that George was not among the players, James took Catherine aside.

James asked, "Have you planned to take supper here or will we be able to dine at home this evening?"

"I have prepared us a meal at home. The boys are there now and I am about to leave this to our newest employee. I need to see just how she handles things without me watching her every move," Catherine replied.

"Very well," James said. "I will meet you at home. I have something I wish to discuss with you, but I do not want to get into it right now. Do you know where George is right now?"

"He went to Denver early this morning and will return by tomorrow evening," Catherine replied.

That evening James sat at his desk at home and reviewed the books relating to the hotel business. Overall, the hotel was doing a good business. Currently, all the rooms were occupied, and all but one of those were long-term men who paid regularly. He was perusing the simple contract that he and George entered into when Catherine came in. She looked over his shoulder. Seeing the document he was holding she stepped back.

"Are you and George having problems?'

"No," he said, turning around to look at her. "Take a seat. We need to talk."

Catherine sat down where she could look directly at James. She appeared worried. James explained to her that there was a man interested in buying the hotel and that he could not consider doing that without her approval. He told her that he must also think of George and Lucy.

Catherine thought for only a moment. "This might well come as a surprise to you, but what you have just said comes as no surprise to me. You know full well that some of your major decisions have made my life difficult at times. You also know that I trust you. I am proud of you as a man and your asking for my advice on matters such as these makes me even more proud."

James let out a little laugh. "Your advice? I am not asking for advice. I am asking you to join me in a mutual decision. Should we, and I mean we, sell the hotel? I am inclined to consider an offer. If you go along with that, I will approach George and tell him what we have discussed and decided on. I think he can work things out with a new owner, should it come to that."

Catherine became more serious. "I love what we have done with the hotel, but I must tell you I am getting tired. I would sincerely like to have some time to the boys, and myself but may I ask you, if we sell, what is next? Do you plan to take off to some far away place? I understand that the United States has now agreed to purchase Alaska.

If you have some notion of going to live with the Eskimos, I say no to selling just to keep you near me."

James laughed again. "I cannot fathom heading for Alaska. I am not sure I even know exactly where Alaska is and I for sure do not understand President Johnson and Secretary Seward's entire motives. I read that the price is over seven million dollars, but I digress. No, I have no plans to head off to parts unknown. For at least the short term, I will concentrate on my duties at the land office. Given the fact that a new territorial governor is appointed every time the moon changes, or so it seems, those duties might well go away at any time. So, what do we do?"

"I think that, if you get a reasonable offer, we should sell," Catherine said.

Two days later James met with George Barrett and informed him of the possibility of selling the hotel. He told George that he would insist on George's agreement to rent the billiard room be a condition of the sale, if that is what George wanted. He suggested that George contact Albus and discuss the matter with him.

George met with Albus later that same week. He met with James at the land office.

"I met with Vincent Albus yesterday," George said. "He and I have agreed that, should he be successful in buying the hotel, my arrangement with you will continue with him. He only needs you to sell. Do you see any problems?"

"I do not," James said. "The more I think about it, the more I like the idea. I have a chance to acquire a nice piece of land down on Twin Creek at the base of the Ute Trail. If I can get Catherine to agree I would like to get that land and raise a few cattle. Every time I meet with the Utes, they tell me how desirable that grassland is. I really do not want to take advantage of the Utes being forced out of the territory, but the fact is that I also want to stay."

By the first week in October, the sale was final. Albus retained the current employees and Catherine settled into some needlepoint that she had been working on for several months. She expressed some reservation about James purchasing the land on Twin Creek, but told him that she would not attempt to discourage him. She knew how much he wanted to once again raise some livestock.

When they last discussed it she simply said, "It is a better option than returning to Missouri, and I am not sure but what you would do exactly that."

A few days after the hotel sold a letter from Charles informed his parents that he and Dora Menke were married on October 6. Charles was still the mayor in Florissant, having been re-elected more that 20 times.

"Well," James said after reading the letter. "Another daughter added to the family. I have this feeling that you are getting old," he said jokingly.

"We will see who is getting old," she said. "Now that I will have more time at home, I will be focused on things that need done around the house. You cannot spend all your time in that office, and this is not the time of year to start thinking about starting a cattle ranch, so just settle down for a while and get old with me."

For the rest of the year James did just as Catherine suggested. He relaxed as much as possible, visiting the hotel and encouraging George to teach him the game of carom billiards; a task that took much longer than James anticipated. During his time at the billiard room he became acquainted with Jack Bandon, the man George hired to keep things peaceful. Bandon was about six and half feet tall and easily weighed 300 pounds. He was not a man to be reckoned with.

The additional leisure time did something else; it caused James to reflect on what his life had been. He had good times and bad. His tenure as the sheriff of St. Louis County had been the time when he started to think how important the lives of others were to him. His unforeseen appointment to the bench, his random friendship with the Utes and his successful business venture in Fairplay had all come to pass in the last ten years. He had watched his children grow and his family expand, but he knew that it was time to take on some other challenges. He knew he had to move ahead on the opportunity to start a ranch near Twin Creek.

CHAPTER FIFTY-THREE

The land on Twin Creek was perfect for a small ranch. James made several trips to the property, but mostly just to evaluate it. Twice he left his horse about halfway up the Ute Trail and hiked to the top of what the Utes called signal peak. The name referenced the use of the high ground above the Twin Creek Valley by the Utes, who used it to send smoke signals to the various bands in the area to warn them of danger or tell them of the presence of buffalo. For James it was a perfect place to get a birds eye view of his new property.

On his second trip to the precipice he sat with a notebook and a pencil and sketched a rudimentary drawing of the land. He included a small house, some livestock pens and a barn. He paid close attention to the flow of the creek and, in his mind's eye, positioned his buildings in such a manner as to be above any high water. From his perspective he could easily see where runoffs of the past had swollen the small creek. A line of debris, not very apparent when one was standing near the creek, but clearly visible from the peak, marked the historical high water of the creek and provided a guide for location of future buildings.

When he came down from the top of the peak on his second trip, he was surprised to find three young Ute Indians walking around his hobbled horse. They were running their hands over the horse, feeling its muscles and looking at its feet. When he approached, one of the lads turned quickly, pulled a knife from his belt and went into a squatting stance, ready to fend off any attack on James' part. James raised one hand and asked the boys if they were part of Ouray's band. None of the boys spoke English, but they readily recognized the chief's name.

In his best Spanish James convinced the boys that he was a friend, not an enemy of the Utes. As a result of the diffused altercation and the thwarting of the likely theft of the horse, James was invited to ride with them to the other side of the pass where they were to meet with some of Colorow's people that were on their way to the hot springs on the east side of the pass. The Utes regularly gathered at the spring where their shaman summoned the spirit, Manitou, in either a good or evil capacity. Manitou was given great reverence by the people. James readily agreed to go with the boys.

James was recognized by several of the Utes present for the ceremony. They trusted him, referred to him as 'Judge,' and invited him to sit in on the ceremony. He was not a stranger to ritual ceremony, having joined the Freemasons when their lodge was organized in Mineral Point, Wisconsin shortly after he and Catherine were married. The Masonic ceremonies were reverent, but did not in any way prepare James for what happened in the steaming waters of the springs.

While he was invited to stay for as long as he wanted, he knew Catherine would be wondering why he was gone so long. The morning after the ceremony he headed back home. He stopped for the rest of the day next to Twin Creek, where he referred to his drawings and paced out possible locations of his proposed buildings. He settled on one specific spot for the house. He continued his trip back to Fairplay with visions of a home on the newly acquired land, but he had some uncertainties as to how Catherine would react to his going ahead with building a house, knowing full well that it would mean an eventual move to yet another remote place. He arrived home and met with the questions he anticipated, and more.

Catherine met him in the yard even before he could attend to his horse.

"Where have you been? I expected you to be gone for four days and I wait for a week. What kept you so long?"

James placed his hands on her shoulders and said, "Let me get this horse some grain and water. As soon as I get that done, I will come in and we will talk."

Catherine hollered at the boys and instructed them to take care of the horse, letting James know that she had no intention of waiting for an explanation. He followed her into the house and went to the washbasin. He splashed two hands full of water on his face and washed the dust from his whiskers. Combing his hair back with his hands he sat down facing his wife and started to explain:

"Well, I had an interesting trip, to say the least. First I simply walked around the new property on Twin Creek and then I walked to the top of Signal Peak, where I could observe the property from a different perspective. I did that twice. The second time I was up there I caught some young Indian boys evaluating my horse. They were most certainly going to steal it as soon as one of them could remove the hobbles. When I confronted them, one of them pulled a knife."

Catherine sat up straight. "Were you hurt?" You did not hurt the boy did you?"

James held his hand up with his palm toward Catherine to stop her from saying more.

"No, I was not hurt. The boys recognized that I was a friend. They then invited me to go to the hot springs where members of their band were preparing for a ceremony honoring the Manitou Spirit. It was a great privilege for me to be invited into this ceremony. Only their native language was allowed, so there was no explanation of the procedure. Their medicine man clearly appeared to be communicating with a spirit and the hot springs was enclosed in a structure that became so hot that I thought we might well be cooked, but somehow it was not uncomfortable. In fact, it was the most relaxing experience I have ever had. I then returned to the property on Twin Creek, where I selected a spot for a house."

Catherine sat back. "So you do plan to go to this place and live there? When, exactly do you anticipate asking me to leave my home again?"

"There is much to do before that time comes, but I do think we could have a comfortable home there and possibly even more than a home. While I was there I noticed several times that people other than the Utes are using the Ute Trail. It has definite signs of small carts and wagons being used, and of course we know that Billy has taken ox carts over the trail more than once."

Over the next several months James visited the property on Twin Creek as often as possible. He acquired a scraper, a John Lane plow and two draft horses. He built a corral and an open front shed for the horses. John and Francis accompanied him on several trips, and when their schooling allowed, they stayed in a tent while James returned to his duties in Fairplay. It was not unusual for a group of Utes to come to the property and a larger tent was added, allowing for a little more comfort when he sat to visit or when Catherine also went along. Catherine was adept in making biscuits in the large Dutch oven and the young Utes who visited were adept in eating them.

James began to think about more than just a small ranch. He envisioned a small trading post and approached Catherine with the idea.

"I have noticed how well used the Ute Trail has become," he said. "I pointed that out to you on our last visit together at Twin Creek. What would you think about investing in some improvements to the trail and establishing a trading post and small boarding house on the Twin Creek property?"

"Well," Catherine replied. "I have known since the beginning of this your need to always expand your horizons and that we would eventually be moving to this new dream property. I will be honest with you. I have enjoyed the leisure I have had since the sale of the hotel, but I also miss it. I enjoy providing for others. Once again, I tell you, where you go I will go. To answer your question, I think it is a good idea and I look forward to helping you achieve your dream."

By Christmas of 1869, the first part of the house was completed, thanks to the help of his boys and his two sons-in-law. Both George Barrett and William Beery were hard workers, but Billy often left without notice. James would find out later that he was simply unaccounted, sometimes for three or four days. Mary did not seem concerned and explained that Billy "had some business to take care of, or some special mail to deliver."

When an opportunity arose to acquire a homestead nearly 20 miles southwest of Twin Creek, James encouraged Beery to file and helped him through the process. He believed that Beery might then choose to settle down and do better as a husband to Mary, who was pregnant and expecting to give birth sometime in the spring.

While it was only 50 miles from Fairplay to the Twin Creek property, it was a grueling trip. Early on, James established a friendship with Samuel Hartsel, who had a homestead and basic trading post about halfway between. The Hartsel place became a regular stop when James traveled to Twin Creek. When Catherine accompanied him, they would spend the night. The Castello family made their official move during a clear, but cold week in January of 1870. They had three wagonloads of belongings, six draft horses, four saddle horses and two dogs when they stopped at the Hartsel place.

CHAPTER FIFTY-FOUR

James and Samuel Hartsel had become almost immediate friends on the day they first met. The two had many things in common, not the least of which was their friendships with several of the Utes. On that cold day in January they became even better friends. Samuel helped James unhitch the horses and provided them with water and a little grain, which was something the horses rarely got.

After the livestock was taken care of James and Samuel engaged in a serious conversation about James' plans to live on the Twin Creek property.

"I know you have not asked for my advice," Samuel said, "But I rarely wait for someone to ask. I figure life is too short to waste time beating around the bush. The distance between here and the hot springs on the other side of Ute Pass is about 60 miles. It may as well be ten times that. The trail is getting used more and more. I believe that a rest stop on this side of the pass would be a beneficial convenience for those using the trail. I also believe that, in the long run, it could benefit me financially. Here is what I propose: You and I should forge an informal agreement to help financially and in-kind to improve that pass so larger wagons can traverse it. You should use your land to establish a trading post where travelers could stop for short periods before you send them on to my place here for another rest."

"You make this sound good," Jams said, "but, before I get started on such grandiose dreams, I want to finish some other tasks, including getting settled in, and I plan to have some cattle by spring. I do not want to bite off more than I can chew."

"I might be able to assist you with the cattle. I deal regularly with a man south of here. He had a good bunch of heifer calves last spring. They will be yearlings by the time you get settled in and ready for them. He will have to get rid of them this coming spring. Then all we have to do is get you a good bull and you will be in the cattle business."

"I am impressed," James said with a grin. "As soon as I get the family into their new home and the weather starts getting warmer, we will talk again. Meanwhile, if you happen to talk to your friend, tell him that I might be interested in some of his heifers."

Early the next morning James and his family left the Hartsel ranch to finish the trip to their new home. One of George Barrett's best teamsters had been hired to drive one of the wagons and serve as a mentor to the two boys. Each of the boys took turns driving one of the wagons. James and Catherine sat up on the third wagon. The saddle horses were tied behind. As far as Catherine was concerned, the wagon on which she sat was the most important one. It contained a brand new Victor cooking range from the Potter Company, or at least it contained the pieces. The range would have to be assembled once they arrived. Catherine had seen only pictures of the cook stove and was anxiously looking forward to having it in her kitchen. The cook stove at the hotel was not much more than a re-designed fireplace with a flat top. This new stove included an oven with big double doors.

As they slowly made their way toward their destination, Catherine spoke up:

"I noticed that you and Samuel were having a serious conversation. What was all that about?"

James had been mulling over what he and Hartsel talked about. Catherine's question fitted perfectly into his thoughts.

"We were discussing the future," he replied, "Samuel has suggested that, in addition to a small ranching operation, we open a full-fledged trading post on our property."

"Why would he suggest that you go into competition with him? His trading post seems to be doing very well," Catherine asked.

"He believes, and I am inclined to agree, that a trading post at the western base of the Ute pass could actually benefit his operation. The pass is being used more and more. He proposes that we could both work on getting the trail improved so bigger wagons can traverse it. If we could provide some goods and services to those people who plan on settling the west, we could recommend Hartsel's place to them as they continue on. He has also given me some information about acquiring some yearling heifers to get our herd started, but I, or I should say we, have a lot of work to do before then."

"Just do not forget that your first task when we arrive is to assemble that wonderful cooking range," she said. "I look forward to having it in my kitchen. Perhaps I could even bake you a pie. We have several packages of dried apples somewhere among all these bits and pieces of our future."

Within a few hours after arriving at the new house, James had a fire going in the fireplace. Barrett's man and the two boys had the horses unhooked and in the corral. They began unloading the wagon that belonged to Barrett first while Catherine made a hasty stew in the Dutch oven hung over the fire. The pieces of the new stove were laid neatly on the floor and a table and six chairs were placed in the soon-to-be kitchen. The beds were unloaded and re-assembled and the group sat down for a meal as darkness fell on the valley.

Early the next morning Barrett's team and wagon were en-route back to Fairplay and James busied himself with assembling the cook stove close to the kitchen chimney so it would not be necessary to move it after it got much heavier. As he placed the double doors covering the oven, Catherine, who was watching closely, rose and stroked the stove as if it were a new lamb.

"This is one of the most beautiful things I have ever seen," she said.

"I can see that we are going to have to cut some smaller pieces of firewood," James said as he took a step back to admire his work. "As soon as I get the pipe hooked into the chimney I will split some kindling and some proper sized wood, then you can fire this monster up and make us some biscuits."

Catherine readily agreed to the plan.

For the next two months not much could be accomplished outside. A windbreak near the corral offered some relief for the horses. The wind blew almost every day and made most of the outside chores miserable. A large pile of logs had been stored on the east side of the house. James calculated that there were an adequate number to add another large room to the south side of the house. He envisioned the addition to be the start of his trading post.

In early April the signs of spring were just beginning to show. There were still large drifts of snow but daylight was sticking around just a little longer. During one warm April day James walked from the house and was surprised to find two of the Ute boys who had almost stolen his horse. The boys were riding colorful ponies and leading a packhorse. Both boys literally jumped to the ground and extended their hands to James. Speaking very broken English, one of the boys addressed James:

"Good day, Judge."

"And good day to you," James said. "What brings you to my home?"

"We are told you are now a trader. We have meat from a ciervo," he said, using the Spanish word for a buck deer.

He stumbled over the next few words, but James was able to conclude that their elders had instructed them to try to obtain a mold for lead balls to be used in a certain rifle. They produced a sample of a .58 caliber mini-ball. They did not have the rifle. After some time, James learned that one of the sub-chiefs had acquired the rifle from a soldier's widow. The description led James to believe that it was probably a Pattern Enfield, but James certainly did not have a mold for the mini-ball in that caliber. The boys were disappointed, but suggested that maybe a piece of the venison could be used to prepare a meal in which they could share with James' family.

Catherine enthusiastically accepted the proposition before James could say anything more. It would give her a perfect way to test her new stove. Within minutes she had a roast trimmed and, while her vegetable stores were quickly depleting, she chopped some onions, turnips and carrots. The roast was in the oven and cooking for over an hour when she mixed up a batch of biscuits. On top of the stove she had a coffee pot and a teakettle. When the dinner was ready she invited the Ute boys to sit. To her surprise, they sat down immediately, but not in the offered chairs, but on the floor. She served them each a plate full of food and handed each a knife and fork. She fully expected them to just pick up the food with their fingers, but they put the plates in their laps, cut the meat and ate as though they were seated at the best formal table.

Frank obviously liked the boys and sat next to them, mimicking their squatted position. Both the Indian boys laughed, nodded their heads and continued to eat everything. Later, Catherine wrapped several biscuits in a linen towel and placed them in a cloth bag for the boys to take back to their camp.

That day began a relationship, not only between James and the Utes, but also what would evolve into a long-lasting friendship the Utes would develop with Catherine and Francis. The friendships were destined to grow stronger and stronger as time passed.

Less than one week later, James arranged for Billy Beery to bring several items from Fairplay. Among the items, which were intended to begin an inventory, was a special bullet mold. Although it would be some time before he would have the opportunity to get the mold to the man that wanted it, James knew that it would be, not only one of the first trades he would make, but also one of the most important.

By mid summer the Castello trading post was becoming more and more popular. Nearly every trip made by George Barrett's company included shipments from Denver, Golden City and places outside the territory. Before long there were others settling in the area. James acquired several heifer calves and four steers from Hartsel's friends and made arrangements for a neighboring rancher to bring him a bull in August. The rancher explained that the bull needed to be culled from his herd. In exchange the bull's owner would get his choice of as many as five calves, depending on how many were born the next spring. In just a few short months James Castello was a rancher, a trading post owner and the husband of a woman that quickly became famous for her biscuits.

CHAPTER FIFTY-FIVE

Governor Hunt had managed to quell an all-out uprising by the Indian tribes, but not many parts of the agreement were upheld by the United States. Being the governor of the Territory of Colorado had a well-earned reputation of being a temporary position. By the time the Castellos were settled into their new home, Governor Hunt was out and was replaced by Edward McCook.

James was increasingly fed up with the political scene and removed himself from it as much as he could, but he was starting to have some thoughts that would surely cause some friction. He watched as more and more settlers came into the area. He and several other businessmen and freight companies were financing the improvement of the Ute Trail. It would soon be a viable passage for larger wagons, which would mean that, in addition to the supplies being hauled over the pass, there would soon be the wagons and oxcarts bringing the people headed west to pursue their dreams. James vowed to be a part of those dreams. He began to explore the possibility of forming a town. The first step was to found a post office, give it a name and then plan a town around the name.

His efforts were thwarted in July of 1871. On the 21st day of that month a package being shipped from Oro City to Denver passed through the Fairplay post office, which was housed in the Jayne store. Jayne was also the postmaster. After attending a party at William and Mary Julia's home, Jayne returned to the post office and found the gold had been stolen. There were three suspects in the theft and Billy Beery was one of them.

James learned of the incident several days after it occurred. He saddled his horse and headed for Fairplay. Once there he learned as much as he could from friends and acquaintances before going to Mary and Billy's home to confront Billy. As usual, Billy was not home. Mary was distraught and confided in her father that she suspected that Billy was the thief. Before leaving Fairplay James penned a letter to the post office department asking that they put a hold on his proposal to establish a post office. He knew that the application would likely be in jeopardy if the rumors of Billy's involvement proved to be true.

John Furay, a detective from the post office department, visited James later at the trading post. He informed James that William Beery had confessed to the theft of the gold and that he intended on prosecuting him. He also confirmed that James had little chance of getting his post office until this matter was cleared up. Within days Billie and Mary came to James and asked for his help. Billy said that he had promised to return what gold he had left, but he had already converted some of it to cash and paid some debts, which included expenses incurred for improvements on his property on Currant Creek.

It took time, but James retained an attorney in Denver who negotiated a settlement whereby Billy returned the gold and James made a deposit in a Denver bank that covered the balance. The deposit was made in Billy's name in order for James to remain somewhat anonymous, although many people assumed that James had rescued his son-in-law from a certain stint in a prison.

Prior to making the arrangement James summoned Billy to meet with him. He explained the plan and told Billy that he would carry it out, but there was a caveat.

"I have literally taken advantage of my many friends and contacts in the legal circles of this territory," he told Billy. "I have, by making this arrangement, put my own reputation on the line. My involvement will likely fade in the memories of many, but John Furay will not forget either one of us. If I am to give the go-ahead, I must have your solemn promise that you will move your family to the Currant Creek homestead, and you will immediately sever your ties with those whose reputations are tarnished. You will, first and foremost, be a husband to my daughter and a father of my grandchildren. I will provide you with some livestock to start a small herd of cattle and you will be a rancher. Are these provisions agreeable to you?"

It was nearly two years later when James applied for a post office to be designated as Florissant in the Territory of Colorado. He explained that the name was in recognition of the town in Missouri, in which his family had a significant role in establishing and in which his son was the current mayor.

The town was platted, and immediately began to grow. The Ute Pass became a bona fide road and was used extensively. The Utes continued to stop at the trading post and were often invited to dinner. They always suggested that Catherine make her biscuits. Late in the year of 1874 Ouray was returning from another of his meetings. The small band that accompanied him was in a poor condition. Just after Christmas James received a short letter from James Thompson, on behalf of the Colorado Territory Executive Department. He read it aloud to Catherine.

"I do not like the sound of this," he said in preparation. 'Tell me what you think. It is dated December 23, 1874. 'My Dear Sir, Ouray, brave of the Utes is on his way to his camp near your place. Should he happen to be short of friends on his arrival, and need anything in the way of transportation or provisions, please accommodate him and send your bill to me.' Signed, Yours very Truly, James Thompson."

"I agree," Catherine replied. "There seems to be something missing in the way of explanation. I am sure Ouray will stop here and will fill you in. Meanwhile I will plan on a meal. It would be nice to know how many he has traveling with him. He surely is not alone."

"I don't know," James said. "I wonder what Thompson means when he implies that Ouray might be short of friends. Well, it is probably a good thing that Frank brought home that deer yesterday. Ouray is fond of venison and biscuits and gravy, but you are well aware of that. It makes me smile when he calls you Little Biscuit."

Catherine smiled. "I do not mind the moniker one bit, in fact I think it flattering, and you will always be known to him as Judge."

Ouray arrived a few days later. Only one brave accompanied him. He explained that the others had gone on to the camp at the base of Mt. Pisgah. He told James that Samuel Elbert, who was the latest Governor, offered to send some cattle to Ouray as soon as spring arrived. Ouray expressed doubts that Elbert would come through.

James told Ouray of the letter and told him that he was welcome to any provisions from the trading post.

"I will take some enjoyment in sending Mr. Thomson the bill," he said.

Francis, who by now was known better as Frank, was elated when Ouray complimented him as well as Catherine for the meal.

"When a young hunter takes game, he must give thanks for being provided, and when he presents that game for preparation he must give thanks to the person who prepared it, and those of us who partake of its flesh must give thanks to all."

Frank nodded his agreement to what Ouray said and thanked the chief for saying it.

Ouray and James talked at length after the dinner. Frank sat quietly and listened as the two men recounted what had happened in the previous two decades. Ouray said that he would likely return to the Tabeguache, where most of his people were. He told James that he was tired and had traveled many, many miles hoping to secure a lasting peace for all the Indian nations and the United States. He left the next day.

Following Ouray's visit, Frank became increasingly interested in the family business. He took on the role of ex-officio foreman and showed a talent for making the right decisions at the right times. James and Catherine concurred with most of his choices and felt comfortable leaving him in charge when they made trips to the Beery ranch or to visit George and Lucy in Fairplay.

In early January of 1875, Frank was taking care of the trading post when a Ute man killed a rancher from Tarryall. The killing was the result of the man accusing the Utes of stealing a pony and the Utes claiming that the pony was stolen from them in the first place. When James and Catherine returned from their visit to the Beery ranch. Shortly after the incident James was visited by an Indian agent and he recounted that the whole thing started there in the trading post some months back when the rancher came to get mail and provisions. He was riding the pony at that time. Some Utes were camped nearby and were at the trading post on that day. They saw the pony, took the saddle off and rode away with the pony. Now, one of the Utes was accused of murder. Ouray was in Denver at the time.

When Ouray returned he met with the agent at the trading post and agreed to look into the matter. It proved to be the last visit James had with Ouray. The other Utes in the area continued to visit the trading post and often used a small campsite nearby.

James took an active role in the post civil war years when Colorado was first proposed to become a state. President Johnson vetoed the statehood, claiming that Colorado simply did not have the population to warrant becoming a state. James did not entirely disagree with Johnson because, had Colorado became a state; it would only have one representative in congress. In early 1876, James once more became active in the push for statehood. He was elated when he heard the news. He came into the living quarters with a special dispatch delivered to him minutes before.

"Catherine," he said, almost shouting, "Look at this. President Grant has said that he will sign off on Colorado's statehood. It will happen before the summer ends. Do you realize what that means?"

"Of course, I know," she replied. "It means another of your dreams has come to pass. It means you helped the people of this territory realize another of their dreams. You said long ago that it was time for you to relax, now relax and pray that Colorado will become a great state. You had a big part in this."

On July 4, 1876, one hundred years after the official formation of the United States of America. Colorado celebrated their statehood. The Castellos held a huge celebration on July 4th, and another on August 1st, when President Grant made statehood official.

CHAPTER FIFTY-SIX

In the midst of the August celebration a coach pulled up to the trading post. James and Catherine made their way through the crowd to determine who else was arriving. They were rendered almost speechless when Charles Castello and his wife, Dora, got out of the stage. It had been several years since they had seen Charles and they had never met Dora.

The couple stood waiting for a greeting of some sort. Charles had his arms partially extended for several moments when Catherine literally ran into them. He embraced her and gently pushed her away to accept a hug from his father. He then stepped back slightly.

"Father, Mother, it is my pleasure to introduce you to my wife. Dora this, as you have probably determined, is my father, James Castello, and my mother Catherine."

Catherine embraced Dora and said, "Well it is about time we met."

By the time James had welcomed Dora, George and Lucy joined them and introduced their ten-year-old son whom had been named Charles after his uncle. Billy and Mary were not far behind. Each was introduced and Frank came running as the news of Charles' arrival spread through the crowd.

"Wow, Charles said, "I assume this is baby Francis."

Frank blushed slightly. "Everybody calls me Frank," he said.

The blush peaked when Dora held him close and gave him a big hug. She ran her hands down his arms, taking notice of his firm biceps.

"This is certainly not a baby," she said, directing her comment to Charles.

James smiled, pulling Frank to his side. "No, most certainly not a baby and he is also becoming an accomplished businessman and trader. He does a lot around here and he never admits defeat."

After a few minutes, James escorted Charles and Dora around, introducing them to everyone. As the sun began its decent in the afternoon, the guests left; each of them thanking James and Catherine for the gathering and many thanking James for the work he had done in the past. Billy and Mary took their leave after being assured that they would see Charles and Dora again in the next few days. George, Lucy, James and Catherine took Charles and Dora into the living room where they all tried to catch up on what had happened over the past years.

As they all took seats, Catherine asked, "How was your trip?"

"It was somewhat amazing," Charles answered. "Things have certainly changed since I first went back to Missouri. A goodly part of our trip, of course, was on a train. I realized just how important the railways are going to be to this country. There were times when we were traveling as much as twenty miles per hour. One does not appreciate that until you compare things. That stagecoach we just got out of has a top speed of about four miles per hour. We were going five times that. Before I forget, I have something for you."

Charles stood up and walked to where one of his cases had been placed near the door. He opened it and retrieved a leather bound folder, presenting it to James.

The folder contained a proclamation naming Florissant, Colorado a sister city to Florissant, Missouri. The signatures of Mayor Charles Castello and his entire city council were neatly done at the bottom.

"I have been instructed by my colleagues to express the honor they felt in being the namesake of your new town, and that is especially true of me. Thank you," Charles said.

Charles and Dora stayed for five days and had lively conversations with the rest of the family.

The first year of statehood brought about many changes. The Ute Pass became one of the most popular routes through Colorado. There were more and more people going west and many of them staying in Colorado. The area around Colorado City was becoming more and more populated and there were nearly thirty thousand people living in Denver. Florissant had a population of about 70 and boasted a blacksmith shop, a school and three sawmills nearby.

James and Catherine had both topped their 60th year and James was beginning to slow down. Catherine had an unexplained energy and she and Frank readily accepted the responsibility of running the business.

Just weeks into the new year of 1878, James suffered the first of several bouts of illness. He was bedridden for most of February. While he seemed to be better in March, he once again became ill and spent another two weeks recovering. Then, on May 17, 1878, James Castello took his final breath while holding onto Catherine's hand.

During the funeral service a man stood, but did not identify himself. He strode to the front of the room, bowed his head for a moment and then addressed the people present.

"With your permission, I would like to address the life of this man whom we are saying goodbye to today."

"I first met James Castello in the Wyoming Valley of Wisconsin about forty years ago. We became close friends and we helped establish the Masonic Lodge in Mineral Point. Through that fraternity, we became even closer and I was there the day he met this beautiful woman, Catherine Hughes. I truly believe that his marriage to her was one of the best decisions this man ever made."

"Based upon my friendship and the many conversations I had, allow me to eulogize for a moment. James' father, Michael Castello was born in Ireland. He moved his family to Pennsylvania, where James was born in 1815. The family was largely involved in the mining industry and, when James was a mere five years old, they made an astounding decision to move to Missouri, where they had acquired some land from a famous French fur trader and pioneer. James' father was instrumental in establishing the town of Florissant, Missouri and James' son Charles is the current mayor of that town."

"Michael Castello was a great believer in the value of education. James was speaking three languages by the time he became a teenager. During those years he experienced the atrocities of slavery and became aware of serious crime problems in the St. Louis area. Owing to his language skills James was often asked to serve as an arbitrator in various disputes. That led to him becoming the sheriff of St. Louis County in

1857. Not long after that is when Charles came to Colorado Territory, along with many others to pursue the riches that gold mining offered. I too, came to Colorado at that time. Charles worked two claims in the Nevada Gulch and convinced his father to join him there."

"James ultimately served a term as a judge in Park County, and although it was a short stint, he managed to impress everyone he dealt with. He was considered a fair and honest man, and to this day, many people still refer to him as Judge Castello."

"Not long after James came to Colorado, Charles left and went back to Missouri. James saw an advantage to staying in Colorado and summoned Catherine and the children to join him here. They opened and ran a successful hotel in Fairplay for several years before establishing his ranch and trading post in, what is now Florissant, Colorado. Just as it has been throughout James Castello's life, he became an influential and respected citizen and his legend will live forever. I am also here to tell you that a Masonic headstone has been authorized and will be delivered as soon as practical so it can mark the final resting place of our brother. Thank you."

As the casket of James Castello was lowered into the ground south of his ranch, Catherine stepped to the coffin, placed a small bouquet of wildflowers on its top and, almost in a whisper, said, "My dear husband, so many times I have quoted the Book of Ruth and said to you 'For where you go I will go.' This time, my dearest, I will again assure you of that, but this time you might have to wait just a little longer. I have no intention of joining you anytime soon."

When the huge headstone arrived a few weeks later, Frank and some friends placed it on the grave.

"It is fitting that this is such a large stone," Frank said, "It represents the life of a very large man, not in stature, but in what he contributed to all of our lives."

THE END

Printed in the United States
by Baker & Taylor Publisher Services